## A HEAVY FEATHER

This is the story of Almayer Jenkin's progress through life. 'You start alone, you finish alone,' she says: 'It's fine to be alone, it's a revelation, truth at last.'

*By the same Author*

\*

*Stories*
**INNOCENTS**
**NOVELETTE**
**LOST UPON THE ROUNDABOUTS**
**FEMINA REAL**

*A story in three parts*
**THE JOY-RIDE AND AFTER**

*Novels*
**APOLOGY FOR A HERO**
**A CASE EXAMINED**
**THE MIDDLING**
**JOHN BROWN'S BODY**
**A SOURCE OF EMBARRASSMENT**

# A HEAVY FEATHER

*By*
A.L.Barker

1978
THE HOGARTH PRESS
LONDON

Published by
The Hogarth Press Ltd
40–42 William IV Street
London WC2N 4DF

\*

Clarke, Irwin and Co. Ltd
Toronto

All rights reserved. No part of this publication may be reproduced, stored in a retrieval system, or transmitted in any form, or by any means, electronic, mechanical, photocopying, recording or otherwise, without the prior permission of The Hogarth Press Ltd.

British Library Cataloguing in Publication Data

Barker, Audrey Lilian
  A heavy feather.
  I. Title
  823'. 9'1F         PR6052.A647H/
  ISBN 0–7012–0452–4

© A.L. Barker 1978

Printed in Great Britain by
Redwood Burn Ltd
Trowbridge and Esher

*To Norah Smallwood, my friend and publisher*

'Man's life is a strange matter
and full of unreason: a buffoon
may be fatal to it.'

                                            Nietzsche

# I

I had only one parent. My mother went away soon after I was born and my father had to bring me up alone. He did it as he did most things, rather badly. I used to believe that qualified failure was the universal norm.

To every action there are conclusions which are classifiable as right or wrong, and these are interchangeable, because right is not right for everybody and wrong is not always wrong, and moral right is not the same as expediency, and disaster may be necessary. My father envisaged certain outcomes and wanted them, if only to keep out of trouble. But it was true of him, as Eliot said of the Hollow Men, that between the idea and the reality, between the motion and the act, fell the shadow.

Father wasn't hollow. He was full of a spirit tremulous and too tender for this world. In the part of the world we inhabited it was practically a holy spirit. He once told me that when my mother married him she was pregnant. He did not infer that it was the only reason she married him, but I did. I knew by then that he should have had doubts about whether I was his.

It's a fact that you need expectations, not so as to have them fulfilled, simply to have something on account. My father didn't expect anything, and no-one, not even Fate, was obligated to him. I certainly didn't feel that I was, although I had most cause. I just felt — right from a baby — that I had to watch out for him.

But when I started school, I started to be critical. I saw that not everybody was in our same boat. 'Not everybody' was an over-statement. Those who were in our boat, I was quick to notice, came low down in the general estimation. They were next to nobody. Shifts which I had supposed were common practice, and the facts of life, I suddenly saw as the ways and means of the under-privileged, a word I was not familiar with, but whose general meaning I grasped.

At first I thought we were in our rightful place, my father and

I, for it was inevitable that some of his diffidence should stick. He thought I was unhappy because I did not like school, and to cheer me, hid Christmas pudding charms in my lunchtime slice of bread and jam. He tried to comfort me by telling me how clever I was going to be, much cleverer than he was. He gave me a germ of hope: I was too young to make resolves, but not too young to stand up in the boat.

He made our living by doing casual jobs of plumbing, carpentering, rewiring, gardening, window-cleaning, whatever he could turn his hand to. It wasn't his willing hand that turned against him, it was the innate hostility of everything. Wood, water, earth, the elements — anything which is not our sort, not flesh and blood, has it in for us. There's a natural law that bread falls on its buttered side and lightning hits the one tree in all the forest under which the traveller is sheltering. I wouldn't be surprised if my father's vulnerability actually set this animus in motion. Why shouldn't the inhumanities have their methods of divining our failures, just as beasts of prey single out the weaklings in the jungle?

He used to take me with him while he was at work. He had noone he could leave me with, and he wouldn't allow me to 'run the streets' as he called it. I spent hours in kitchens and basements and in the gardens of other people's houses watching him at his jobs. In winter I suffered from the cold. So did father, but he at least had a purpose. I had none. I stood miserably in shrubberies while he cleaned windows or mended gutters. He used to tell me to go and play as if I could do it to order.

I tried. I caught the drops of rain from the railings on my finger, every drop was to be a pearl. If they were frozen drops I broke them off and they melted in my palm. Sometimes I found a bush to crouch in and pretend it was my house. But there was always the cold. It pinned me and I could do no more than turn a few times on the pin and then stand among the dank laurels or on the frozen grass, and wait.

People tell me they do not remember feeling cold when they were very young. I remember being half obliterated and hanging on to a shred of myself by endlessly repeating some thought or word, or by some small voluntary hurt such as biting on my lip or on a loose tooth. I remember the sight and odour of that particular cold. It was yellow, a mouldy yellow that smelt of railways. In summer, in warm summer rain, the iron railings smelt to me of winter.

One day when my father had taken me with him on his rounds a woman told him that I should be wearing gloves.

"Gloves?" His mind wasn't on me, he was thinking about the slates to be replaced on the roof.

"The child's hands are covered in chilblains."

I put my hands behind my back. Father looked at his own hands which were dark blue and split.

"We're thin-skinned."

"Tell her mother to get her some gloves." The woman shut her door and went back to her fireside.

"Keep your hands in your pockets," father said. He was shoving at his ladder when the upper part slid down and caught him a blow on the wrist. He did not swear. I never once heard him utter a curse, though he frequently had cause. He sucked his wounds and picked up pieces and mopped up messes with the same uninvolved air. "Go and play," he said, putting his wrist to his mouth. How could I play with my hands in my pockets? Even he couldn't expect that. "But stay where I can see you." He went away up the ladder into the mouldy yellow.

Next day he bought me gloves. They were brown woollen, and too big.

"You'll catch up," he said when he couldn't get my fingers to fill empty inches. He always said that, but I never did catch up with my clothes: they wore out and got torn — I tore them myself if I didn't like them — and were discarded while they were still too big for me. But I was pleased with the gloves, deeply and fundamentally pleased by them. Believe it or not, I had never possessed any before, probably because father hadn't either. He was so unaspiring that anything he did not own and recognised no immediate practical need for was beyond him. He did not lift his eyes for himself, or for me. I think I always knew that, and had started to regard it as a kind of bondage. Later I actively resented it as misjudgement and misprision.

Putting on the brown woollen gloves was a satisfying experience not all to do with their comfort and very little to do with their symbolism. I don't know how much they meant to me, what variety of meaning they had. It was a time of primary need and they were seized on and made to fulfil it. I can usually find what I want when I want it.

In the first days of January, before I went back to school after the Christmas holidays, father took me to a house in Rosamund Road. It was a small mansion, Victorian Gothic, enriched with fretted stone and four turrets. Paddock gates led into a path of pink brick which rang underfoot like the top notes of a xylophone.

A uniformed maid opened the door. It was not the first occasion I had encountered one of these officials of another world. They made an impression on me so deep that I have ever since been hard put to dissuade myself that a uniform, any uniform, is a cloth of virtue. She told father that the pipe which was leaking was in the cellar and he would find steps down to it at the end of the passage.

"I have the child with me," said father.

She scarcely gave me a glance. "Keep her with you then."

I didn't like that cellar in Rosamund Road. It became established in my memory as the archetype for all sinister settings of crime and abomination. It was a place of iron doors and sweating stone. There were mountains of coal and coke, and shapeless things shrouded in cobwebs. When father lit the one gas mantle it shrilled like a tiny orchestra, but did not illumine the depths. All round us a monster of black shadow bided its time.

Father went on his knees to a congerie of pipes. He was anxious to find the leak, hoping, no doubt, that it wouldn't be too much trouble. I heard him whistle into his teeth and very thoughtfully, as if fearing to disturb something, he stretched a hand behind him towards his bag of tools.

There was nowhere for me to sit. I had on my new gloves which were causing my chilblains to itch. I stood as close to father as I could, rubbing first one knuckle, then the other. I was discovering subliminally, sub-rosa, and for the first time, that pleasure can co-exist with pain and be enhanced by it. After a primitive fashion I was experimenting with the border between.

"You shouldn't do that," said father. "It makes them worse."

He adjusted his spanner and began to work on one of the pipes. It wasn't long before the spanner slipped and fell from his hand, ringing like a bell on the stone. Father sighed and lay down with his knees in the air for a closer examination of the pipe.

It came to me then that not everyone's father had to get his living cramped under water systems, crouched in cupboards, spreadeagled on roofs. It came to me that mine was a singular misfortune. Sympathy for him I had none, any more than I had for a tabby cat for being born striped. It was the indissoluble conjunction between us which appalled me, the arbitrary commitment to his world, the inescapability. I rubbed my chilblains until tears of anguish ran down my cheeks.

Poor father, I see him now with his grey underpants tucked into his boots. His overalls were shrunken and shot up his calves when he bent his legs. Flakes of wet rust like old brown blood dropped on his face and hair.

"There's only one thing to use against water, Almey." He was getting out his blow-lamp and some stocks of solder. On his modest terms he was an optimist. He had to be, because he asked more than the rest of us in asking for things to go right for him. It wasn't his fault that he influenced them the other way. "And now I come to think, we use water against fire. Funny, isn't it?"

I looked at him in dismay. I did not see anything comic or strange, and did not expect to ever again. My life was now and would be just as it always had been. It seemed possible — yes, at six old — to be in for no more surprises.

But for the time being, father was not bothered. He was at the beginning, not yet prey to the doubts and certainties that afflicted him once a job was done. His lips were pursed as he set to work, he was probably whistling again. I couldn't hear because of the roar of the blow-lamp.

At school I had made friends with a dimpled little girl named Margo. She had a pretty mother and a baby brother. Her father came home to tea at six o'clock in a grey flannel suit. His shoes were the colour of violins. His tea was different from ours. He had meat and vegetables freshly cooked, and with them he ate slices of thin bread and butter. Afterwards there was steamed treacle pudding, and custard. I rarely saw that sort of food. Father wasn't good at cooking and we ate a lot of fried bread and bacon. My idea of Sunday dinner was a pork chop and Lyons Kup Kakes.

It had come as a profound shock, and I was shattered, not so much by the discovery of dimensions other than mine, but by the thought that I couldn't get into them. At first Margo caused me to suppose that they were for the chosen few, and that her dimples her curls and her white kid shoes were the essence, as gold was the essence of a crown. To be like Margo was to look like Margo: certainly nobody could look like me and be like her. I accepted that.

While I had thought of ours as the only way to live I was happy, living that way. When I found it wasn't the only way, I was less happy. But as long as I could believe that Margo had been made better *for* better things and not because of them, I was resigned to going on living as I always had.

Then one day in class she was asked a question which she could not answer. The teacher grew impatient and banged on the blackboard. Margo wet her knickers. I saw the trickle run over her white silk socks into her white kid shoes. I couldn't have been more surprised if it had been a trickle of sawdust.

But I realised what it meant. It meant that she was no better than she should be, certainly she was no better than me. I experienced a rush of exaltation, but only momentarily, for I at once asked myself, if there was nothing for God or a Grand Design to choose between us, why was Margo so blessed? Then I saw that the question was not why she should have so much more, it was why should I have so much less. I knew the answer. I was six years old, but I had the genesis of an older knowledge to guide me.

As I watched the black cobwebs stirring in the blast of father's blow-lamp I thought of something that had been said to us at Sunday school about living in the station to which it pleased God to call us. It had puzzled me that God should want us to live in stations, but now I saw the relevance, for had I not been called to stand and wait? God did not mean me to go away. He was not going to send any trains.

"Well," said father shutting off his blow-lamp, "that should fix it." He came out feet first from under the pipes and then had to crawl back to look for his cap. He brought it out covered with coal dust.

"I want to go away," I said.

"We will. As soon as I've packed up my tools."

"On a train," I said. "I want to go on a train."

"At this time of year? It wouldn't be very nice. Nothing doing at the seaside. In the summer we'll take a trip." He picked up his toolbag, a wistful look coming into his face. "It's the best I can do." He was talking about the pipes.

When he went to report that the job was finished the maid asked if he would like a cup of tea.

"I have the child —"

"You can bring her if she's quiet."

Going with him into the houses where he worked I liked the kitchens best, they were warm and smelt of food. Once, in an attic, there was a rocking-horse. Father lifted me into the saddle but would not let me stay and ride it. When I cried, he said, "It isn't ours," with a finality rare for him.

This kitchen was very large and very warm. In the huge range the fire burned without flame. It had reached the liquid stage and would have run down the sides of a volcano. As I drew near I felt secret places in my body stirring. I always feel those stirrings on coming in from the cold: I am different in the warm, I am whole.

The range held the fierce heart of the kitchen and it was as shiny as the back of a beetle. I remember the silver dish covers, and seeing myself reflected in them, globular, my scarlet tammy rising to the ceiling. On the dresser the plates stood in rows. I counted them; I reckoned if there was a plate for each person there must be fifty people living in the house.

"Sounds travel up these pipes," said the maid. "I hope you haven't disturbed the old one."

Father stood uneasily rubbing his hands over the seat of his overalls. She asked him his name.

"Peter Jenkin."

"Well, Peter Jenkin, I'm Irish and have the soft tongue. But if you've woken the old one you'll have Nurse here directly and her tongue's as sharp as her scissors."

"Is somebody sick?"

"It depends what you call sick. We took to our bed twenty years ago and we've laid there ever since, letting the world go by. I'd say we're disinclined more than sick."

"We?"

"Mrs Manchester." Irish wore a starched apron which kept up a constant background fuss — what father used to call 'static' when it happened on his wireless. "This is her house and you'd think she'd walk round it now and then. Not her. She stays in her bed tidy as a china doll and there's us down here running to pick up after ourselves." She handed father a cup. "Sugar's in, if you don't take it, don't stir."

"It doesn't matter — "

"What about her?" She nodded in my direction.

"A little tea and plenty of milk and two spoonfuls of sugar."

"Orders, orders! I can see you spoil her. She's a footy little thing." As a matter of fact she never did give me any tea, but she pushed a plate of cakes across the table to me. "You're a footy thing yourself."

"Footy?"

"This way." She put a hand on his chest and the other in the small of his back. "There's no substance in you, you're a footy pair."

I deliberated over my choice of a cake. It was important because some had cream in and some had jam, and I wasn't sure I would be invited to have two.

"Like father, like daughter, you don't know what you want. Sit down, Peter Jenkin, and drink your tea. I won't bite you. Cook might. Nurse don't bite, she snips."

Father sat down. "I don't think they'd hear much upstairs. A slight reverberation perhaps, no more than the trams."

"Trams is it, in Rosamund Road? " Irish stretched herself, lifting her arms above her head. I was awed by the independent way her bosom swelled. It looked threatening, I didn't trust it even after it had subsided. I thought it must be her bosom which made the static noise. "It's my day off tomorrow. I'm going to Brighton with my intended."

I had seen a cake containing both cream and jam, and I stood on tiptoe, fingers wide to encompass it. I had not forgotten that I still wore my gloves: they had been a comfort and I was not disposed to part with them, even for the cake. Father, for whom the bosom was insolently performing, appeared to be looking directly at me, but his concentration must have been in the corner of his eye for he made no comment about the gloves.

"The last time I was at Brighton it was all stones."

"They're still there. You poor man, have you never been to the Pavilion or the waxworks or to Black Rock on the little railway?"

The cake was large and sticky. I carried it down to my level, below the top of the table. I had not been asked to sit, so I squatted on my heels. When I was out of sight I took a bite. Cream welled into my teeth, and the sharp sweet taste of jam.

"Mrs Manchester lies up there, the soles of her feet so tender they'd bleed, Nurse says, if she was to tread on the carpet. There's nothing wrong with her, she's got all her organs, she's got her eyesight, she's even got her teeth. What a waste!"

"Some people like to save themselves."

"Now who in the world would she be saving herself for?"

"It might be the best thing. We're not all made the same."

"How do you think she's made? Of sugar and spice? There's no-one waiting for a whole helping of Mrs Manchester, I can tell you. But there's her money in the bank, thousands of pounds, and she in her bed never getting a farthing's fun. Holy Mother, it should be mine!" Father's feet stirred under the table. "I know what I'd do." One of her square black shoes nudged him ungently on the shin. "I'd have the fun and all!"

Out of the bite-shaped shell of cake, jam and cream burst over my gloved fingers. I knew that I was looking at a wickedness, a cardinal sin which I had never before had the chance to indulge in. I was as deprived of felonies as I was of benefits. I closed my fingers on the remains of the cake, and squeezed.

"Thanks for the tea," said father. "I ought to be getting along."

"What would *you* do with a few thousand?"

"It'll be five and sixpence for the job. I trust it will be satisfactory."

I knew myself to be both radical and guilty. As I opened my fingers it seemed to me that there was no answer to what I had done, no utterable syllable. I was appalled and delighted, for it meant that I should never again be accepted. Salvation is where you find it.

"What I'd do," said Irish, "I'd go to gay Paree. I'd show Mrs Manchester. I don't need teaching how to spend money, I am naturally gifted with the knowledge. In bed at night I think of what I'd do if I had it. My intended declares it would take Henry Vanderbilt's as well as Mrs Manchester's. When I go to sleep I dream about it. There's no harm."

"There's no good either."

"It's well for her she hasn't left it all to me." She giggled. "I'd be entirely willing to help her save her breath for the next world. Don't you want to better yourself, Peter Jenkin?"

"Not with other people's money."

"Then it's your wife I'm sorry for."

"There's no need."

"If a woman's not encouraged she has to use herself in other ways. Would you know that?"

"Encouraged?"

"I'd rather a man gave me the back of his hand if it showed he cared. Do you ever give her the back of yours?"

"No."

"Or the front? The tender touch of the fingers? Don't you ever stroke her hair? Or her neck? Or her —"

"Almey," said father, "Where are you?"

"Don't you," said the maid, edging forward in her chair so that her apron touched his knees, "use your hands at all?"

"Almey! Come out of there!"

I heard the note of panic but I hardened my heart and crept deeper under the table.

Irish burst out laughing. "You're a bloodless man, Peter, and your wife will end up as a cats' home."

"Cats' home?"

"She needs something to love."

I began to eat the abominable mess in my palm. How shall I describe the sense of pure wickedness it gave me? Or absolute alienation? I knew that father was good, so was everyone else. Everyone had the qualifying degree of goodness. Some people had more, but none had less, not even other sinners, for they had not chosen to sin, had not sought it out and preferred it, as I had.

"Why do you think that I —" Father cleared his throat — "that she —" He said bleakly, "I am not bloodless."

"If you're asking why your wife doesn't love you —"

"I'm not asking that."

"If you want to know what I think, I think when she chose you she got the haulm and left the tatie."

"We were the same age."

Irish laughed. "Boyeens in their prams have the way with women. It's given to every Irishman with his mother's milk. Who better than his mam to tell him what a woman wants?"

"My wife left me," said father. "She is living in Norwood. I daresay — I hope — she is happy."

"Glory to God, I wouldn't wonder!"

I was first to notice the water. Being on the floor I was better placed to see it than those two were. It was advancing across the red tiles from the direction of the kitchen range, a tide about an inch deep, and steady, except for an occasional quick sally from points on the perimeter. These sallies were immediately overtaken and reabsorbed into the apron shape which spread, as I ascertained by going on my knees and putting my cheek to the floor, from beneath the range on one side of the kitchen to the pillars of a stone sink on the other.

It was so clear and silent, I fell in love with it at once. At once I feared it would vanish, or prove never to have been. I closed my eyes hard. When I opened them a little swell of water, no more than the drawing of a breath, was slipping towards me. It magnified every crack, every grain. I have never seen a fly in amber, but I have seen a floor through shining water. It is what I remember as my eye of childhood, a vision crystal clear and scrupulous. I like to think I saw everything like that. It is sentimentality of course, for I had learned already to look without seeing.

I pulled off my gloves and went forward on hands and knees. The maid caught sight of me, and the water. She screamed, I swear the tide ruffled with shock. Then, taking heart, and supplied from its secret source, it rolled into my outstretched hand. I was enchanted, I broke the edge with my fingers. Once, at the seaside, the sea had come across its enormous shore to break a little foam, like egg-white, over my feet. But the sea was cold and vast, this was warm and private.

Irish spoiled it. She screamed and flapped her apron as if she would shoo the water away. She hopped like a bird that couldn't get off the ground.

Father rose slowly to his feet. I don't think he believed what he saw, although he wasn't surprised. I think that purely as a preventive measure he had seen it already, or something like it. I do that myself sometimes: I get in first with disasters. That's how father tried to take care of things, he had a quick peek at the worst and hoped against hope for the best.

He was inching back from the advancing water and when he found that he was caught between it and the table he drew his feet and his knees together in a prudish way. Father was never manly, his clothes did the identifying for him; in drag he would have looked androgynous, like those raw-boned women who seem to have come down with a foot either side the sex divide. He also had a mannerism of pushing the air with his hands and turning his head aside from anything he disliked. It was not only feminine, it was Victorian.

"It must be a fractured pipe."

"Fractured, is it? Mary Magdalene, it's cut in two!"

"Behind the range?" Father said miserably, "There has to be access —"

"We'll all be drowned!"

Another little surge, the water reached her shoes. She too was caught between the table and the tide. She turned round and round on the spot and finally scrambled on a chair where she stood battering her apron and squawking.

I was on my hands and knees. My hands reminded me of crabs seen at the fishmonger's. I walked them up and down in the water.

Father lifted one foot, then the other. He was worried for his boots which were his only pair. I suppose he was undecided as to which one to keep dry.

"Do something, you poor man!"

Father came to a decision. He picked me up and sat me on the table. Then he unlaced his boots and put them beside me.

He had no sense of the absurd. Although he could not save his face he never lost his conception of the seriousness of his situations, however ludicrously they turned out. He had a knack for turning the funny side out. But he didn't see himself, kneeling like the faithful to a blocked drain, or marooned on a roof with a chimney pot in his arms, or juggling with a pane of glass on a shaky ladder. I saw him, and heard other people's laughter.

But I was bewitched that day in the kitchen in Rosamund Road when he rolled his pants up over his ankles and tried the water with his toe.

"Paddling, is it? Oh, will you look at the man!"

I noticed an extraordinary thing. From a point at the base of a cupboard along one wall the water was issuing a rich cobalt. This colour spread rapidly, the clear rose reflected up from the tiles became a beautiful cerulean, the colour of summer seas.

"It's got to the Reckitt's!" cried the maid. "All our Reckitt's bags are in that cupboard!"

Enchantment was complete. I had never seen anything so strange, so lovely, so exclusive, as that pure blue tide. Tears came to my eyes with the poignancy of it. I had my first intimation of the fortuitousness of beauty. Father's feet woke it to wavelets and eddies, trailed delicate plumes with every step. Rose pink at its rim, shot with green and azure, the magic sea broke out of its bonds and surged to meet him.

"We'll all be drowned!" shrieked Irish.

Wild with longing I watched as father turned and came splashing back. He had forgotten his tools.

"Can you tell me where the stopcock is?"

"Mary of God, how should I know?"

"I'll have to turn off the mains supply. Until I find the leak. It mustn't be for long, not with the boiler dry and a big fire burning."

"Is it the hot baths we're waiting for!"

"The boiler might burst," father said sombrely. He took his spanner and splashed across to the range. He turned on the brass tap set beside the oven door. A trickle of water ran out.

Snatching up the teapot, Irish emptied it into the flood. "You'll be needing every drop!" She sounded hysterical.

They weren't paying any attention to me. Leaning perilously down, I unbuttoned my shoes. I knew that I couldn't have everything I wanted, but was still in the dark — in the blackest night sometimes — as to why so much was refused. When circumstances allowed, I did not risk refusals, I went ahead and took or did what I wanted, hoping — with father's same optimism — that it would turn out all right.

I lowered myself from the table. When my feet touched the water I knew that this did not come into any of the categories of refusal that I was familiar with, i.e. that it couldn't be afforded, that it would make me sick, that it wasn't mine. This pretty tide pearling round the legs of the furniture, the blue-and-rose-mottled shawl of water now completely covering the kitchen floor, was in fact mine.

"Holy Virgin, will you look!" prayed Irish, lifting her eyes. "Paddling, the two of them!"

Father turned a little wheel under the sink and a warm wave ran towards me and slipped over my ankles.

## II

When my father thought of marrying again he did not say so, but he made uncalled-for remarks about how much better women did certain things, things he had done himself for years, or which had not been done and which we had not noticed the need of. It was a sign of the way the wind was blowing, a breeze in evidence. He was a dreamer after his fashion, and since he was content with so little he would not have taken what were, for him, direly practical steps if he had not been stirred to his depths. He must have reached a point where dreams were not enough.

It came as a surprise when he said he wished me to learn to play the piano. Just that once, I think, he used me to further his own ends. We had little money to spare for extra-mural tuition. No doubt he told himself that come what may, and if nothing at all came of it for him, I would profit from the extra refinement.

I was never to find out much about her. She tried, with some success, to keep herself to herself. She wore her weird grubby clothes with an air, even a flair. Her features were fine and regular, the skin without pucker or crease, smooth as ivory, and much the same yellow as her piano keys. She wore big dusty hats and black dresses sewn with steel beads and ruching at the wrists. Father said she was a lady, and I still think of a lady as someone who smells of old facepowder.

She lived beside the railway. The windows of her house were bloomed with smoke from the sidings, the tossy grass in the garden was full of tram-tickets. The first time I was taken to see her, father made me brush my hair and fasten it with a slide. He himself shaved and washed and put on what he called his 'sports' jacket. It had a bold dogtooth pattern and I asked him what sports he was meant to participate in when he wore it. 'Draughts,' he said, with a shamed smile at his joke.

Miss Velva, when she opened the door, gave us a lightning comprehensive glance and put the brim of her hat between us. I thought she must be on the point of going out: afterwards, I found that she wore a hat all the time.

"You won't remember," said father, "but I came to repair your roof."

"You will be paid."

Father cleared his throat. "I'm not here about that. This is my daughter, Almayer. I want her to have piano lessons."

She stood in silence, her great hat drooping to her shoulders. Then, reluctantly, she drew open the door and I had my first whiff of the house, bitter-sweet, of dust and decay. I have always believed that the sweetness came from her, that she was powdering away beneath her rusty black and her limp organdie.

She ushered us into what she said was the 'music room'. The chairs stood shoulder to shoulder round the walls, on each was a lace mat which I regarded as a warning, a deterrent, and never sat on any of them. The piano wore a silk shawl — to keep it warm, I supposed, for the room was icy. There was a tinted photograph of a lady in evening dress gripping a 'cello between her knees.

Miss Velva, seeing me stare at it, said sibilantly, "Suggia!"

Father looked anxious. "She doesn't know any music at all."

"The world-famous 'cellist. We were students together at the Conservatoire."

She did not ask us to sit down. She herself stood with one hand on the keyboard and now and then she struck a chord. This lent emphasis to everything she said and I wondered if the purpose would be to teach me to communicate entirely by means of the piano.

"I am not sure if I can take another pupil. There is no limit to one's best and I regard it as my duty to give no less. But there are limits to one's capacity to impart it. At times it is like getting blood into a stone. Is she musical?"

"Oh yes," said father.

She struck a note and told me to sing it.

"I'm not going to learn singing, am I?"

"Do as you're told, Almey," said father.

I drew in my breath and produced a squawk.

"She has no ear," said Miss Velva.

"She has for some things. She can tell you the name of every church bell in the district on Sundays, including the convent."

"The convent bell only rings twice a year," I said. "The day

St. Philomena was born and the day she was sainted."

Miss Velva said to father, "Did you leave a ladder on the roof?"

"A ladder?"

From under her hat she flashed him a look. "I have thought sometimes that someone is walking about up there."

"Oh no. I only have one ladder and I need it for my work."

"Very well, Mr. Morcom. She may come on Thursdays."

"My name's Jenkin —"

"Thursdays at a quarter to five. I shall start with fingering and theory, and she must practise an hour every day."

"We haven't got a piano," I said.

"She can use the one in the church hall," father said quickly.

"No piano?" Miss Velva hooked her fingers and struck a discord. "She wants to learn. Don't you, Almey?"

I heard the appeal in his voice and answered it from force of habit. "I have always wanted to play the piano." It was true insofar as I saw myself in key situations — in the very wards of the lock, so to speak — and in one of them I was bowing beside a concert grand to the standing ovation of a delirious audience.

"She must practise. I cannot teach anyone who is not prepared to work."

"She will, won't you, Almey?"

"Music is the highest human achievement. I have affiliations with all the major schools of music, and diplomas too numerous to mention. I have given public recitals and adjudicated at more music festivals than I care to remember. The fee is one shilling an hour."

"I want her to have the best."

"For extra tuition I charge accordingly. The higher the grade the higher the fee."

"She'll get on like a house afire."

"She will require coaching for local festivals or accredited examinations and I could not prepare her without adequate remuneration."

"Of course," said father stoutly. "Extras are extra in my line of business too."

She put up her hands as if to take off her hat, but instead she drove her hairpin deep into her skull. "Everything has its price. Instruction in the greatest of the arts, in the participation of the purest joy, is one penny per five minutes."

"I wasn't thinking of the money," said father. Miss Velva, who could then have seen no reason to think of anything else, folded herself over the piano stool with a motion at once sensual and virginal. "Just of her getting the best. Which you'll give her." She poised her hands above the keys. "I could look at the roof, it may be birds getting in under the eaves."

"Ostriches," she said, and began to play dreamily, and, I think badly, something which could have been the 'Melody in F'.

All the way home father worried about how she was to be paid, about the transaction, the actual passing of the shilling from my hand to hers.

"I'll give it to her after I've had the lesson."

"Not after — before. And never hand her the money. Deposit it on the hall table as you go in, and let her see you do it."

"Why?"

"She must never have to ask."

"Why? You don't get paid for anything till you've done it. Sometimes not then."

"She is not a common tradesman." Common she was not. Who else have I known who paced about crying 'Diminuendo! Dolcemente pianissimo! Oh non brutamente!' "She is a lady," said father.

"I don't like her."

"You don't know her, you've only just met her."

"I like not liking her." This was true: I liked her as a source of morbid interest and speculation.

As well as the Suggia portrait there was in the music room a framed snapshot of a horse in a field. I studied it from all angles, remembering puzzles of my earlier days when one was required to look carefully at Red Riding Hood and hidden in the picture would be found Grandma, the Wolf, and the Woodcutter's axe. I asked Miss Velva if the horse was hers.

"Horse? It is a photograph of my old home."

"I can't see any home."

"It is behind the trees."

I had no gift for music. Scales and fingering exercises bored me, the insistence on accuracy bored me, all I wanted was to make a joyful noise. Miss Velva would seize the keys from me, as shocked as if I was about to bounce eggs. 'D, G, B flat, D natural — can't you hear the *colour* of the chord?' I could certainly smell it. The bass notes of her piano had a pungency which caused the small hairs in my nostrils to recoil: the treble pierced to the root of my nose.

To practise I had to use the piano in our church hall, an ornate instrument with a bodice of crimson satin under a fretting of walnut. In winter I lit candles in the brass sconces because by then the caretaker was my enemy and wouldn't let me have electric light.

The instrument was out of tune, but its dampers gave it effervescence which in my opinion greatly enhanced the sound. At first the caretaker took an interest, and saved his cleaning so that he would be there to hear me play. We agreed that scales were dull, and together managed to pick out such tunes as 'Sally', 'Keep Your Sunny Side Up', Love is the Sweetest Thing', and the Blue Danube waltz. We were happy with an approximate noise, and I learned a safe sequence of chords to fill out the left hand while bringing up the theme in the right. We had rollicking times. The caretaker sang to my accompaniment and danced with the church chairs, first formally requesting them for the pleasure. He was a pretty old man with silver curls and roguish blue eyes, quite a clown.

In return for my use of the piano father did several repairs to the church house, for which the caretaker received a maintenance grant. Father had to do the work free of charge, but he didn't mind. He didn't fall out with the caretaker — I did.

One day I was extemporising on my version of the 'Can-Can': it wouldn't have been recognisable to a danseuse of the Moulin Rouge, but the caretaker had a chair on each arm and was kicking up his legs and shrieking like a lady when a minister of the church walked in. He wasn't the incumbent, he had happened to be passing and heard the secular noises. He reprimanded the caretaker who cheeked him. The minister went away and reported him.

I don't think he suffered more than a dressing-down, but he had an unblemished reputation and blamed me for spotting it. He locked the presbytery door so that I couldn't get to the masterswitch to put on the lights. He took the peg out of the piano stool so that the seat shot down when I sat on it. He left a dead mouse on the keyboard. He might have done more, but he wished to retain father's unpaid services and couldn't risk frightening me away.

"There's something wrong with your Miss Velva," I told father. It amused me to call her his.

"Wrong?"

"She can't look me in the eye."

"She will when she knows you better."

"She keeps her hat on so that she can hide under it."

"So that she can be private."

He must have hoped to be invited into her privacy: he offered to do some jobs on the house. It was an act of courtship: another man would have proffered a bunch of flowers, father offered her lead paint and putty.

\* \* \*

Peter knew that some people ate toast with forks, which he took as indication that they were superior. He was accustomed to encountering obscure qualities and powers. Mostly they were hostile, and although he did not presume to oppose them he did, at a fairly lowly level, venture to dig himself in. There were limits below which he could not go if he was to maintain his existence.

To avoid doing the thing which other people did differently he might have waited outside and upset nobody. But he decided, simply as a personal provision, that it would be permissible, if he were required to eat toast, to take it up in his fingers.

She was sitting in the window of the tea-shop, framed in a hole in the steam. She wore a fox fur and her chin rested on her hands, the fur of the fox splayed between her fingers, the fox's pointed muzzle biting deeply into her shoulder.

The place was full of people. Their mouths stopped chewing when they saw him and he almost turned and went out again. As he passed between the tables, his tools, which he carried in a carpet sling, dislodged someone's umbrella. It fell, bringing down a cream horn. He was too late to stop his foot descending.

"Excuse me — " perhaps she was asleep under the brim of her hat — "I don't want to disturb you." He could feel the cream horn newly dead on the sole of his boot. "It's about the noise you complained of in your roof." She looked up, the tip of her nose shone as pale as a pearl. "The bottom row of tiles, above the gutter, they're loose and the wind gets underneath. Makes a chattering noise."

"Chattering?"

"The cladding's gone."

"The what?"

"I've known old roofs ruffle up like the feathers of a bird."

An argument started at the table behind him. The waitress who was making out the bill said that three cakes had been eaten. The customer maintained he had only had two.

"Where's the other cream horn then? There were two chocolate éclairs, two jelly meringues and two cream horns. I should know, I set them on the plate."

"It went on the floor."

"Went?" the waitress said sharply. "It walked off the table?"

"It was knocked off."

"Where is it now?"

"How should I know?"

"Very well, I'll call the manageress."

"Call the police if you like."

"Someone's got to pay."

Peter said to the waitress, "It's on my boot."

The faces all turned towards him, he could feel himself reflected in every one.

"Let's see," said the waitress. He was obliged to hold up his foot like a horse to be shod. "Phoo, what a mess." She handed him a paper napkin. "Here, wipe it off. Are you going to pay for it?"

"Put it on my bill," said Miss Velva.

"No, I can't let you do that."

"Why don't you sit down. Waitress, bring another cup, please."

"I'll take the cake." said the waitress, "what's left of it." She poked Peter in the back. "What they call shoe pastry!"

He stowed his bag under the chair and sat down. "I must pay for the cake."

"Cream horns are fourpence."

They were all watching to see him pay up. To be done with it, he counted out the coins and pushed them across the table. Two went under Miss Velva's plate.

She picked them up. crooking her smallest finger. "I don't tip the waitress, she earns more than I do. I would be prepared to work eight hours a day for six days a week if 48 people wished to learn to play the piano. Or if 24 would come twice a week. Or I would prefer the same 12 to come four times. Knowledge is like jam, the farther it is spread, the thinner it gets."

"Would one and sixpence — "

There was steel under her hat-brim, and it laid him open from head to foot. "Music is a gift of God, money cannot buy it. You think, no doubt, that I am obtaining money by false pretences. But I tell you I give value for money. If there is a spark I blow upon it and perhaps a fire is lit and someone may learn to listen. I do not go so far as to say someone may learn to perform. You see how little I can do! Is it enough for your shillingsworth?"

"I'm satisfied."

"Con brio, con fortimento rallentando? Non pui e crescendo!"

He said doggedly, "Almayer is getting on nicely."

"Why did you give her that name?"

"Almayer? It was her mother's idea."

"So she is romantic."

"No," he said, "she wasn't."

"She is dead?"

"She went away, left us."

"Why?" Peter shook his head. "She must have had a reason. For me it would be another husband — richer and stronger. Only for that, or death, would I leave husband, child and home."

"She wasn't happy." She had said that was why she was going and he thought of it now with the same degree of surprise. It was as if she had said she was leaving him because she wasn't warm enough. It seemed so remediable. "It meant a lot to her — happiness."

"What a greedy lady to expect that too!" Miss Velva laughed and the fox's snarling muzzle fell on her breast.

\*     \*     \*

If women were all made the same there could be no getting through to them, no knowing and no satisfying them. It meant that Miss Velva hadn't taken sides, she had been already ranged against him. But it did not help to think that his problem was general, for had she taken solely against him and not against all mankind he could have tried to win her over. 'Excuse me for embarrassing you. It's my toolbag — you see, I have to carry my tools with me between jobs — and the umbrella which was left in the way — my toolbag knocked down an umbrella and the umbrella knocked down a cream horn and I trod on it. It could happen to anyone but it will never happen again to me —"

But she was not embarrassed, and allowed him to pay for her tea.

He questioned Almayer about the music lessons, he wanted to know everything that happened.

Almayer was having trouble with her arpeggios, she thought it was because of the skin between her fingers.

"My hands are webbed like a frog's. For me, three-quarters of the world's great music will be unplayable."

"You'll manage."

"No Mozart, Tchaikovsky, Beethoven, and not much Chopin. I can't play sustained octaves because my thumb or my little finger will keep slipping off the keyboard. Should I have an operation to split the skin between my fingers?"

"I don't care if I never hear an octave. Just play what you can."

"According to some people, hands are an expression of personality."

"What does she do? What does she say?"

"She hits my wrists. You've no idea how strong her hands are, strong and lizardy."

"Now, now. Don't start something you can't finish."

"I can finish. It's the way they move and their yellowy colour. If they were any other colour, if they were black or brown, I don't think I'd mind."

"Colour doesn't matter, she's a fine teacher."

"I'll tell you something odd, not to say suspicious, about your Miss Velva."

"Mine?" He wanted to come gently to that, and perhaps to turn aside to savour the sweetness. He didn't want to bounced into it.

"This afternoon while I was having my lesson, a man came and looked through the window."

"What sort of man?"

"A bad sort. He pressed his face to the glass and I could see right up his nose. It was full of black smoke. I screamed, and what do you think she did? She pretended there was no-one there."

"She was frightened."

"Not her. He wasn't looking at her."

"Did he try to come in?"

"No, he went away. When I told her he looked as if he wanted to eat me — which he did — she said, 'If I thought you'd tempt his appetite I'd serve you up with mint sauce.' "

"She was pulling your leg." She had a way of piercing to the heart of the matter. She tended to pierce to his heart also, but he had promised himself that soon he would be there, on her lip, sharing the joke.

"She knows who he is allright," said Almayer.

"I must go to her and let this fellow, whoever he is, see that there's a man about."

There had once been a girl in a chemist's shop whom he loved for her glossy white overall and her smell of soap and sealing-wax. He thought that she would change his life, bring to it her purity and efficacy, dispense sealed packets of betterment and healing.

Later he had met the girl who became Almayer's mother. He married her believing that she would comfort him. And she did. He was cosy while it lasted, but then she told him how bleak her life was and she chilled all their past time together.

Miss Velva was so capable of setting aside what did not suit her: she could set aside anything under the sun. If he was included, he would learn to suit!

He ran past the siding. On his way to her, about to see her in the flesh — a need which had been with him ever since he had found her framed in the teashop window, mysterious, reserved, her fox fur snarling on her breast — the shunting of the railway trucks was music. That sight of her mapped itself on walls, the promise of her ran out of taps.

But when she stood before him he could not think what to say. He had come because he must, but forgot what his excuse was. His mouth opened and dried, he was dumb.

She turned away as if she had been expecting him, and led the way to a room overlooking the garden. She was wearing a printed shawl over her shoulders, and a great red hat. From under the brim she kept an eye on him whilst pinning up her knot of hair. Her hair was as dense as smoke. He thought dizzily of suffocating in it.

"Dear me, I've forgotten your name. I call all men Stanley

Morcom, it is the only name I remember."

"Who's he?" There was no fire in the room and no sign of human occupation. On the table was a conch shell of a blushing, intimate pink. To Peter, not normally receptive to such thoughts, it made an immediate and explicit suggestion. He said faintly, "Is he the man who looked through the window?"

"What window?"

"I want to hear about that man."

"Want is everyone's master." She put a hairpin in her mouth. "We hear little of gratitude."

He could of course have spoken of that. Of course he should. "I am."

"What are you?"

"Grateful."

"For what, my poor soul?"

"For you."

She put up her face and laughed, a single snatch of laughter. "I am not aware that I have made you a present of myself. Have I given myself to you?"

He gazed at her with the old desperate weakness, feeling like the child arrived at the sweetshop to find that he has no money. "Was it Morcom that frightened the daylights out of you?"

"No-one has frightened the day or the night out of me."

"It takes something to frighten Almey."

He could swear the catch of the door clicked. He looked round and the door stood ajar.

"The roof," she said. "I told you there were noises on the roof."

"I can put that right. It only needs a dab of cement under each tile. There'll be no charge."

"You think you can buy me for a dab of cement?"

"Buy you?" He said confusedly, "It's the other way round."

"I should buy *you*?"

"What's this talk about buying? I don't like that — "

"Mr Morcom, will you stop wringing your hands!"

"My name isn't Morcom."

"It is a sign of inconstancy." She said briskly, setting her hat straight, "You say your wife left you. Did you ask her to return?"

He shook his head.

"You should have gone after her. It would have shown

charity and strength of purpose."

She had slender feet and wore black silk stockings with white clocks. He longed to take her ankles, to move his hands up her calves to her knees. He had the feel, the dream, the ghost of those silken legs in his hands.

"There was Almayer to look after."

"Do you know where your wife is now?"

"I've got an address. I don't know if she's still there."

"You never tried to find out?"

"No." He might have tried once, he might have looked at the place she had gone to in the hope of seeing what was so different about it. But by the time he knew where she was, he had realised that the difference was simply that he wasn't there. "She was right to go."

"She was not right. A woman is but a rib and it is not right for the rib to desert the body. A woman, a wife, is sworn to the man and to his progeny and to his home. And when he and all that is his has gone, and he is no longer remembered, it is her duty to regard him always in her heart."

"Is that how you stick by Morcom?" He could hear his anger and so must she, but she did not know about his despair.

"I am a virtuoso."

"Yes." He felt more hopeful. He thought that so much virtue must do away with Morcom.

"Pure in spirit. If I am not that, I am nothing."

"I would always respect you."

"Single in mind, whole in heart, deaf to reason. Dead to love."

"Dead?"

"Dedicated to music."

\*   \*   \*

I always supposed she lived alone. It did not occur to me that she might have family or friends. Or even that she must have been born. So far as I was concerned she had arisen complete, her hat on her head, already powdering into dust. She was not the sort of person to have relations. At no time did I see her anywhere except in that house which bore no imprint, no relic of her occupation. In fact it looked as if I had been the first to enter it for years. Once I tried an experiment. After my lesson, when she closed the front door behind me, I pushed a tiny screw of paper into the jamb. It fell out the next time she admitted me, a week later.

Then, one day, hands poised above the keyboard, the piano throbbing with my onslaught, I heard the distant but unmistakable sound of water flushing.

"Someone," I said to the rose on her hatbrim, "just went to the lavatory."

She had a technique, she could strip to the bone in the time it took her hat to travel ninety degrees. She spoke no word, just lifted her head and aimed one of her lightning looks.

I told myself that father ought to know there was someone in the house with her, and it was up to me to find out who. I contrived to leave some of my music behind and late that evening, when father supposed I was in bed, I let myself out of the back door, got through the hedge into the next garden and dropped over their wall into the street. It was dark, the lamp-posts stood in saucers of light and beyond them was the secret liveliness that goes on after you have looked and turned away. I made the most of being out. The air smelled of cold beasts, of snakes and toads. I didn't like it and knew I wasn't meant to.

There were no lights in her house. The other houses had orange windows aglow, hers was solid from cellar to attic: cupboards, firegrates, chimneys and taps all packed with dark. She was inside, wearing her hat and holding on to what I hoped was an atrocious secret. The plan was to catch her unawares, when she was not expecting me and I might surprise something which hadn't been removed — or someone who hadn't dodged out of sight.

There was no reply to my knock. Indeed, it sounded hopeless as a summons and spread itself rather than penetrated.

I tried a sharp rat-a-tat-tat which was swallowed by the noise of a train stamping out of the station.

I was about to peer through the letterbox when a bolt was drawn, the door opened a crack, and I looked into an eye, a yellow eye like a cat's, at the height a very big cat's — a monster cat's — eye might be. I felt a qualm in the pit of my stomach.

"What do you want?"

"To see Miss Velva."

"What for?"

"To get my music."

"What music?"

"Czerny's Studies and 'The Robin's Return'." I had seen that eye before. "I left them here this afternoon."

"She's gone to the pictures." The door opened a few more inches and I saw the other eye. "You'd better come in."

I questioned that statement. On the doorstep, with the house of darkness solid before me and the lights of human habitation at my back I wondered — better for what?

He stooped — his eyes had extra rings in them — and peered into my face. "Are you coming or aren't you?"

I went. He switched on one small bulb which leaked light into the hall and went before me along the passage. All I could see of him was the empty seat of his trousers. Either he had once been a much bigger man or they had been intended for somebody else. I couldn't see anything to be afraid of. But some things, I knew, did not have to be seen to be believed.

"Come on, come on."

I followed him into a part of the house where I had not been. I lifted my nose and sniffed. Smells have always meant a lot to me, and coming from him was an odour which was more of an air, it was so lively. When he opened a door at the end of the passage the odour romped out like the breath of an oven.

The room was intensely hot, he had just about everything in it for his needs and I suppose as much as he could get for his pleasure. It was so different from the bleak music room that I could hardly believe I was in the same house.

True, he had only a few bits of furniture — a table, a camp-bed and two baggy armchairs — but everywhere else there were newspapers, bottles, crockery, clothes, tools, wireless parts, food, and sawn-up railway sleepers. A fire — the first I had seen in that cold, still house — was literally roaring up the throat of the chimney.

He pulled me over the threshhold and kicked the door shut. "Now," turning his yellow ringed eyes on me, "let's look at you."

"You looked at me," I said boldly, "through the window, while I was having my lesson."

"Was that you? You look different. Are you alone or is someone waiting outside?"

"Why?"

"I don't want you fetched away now you're here to talk to me."

"I'm here to get my music."

"Take your coat off."

The sweat was beginning to gather in the backs of my knees, but I pushed my hands into my pockets and held my arms tight to my sides. He locked the door.

"Whose return was it?"

"The robin's."

"When you play it, it sounds like the elephant's." Grinning, he aimed the door-key into a sugar-bowl on the table. It fell on the floor.

I looked at him critically, not disposed to make allowances. I had been ready to be impressed, but now he disappointed me. I could not summon up real fear: all I saw was that his clothes no longer fitted and there was room for another man inside them. Long ago I had had a teddy-bear which leaked out of its skin. The head had yellow glass eyes like his.

"Are you Miss Velva's father?"

"What gave you that idea? We grew up together. She was three years old when I first saw her, no bigger than an organ grinder's monkey, and I was ten."

"Was she wearing her hat?"

"Hat? What hat? I used to carry her on my shoulder. She twisted my ears to make me go where she wanted."

I could see her doing that. "If you're not her father, what are you?"

"*What* am I?"

"You've got to be something."

"So I have. I see your point. Is it yours, though?"

"Are you her brother?"

"She's got no family. The mould broke when she was born."

"Are you the lodger?"

"Who wants to know? Your mother? The neighbours?"

"I want to know."

"I'm her biscuit. Full of weevil!"

"My father thinks she's holy."

"Is that what he thinks?" He kicked over a stack of wood and with deliberation chose a piece. "She's a fixer."

"Does she never take her hat off?"

"She fixed this house. She fixed the joyful noises." He weighed the piece of wood in his hand, holding it with a satisfaction I could not miss but could not identify. "Sit down, make yourself comfortable. Are you hot?"

"No, I'm cold." I hugged myself, tasting the salty sweat on my lip.

"I can't get warm either. You brought the cold in, you must have lowered the temperature a good ten degrees." He turned away to throw the wood into the molten heart of the fire. While his back was towards me I picked up the door-key and put it in my pocket. "I've never been warm since the Armistice. There's no marrow in my bones, just mud. Bring up a chair, we'll roast ourselves."

"I'd better get my music. Miss Velva won't like to find me here."

"Are you afraid of her? She used to be a gentle creature. When I raised my voice she'd tremble. Before the war that was." He thrust his hands into the flames. "Now she's sharp as a knife. She lays me open like an onion, enlightens my ignorance. Ignorance was the only thing that kept me going. I look into my onion and I don't see myself there. Just layers of this and that, and in the middle a weeshy-wee hole. Better not to know."

"She doesn't frighten me."

"Ignorance makes the world go round. She did me a big disservice." He looked at me over his shoulder. "I never should have known about that hole."

I wondered how much I should tell father, how much I should be able to tell him. There was a lot I could not put into words, not the lock, stock and barrel words he would accept.

"I got what I deserved. I killed the little soft creature, I starved her."

"Starved her? You mean you didn't give her any food?"

"I didn't give her any love."

I did not think that such deprivation. I was edging towards the door, the key ready in my hand. He had been crouching over the fire with his back to me, but he seemed to know what I intended because he whipped round and ran to the door. "We haven't had our talk."

"It was your talk, not mine."

"If she would fix me, we could stop the war." The fire roaring up the chimney cooked the smells of his past and present needs, his clothes, his food, his newspapers, his tarry wood. "It's the only way — she's got to fix me."

I said, "I want to go home."

He was between me and the door, gazing at me with a cunning which I found awful and squalid. "Then you'll be clean gone, won't you? You'll be all over and done with. If you can do it, why can't I? I believe if I was to come with you, if I was to walk out with you, I'd be over and done with too."

"You couldn't be." The last thing I wanted was to take him with me.

"Why not?"

"Because there'd be nobody here for you to be over to."

"I want to be clean gone. Like yesterday's dinner."

"You'll have to wait for Miss Velva to come back, then you can clean go any time." Something advised me to keep my hand in my pocket and not let him see I had the key.

"She'd like to herself," he said. "She flies to her piano and strums for hours, but that's only pushing it back. Do you wake up sometimes and find you've got into a vacuum, floating free, no ties, no troubles, nothing? Then the valve opens and it all rushes in and down you go with weights on your feet. You will when you're older, you'll wake up and be free. Just for a minute."

Sweltering, I drew my coat collar round my ears. "There's a terrible draught."

But he did not move from the door. "She never misses one of Norma Shearer's pictures. They were born the same day, the same year. They're twins, you see, and the spitting image of each other. Like as peas, her and Norma Shearer."

I was struck dumb. I couldn't even smile at the absurdity of it. I was ashamed, and alarmed. It was probably the first intimation I had that other people, besides my father, could fool themselves.

I went across to the mantelshelf and picked up a framed photograph. "Who's this?" I wanted to get him away from the door.

"When I was in the Army."

"What's that behind you?"

"The photographer's idea of a Bofors gun. Looks more like a rickshay."

"No, in the corner. I think it's a rabbit in the corner."

"More likely a rat." But he came over to look. "That's my shadow. I was in the Green Howards, a strapping great chap, with a shadow as thick as Army socks."

"Green? You're brown, everything's brown." Those old sepia photographs of men in uniform always raised a yawn in me. They didn't look as if they had ever been alive. I supposed that everything, air, sky, water, men, women, children must have been the same old brown. World War I was an old brown time to me.

"I was a good soldier, I was made up to Sergeant in 1917. Do you see my stripes? I put white paint on to make them stand out for the picture."

I looked back at the door which he had left unguarded. "I've got to go."

Concealing it in my hand, I drew the key from my pocket. He watched with a repressed excitement which I sensed had little to do with me.

"There's no guarantee that time always goes forwards, there's no law — I never heard of any — like the law of gravity. I'm cutting up my dinner with an ordinary dinner knife and I think of my bayonet, the thought of it slips into my mind, like you might think of a chicken when you're eating an egg."

"I wouldn't," I said. "It would make me feel sick."

"Or I think of my Army mess-tin. If I had a pound note for every meal I've had out of that old tin I'd be a rich man. But I've turned my back on all that. It's twelve years since the Armistice — out of sight, out of mind — if time goes forwards. If it does — " he said, widening his eyes so that I saw scarlet threads among the yellow — "why is my bayonet and my mess-tin at the head of the queue to get back in? And then there's my boots. When I'm putting on my rubbers they turn into Army fieldboots, hard as iron and covered in mud." It wouldn't be easy to get the key in the lock without his seeing. He was still over by the fireplace with the photograph in his hand, but if he made up his mind to stop me, he could. "I didn't think about it while it was going on. My C.O. said if every soldier in the British Army was like me, the war would have been over in a month. An order was sacred, I jumped to an order, never asked was it right or wrong."

Although he had not taken his eyes off me I was beginning to think he was not seeing me. I tested by making a face at him, several faces, each one different so that he wouldn't think it was just a twitch. Finally I put out my tongue.

"I had the time of my life. I had everything. I didn't have to enjoy it all, but I had it. You know what I mean? I was good at

37

forgetting what I didn't want to remember. I was a young man, and Christ, I could choose!"

I put the key in the lock. He went on talking. "You can't get away unscathed —" For a moment I thought he meant me. "If you weren't scathed at the time, you will be afterwards. You'll get your scathe."

He made no attempt to stop me as I unlocked the door. I was beginning to understand that when he said 'you' he meant himself. He wasn't thinking about me, there was no point in reminding him that it hadn't been my war.

"I can't choose now. I'm obliged to remember everything now. It takes some remembering!"

"Don't tell Miss Velva I left my music," I said. "She thinks I don't practise enough anyway."

"There's no rhyme or reason about the way things come back, no order. It's not first to last, it's not even one turn each. Some things I remember over and over again. Like the feather, a little white breast feather."

I stood outside the door, looking back at him. It struck me that there was no way to describe him, except to say that he was old.

"It was shaped like a boat. I was sitting in a shell hole and it came floating past. The breeze carried it towards the wire. A Cameronian was spread out on the wire, dead as a doornail. The feather touched his shoulder, just touched him and floated on again. But that touch turned him right over. He hung upside down. Three days and nights he hung there with his kilt round his neck, showing his Sunday face, till a shell blew him to smithereens. It must have been a heavy feather."

I made up my mind then and there that if I came across my old teddy-bear's head I should pull out its yellow glass eyes.

## III

She wished it had been done with more style. Coming as it did, while she was at the stove, tilting the pan to melt the fat, it could have been fried egg he was asking for.

"What about it then?"

She was human and she was being asked for all she humanly had to give. Hands clasped under his neck, his chair tipped, knees jammed against the table, Sol was watching her through his glasses. She had told him the glasses put years on him and he said he wore them to read the back pages. "What do you wear to read the front then?' she had asked. He didn't read the front, he said, only the football and racing results.

"What about what?"

"Shall we, Mrs Jenkin?"

Her heart jumped in her chest as promptly as if it had been waiting for the words — get ready, get set, go. "Are you trying to make a fool of me?"

One day the width of his grin was going to split the frame of the glasses. "I'm old-fashioned, and you're a married woman."

"Not any more."

"Until someone puts you asunder."

"He'd never divorce me."

"Then it's up to you, isn't it?"

She nodded because it always had been up to her. Peter just used to stand and sniff his hands and wait for her to tell him what to do.

Sol unhooked himself from the chair. She had the pan still in her hand as he gave her the first instalment, a kiss that caused her blood to sing louder than the gas jet.

He drew his hands down her hips and thinking he was about to start the second instalment, she said, "There isn't time." He smiled and suddenly she felt like a parcel in his hands. "We've waited so long," she said furiously, "we can wait a bit longer."

"I haven't been waiting, I've been getting on with it." She

tried to push him away but he rubbed her nose ungently with his. "Haven't you?"

"What if I have?"

"If you have, then it's jam yesterday, jam tomorrow and I shall give you jam today."

"Jam? You flatter yourself."

"Nothing lasts forever." He let her go. She leaned against the stove and was mortified at her weakness. He said soberly, "I want you to know that at the outset."

"Did I say anything about forever?"

"I don't want you thinking I'm a steady number."

"Perhaps I'm thinking better of it!"

He put the glasses in his breast pocket. She was always struck by the difference they made, his big spreading features were gathered and alerted behind those little steel rings.

"I'll be back about eight." He kissed her again and she didn't try to stop him: she reasoned it would serve him right to go away thinking he had won, and then find that he hadn't.

He went out of the house in his shirt sleeves, his jacket over his shoulder. He was always warm, she could go into a room and know he had been there and just gone. He left the air warmed. On winter mornings he breathed white smoke. Once she watched him take a handful of snow from the railings and rub it over his face. The snow melted and he smiled at her through a blur of water.

She went to the window. She always did, because she liked to see him go, because of the way he went. There was something about it, about his walking round the lorry, kicking the tyres, rattling the tailboard, swinging into the cab. Like a gorilla swinging into a tree! She smiled at her scorn: of course that was it — he was a free animal, there was freedom in everything he did.

He waved from the cab, not turning to look, taking for granted she would be there, not to take it to heart if she wasn't.

She thought she was damned if she would, then! His talk about not being a steady number showed he thought she was trying to pin him down. Forever, indeed! What had she done to deserve that?

She knew what she had done. He had said 'Hup!' and she had jumped into his arms like a little dog, a little bitch, all four feet off the ground. The idea made her laugh. She had a short-lived temper, people didn't take her seriously, they thought they could get away with anything. *He* thought he could get away with everything. She threw in the bacon and shook it round the pan.

Philly's head appeared round the jamb of the door, half-way up. He always stopped before he came in — to look through the keyhole she had told him, but he said how could he when the key was in it.

"You can come in, he's gone." Philly stepped from behind the door. He was wearing spongebag trousers and what appeared to be a pyjama jacket with a bow tie and a wine-coloured blazer. She watched him skip across to the table. "Are you afraid he'll eat you?"

"He overwhelms me. My poor little flame's put out by all that electro-magnetism." Her dressing-gown had gapped open to the waist, and following his gaze she saw that her pair were aimed straight at him. "It's allright dear, the sun does put the candle out."

"I don't mind you looking," she said, "It's the way you look, as if they were two pounds of sugar."

"Another man's sweetness."

"Don't be a fool." She pinned her dressing-gown across. "What's it to be? Bacon and egg?"

"Toast and a cup of your delicious stewed tea."

"The tea's fresh, I made it for Mr. Spreckley."

"Fifteen, twenty minutes ago? An informed guess based on the state of his plate — congealed egg and curded fat. It brings the farmyard right to my nose-hairs."

"If you feel like that why don't you have your breakfast upstairs?"

"I should miss our tête-à-têtes." He pushed aside the greasy plates and propped his elbows in the space. "The point I wish to make is that one of the disadvantages of tea, one of the several disadvantages, is that it remains potable for a bare three minutes after infusion. After that it becomes a dye. Your pretty pink stomach lining must be dyed dark brown, Queenie."

"Nobody sees my stomach lining."

"Don't you want to be pretty right through? For him?"

"For who?"

"Ah, Queenie, you know you can take your choice of us — a new one every day."

"I'm not a tart."

"In one sense no, in the other sense yes, and very delectable too. What I mean is that the men will stand up and be counted for a girl like you."

"If I thought you meant anything else I'd throw you out."

"To become a wanderer on the face of the earth."

"You'd wander as far as the first bar."

"This is my home, the only one I've ever known. All I ever had was somewhere to flop but no-one gave a damn whether I got up again." His ratchet nose softened. "Until I came to live here with you there was no place I could be myself, take my girdle off, so to speak. You know how it is when you get into your very own place and shut the door? Home is where the heart is – Queenie, you don't have to accept my heart, just let it lie around."

His smoke-screwed eyes were wet. She laughed, not knowing what to make of him. She made something different every time: a Brain, a Charley, a devil, a lost soul. But she had never been able to talk to anyone as she could to him. Often they sat in the kitchen half the morning, talking, and she did not recognise her own mind, certainly she did not know where some of her thoughts came from. They were subconscious thoughts Philly said. He knew a lot about her but she had noticed that for all his talk she had learned very little about him.

"You should find yourself a girl friend."

"I had one once. We loved each other. We used to meet in the park. She didn't hide her feelings. It was wonderful, she'd run to me, her arms outstretched, her face all lit up, and I'd catch her and hold her and spin round and round till we fell down on the grass together. Then she'd kiss me, butterfly kisses, all over my face."

"Well!" said Queenie. "What happened next?"

Philly lowered his eyes. "We used to sit in the rose-arbour and I fed her with peardrops."

"Peardrops!"

"Those nice boiled sweets with sugar outside. First a red one, then a yellow. She was very fond of them. Sometimes we just sat and whispered to one another, sometimes we walked round the park pushing the pram. We made rather a pretty picture."

"Pram? Was she a nursemaid?"

"She was eight years old. It was her doll's pram."

Queenie threw a piece of toast at him. He caught it, pierced it with the point of his knife and inserted jam into the slit. "The bread's rather thick, dear."

"You're not getting any younger. You should seriously think about setting yourself up with someone half your age."

"I'd rather it was someone a quarter my age." He nibbled wistfully at a corner of toast. "I can't afford it. Young people are so mercenary. One has to spend money on them, show them what they call a good time. They won't do it for love."

"Do what?"

"Ah Queenie, don't tease. I don't expect a grand passion, just a little kindness, a little sweetness, a bright face bringing my Ovaltine."

"Why don't you get a job?"

"My job is keeping body and soul together. I have to work at that, it doesn't come naturally as it does to you."

"I believe in being natural." She yawned and stretched herself. "I don't know how to be anything else."

"That's the perfect synthesis of matter and mind, never to feel torn between the loaf and the lily."

"If I did know, I'd be something else."

"Queenie, you choose the loaf every time. There's no question, no shadow of doubt in your mind." He propped his chin on his hands and gazed at her. "You've chosen Spreckley, haven't you?"

"If he's the loaf, are you the lily, Philly?" He laughed with her. She always warmed to people who could take a joke against themselves. It was a rough and ready rule, but she felt they could be trusted. Sometimes she thought Philly was the best of the bunch — the two-fisted bouquet — of men she had known.

"Keep your lily. I'll take a slice of Sol Spreckley."

"You're not expecting the whole loaf?"

"I don't want it."

"Such sturdy independence. If only I had a little of it, but I'm so tied up with everybody's troubles. I hear people crying for help. People walk past me in the street with their mouths shut, biting their tongues, or people miles away are crying out for a friend. I'm on a private wave that picks up vibrations from their hearts. It's worse at night when I'm trying to sleep."

"I'm the same. I can't eat if I see pictures of starving children. If you were to pin the pictures up in front of me I'd have to starve too. I could die of those Indian famines."

"That's not empathy, that's your woman's heart. I feel their torment but that doesn't help a single soul. I can't take over one little disappointment, shed one single tear for someone else. No one's going to be let off a grief because I'm suffering too. All I'm doing is making a carbon copy. What sort of vocation's that?"

"You should have been a parson."

"I know I talk too much." He lit a cigarette, swallowed the first smoke and passed it to her. "Not like you, a still unravished bride of quietness."

"Me a bride?"

"You were once, and there's never been duress, has there?"

"You mind your business and I'll mind mine."

"Oh you do! If only I had your acumen. I'm too diversified for material success. If I tried to run this house — "

"Hotel."

"This home of the hearts — mine's not the only one, you know — this private world, this blessed spot — I couldn't. I wouldn't even know how to keep the books."

"What books?"

"You don't mean to say you do the sums in your head? Those complicated long divisions? Those vulgar fractions? It isn't fair that a woman so substantially endowed should have invisible assets as well."

Ash from the cigarette fell into the folds of her dressing-gown. She opened the front and flicked the ash off her breasts. Philly averted his eyes. "It's all very well for you," she said, "you don't have the worry of it."

"You have this beautiful private house, let at realistic rents to gentlemen who go about their business all day and require no service, no meals, use no gas, electricity or water, inflict no wear and tear. You're bound to make a profit."

"You think so?"

"You should listen to me. I warned you about that Chinese, I told you he'd skip without paying. Their religion forbids it, you see. Confucius taught that a man cannot owe anything to a woman, not even if she's his mother. She is in *his* debt. Pregnancy is a mark of privilege."

She lay back, lifting her legs in a gust of laughter.

"Your toes are like the pipes of Pan," he said, "your instep is like Eros's bow. Such classical feet should be washed in asses' milk."

"And where would I get that?"

"You could try the tap."

"There's only water in the tap."

"You could try it. And some soap."

"You've got a nerve." She reached out with her bare toes and hooked them over his knee. "Privilege!"

He jumped up. "I've got to see a man about a horse," and ran from the room. He couldn't bear to be touched. Any time she wanted to stop him she only had to lay a finger on him. She laughed at the thought. It was such a queer thing — marvellous really — but if she were to hold Philly in her arms it would be the death of him. But it was going to be the making of Sol, and of her.

She stubbed her cigarette into Philly's crusts and went upstairs to look at her bed. It was a double bed, she had meant to let the room as a double, but no loving couple had come as boarders. She splashed the sheet with eau-de-cologne. The quilt was stained with ironmould and she looked for something to put over it. Sol wouldn't notice, but she couldn't be sure that those marks wouldn't remind her ever after when she got into bed alone. She tried the sheepskin rug from the floor but it looked as if a sheep was on the bed.

She examined herself in the mirror. She could not see what other people saw because although she might forget who she was looking at, it would always be herself who was looking. Was her nose too big? It could be said it was too small. She would have liked it longer and thinner, but that might not suit her face which was short and wide. Philly said she had a face like a rose, 'the old-fashioned cottage rose, not one of the florist's variety, all whorled like a whelk shell'. She should do something about her hair. Like washing it. With its natural grease it was the colour of brass: without, it was the colour of straw and straw was definitely wrong for her face. Newly-washed hair made her look older.

If she was honest with herself — Why should she be, who was listening, where had honesty ever got her? Which was preferable, to be lost or to be trapped? Was there another choice? Was there even that choice? She put her arms around her shoulders and cuddled herself. Honesty had got her as far as Sol Spreckley.

\* \* \*

She firmly believed that she always knew what was going to happen. She remembered waiting, she could even remember working out when it was likely to happen – when *from*, because of course for a long time it couldn't. She believed she had said to herself one day, 'It could be any time now.' At night, sometimes, didn't she say to herself, but not in words, 'It wasn't today then'? And as she went to answer the door, didn't she think, 'It's now'? She thought that she suddenly felt cold and it was the same old creeping, laying, cold.

She opened the door and looked. There was really no need to confirm that it was happening, the knowledge had already opened up inside her. But there was need of another kind, and she couldn't get to the door fast enough.

"Yes?" she said. She had never spoken a truer word. She thought with furious amazement, and could hardly believe her belief in it, of the space she had put between them, thinking - as she must have done – that that would be all she needed to do. And all those years, all the time, there was something that couldn't be got through or to the bottom of, that had been between them since they were born. She almost cried out No! it must have been since *he* was born. For with another man, with any other man, it would have been different.

"Who are you?" she said, to get it started, like a game – or a fight. Perhaps she should have said, 'Who am I?' The girl's lips moved. They were mauvish, with cold probably. She had a thin skin. Like his. Her long hair blew about in the wind and when it whipped across her face she made no move to put it aside. "You'll drown in all that hair."

Queenie felt she was drowning too, and would have welcomed it as an end, the only available end, to a moment which had begun years ago.

She held the door wider. The girl hesitated, her eyes shining through the strands of her hair. Shining with what? What was she thinking? What had she been thinking of all this long moment? What did she expect? In coming, what had she decided?

Queenie shivered. Yes, it was the same old cold that crept into her bones and lay on her heart.

She had some idea that whatever had to be done, the doing could be kept from the rest of the house, and took the girl into her private sitting-room. She was in the habit of leaving things there which she had stopped using, and she never sat in it, but the girl was entitled to courtesy. For all the girl knew, courtesy was all she would get.

Queenie, who wanted not to look at her again, was obliged to look instead at a broken chair, a cracked washbowl, a bundle of soiled curtains and some Christmas paper chains. Well, I didn't see them before, she thought, they didn't matter before. From now on everything will matter. God, I can't live like that!

"What's this?"

They were the girl's first words. All the others that had gone before were lost to Queenie. These were the first she had heard her speak and she marvelled, she could not help it. At the same time she mocked herself. You think you put the tongue in her head? You thought it was your doing entirely that she had ten fingers and ten toes. The first time you saw her you thought you were God.

"It's a drum," the girl told herself. She did not seem to expect any other answer. "The taps should be screwed tight, it's bad for the skin otherwise."

Five minutes after feeling like God, didn't she think, anyone can do it? Yes, already, at the rate babies are born, hundreds of women — black, brown, yellow — have done it since me. Didn't she get a needle in her arm for saying so?

"It's a musical instrument," said the girl. "It ought to be treated with respect."

Queenie looked at the girl's feet. They had been perfect, she had made sure, unwrapping the child and counting the toes as soon as she was alone with it. She had a horror of deformity and of course she didn't expect anything of his to be right.

She was reassured to see that the girl wore sensible, round-toed strap slippers. But the welts were coming away from the stitching.

"I'd play it, I'd walk in front of the band throwing up my drum-sticks and spinning them on my finger."

"You can have it."

"Oh no," the girl said quickly.

"I don't want it. Someone left it here."

"They might come back."

Queenie almost said, "Owing six weeks' rent?"

"Are those yours?" Queenie's flesh-coloured corsets lay under a chair. "Pink shoes?"

"They're not shoes, they're stays."
"They've got laces."
"Stays have laces."

Had she never seen a woman undress? That's my fault, thought Queenie, that's something she's missed, one little thing. What else had she missed? Wouldn't it be quicker to count what she had had?

Asked what she wished to call the child, nothing would come to mind except the title of a book. She had had a bad time, so had the child, and she knew that neither of them was expected to last much longer. 'Folly,' she had said, and the nurse, putting her ear down, said brightly, 'Polly? That's a nice name, dear.' 'Almayer's Folly'. She could not remember what Almayer's folly had been, but for a woman there was only one.

She said to the girl, "Who sent you?"

"No one."

The girl stooped to look at a Bateman cartoon – 'The Guardsman Who Dropped It' – which had itself come off its hook. Philly had brought it home, he said it illustrated the human dilemma. 'In the picture the two basic elements are conformity and death. That covers our lot.' 'Death?' 'They're soldiers, dressed to kill.' 'That's morbid,' she had said, 'I'm not hanging up anything morbid.'

"We have a picture of King Solomon splitting the baby."

Queenie did not know whether to laugh or cry. She should cry, remembering the picture over the sideboard of a man with a towel round his head holding up a naked baby by its foot, wondering, she had always said, whether to chop from the top or the bottom.

"Who gave you the idea of coming?"

"It was my idea."

"If your father doesn't know where you are he'll be worried about you."

Almayer stooped to pick up a bead from the floor and laid it on her palm. "He doesn't mind."

"Why do you say that?" Give one good reason – Oh no, she cried silently, don't. I can't talk to you as a child or as a person. Only as a conscience. Your long hair and those thin legs, and God knows what else, make me a conscience.

"I can go where I like. He doesn't stop me."

Had he tried? Would it occur to him that there were things a young girl should not do? Would it occur to him that there were things which should not be done to her?

Almayer raised her eyes. "I found this address in his waistcoat pocket."

Imperceptibly it was a question. *The* question. She must have asked herself — how many times? — and now she had come for the answer.

"Would you like some tea?" Almayer nodded and Queenie realised that she would have to go to the kitchen to make it. Should she leave Almayer alone? She would certainly turn the room over, and there was no knowing what she might find. "You'd better come into the kitchen."

Queenie knew that she would regret it. The kitchen would not be a place where Almayer had not been. From now on, she would see and feel and taste Almayer there. Her presence would go on working on every cup, every crumb, Queenie would never find anything in the kitchen as she had left it.

Almayer was concentrating on the bead in her palm. She was stiff with discomfort. The big bones were very noticeable at the base of her bent neck. "Are you happy?" It slipped out — after twelve years was it, or thirteen? She didn't even know how old the child was.

"Do you mean now?" There was bravado in the question and in the wide eyes she raised to Queenie's face.

Queenie turned away. She almost ran, blundering into the kitchen like an animal going to ground. There was no sanctuary, the kitchen was as unready as she was, breakfast plates still on the table, crusts and cigarette butts, the curlers out of her hair, the tap whistling into the sink, white fat in the frying-pan, and the smell of Philly's hair cream.

She filled the kettle, noticing the potatoes in the sink and requiring an effort of memory to recall that she had been going to peel them. Every old mucky thing was as new as if she was seeing it for the first time. Seeing and suffering it: she might look through Almayer's eyes, but the muck was hers to suffer. Was this what their relationship did to her? Was she now where nature intended, under Almayer's skin?

With no effort she remembered Sol. He smacked back into her thoughts as if to punish her for being kept out so long.

"Nobody can be happy all the time." Almayer had followed

her. She spoke crisply, secure in words said to her — at what moment of disappointment or despair? — and which she now found a use for. "You'd look silly, wouldn't you, keeping on laughing and singing."

"You don't have to keep on."

She told a lie: with Peter she had to keep on. With him she had had to crack her face or welter in tears. She remembered him saying, 'I thought you were happy,' whispering, as if he was talking about sex.

"If you mean this minute, I'm not," said Almayer. "I expected to be happy, but I find I'm just the same."

"The same?"

"The same as if I hadn't come."

When her case was packed and her hat was on her head, 'I'm not taking the baby,' she had said, and she was ready to cry, 'Keep her, she's yours!' if he so much as opened his mouth. She understood that if she took the baby she would not be going anywhere. With the baby she could not get away from him. She understood that if she stayed she would die privately, in her shoes, and continue to walk about, all there as far as could be seen. What more would be wanted? He, certainly, would never miss what he had never had, he did not know how to have it, God help him. She had perfectly understood that God would not help them if they stayed together.

Queenie turned her back on Sol's potatoes. They were his, whether she peeled them or not, whether he ate them or not. Even a potato can be lucky. As for her, she was being given something to get on with for the rest of her life.

She took down the black and gold cups which Philly had got with cigarette coupons. She hadn't used them before and she wouldn't use them afterwards, because each time she took down those cups she would have to live this moment over again.

When she offered biscuits Almayer shook her head. "I don't like gristy things."

"Gristy?"

"They're coconut."

"I haven't any others." There was no cake, no buns, no potted meat, she had left it too late to go to the shops. She stood like a fool and the plate in her hand began to shake and the biscuits fell to the floor.

Almayer picked them up. "It doesn't matter. I'm not hungry."

"I could boil you an egg."

"No, thank you."

"I'll make a banana sandwich. Do you like banana?"

"You don't know anything about me." It seemed to strike Almayer as funny. Queenie had believed that the less she knew, the better. For her, of course. Could she tell Almayer that? "You don't even know when my birthday is."

"Yes I do. I do know that."

"You don't send me birthday cards."

Queenie had not asked what he was telling the child, knowing that once she knew, she would start thinking for her, making up a world for her and, very likely, highly likely, living in it for her. She had preferred to think she was as good as dead to Almayer. Surely it was better to be dead to Almayer than dead to herself? That was the principle, and she was holding on to it.

"Or birthday presents. Or Christmas presents."

"Is he good to you?" She had no right to ask, let alone care. If she was going to ask, and care, she had thrown out her principle. They looked at each other, Almayer with calculation. Queenie could see her putting two and two together and not being able to make the sum come out. That was something Queenie had to see, something she had coming to her.

"He's going to marry my music-teacher."

"You're learning music?"

"I came to tell you he's getting married."

"I used to play the piano. But not properly, I never had any lessons."

"You ought to know. He's madly in love with her."

Queenie, mashing banana for Almayer and finding pleasure in the task, thought bitterly, what happened to all the tasks, over all the years?

"He's burning up for her."

Queenie put down the fork. It was no time to laugh, but laugh she did. She didn't want to, she didn't enjoy it. She couldn't help it. She relayed that laughter like a gramophone horn, knowing full well that she was doing herself an injury. The more she laughed the more harm she did. She wouldn't have thought that there could be any left to do.

Almayer's face sharpened. The bones glittered. She thrust back her hair, shaking it off her shoulders as if it were something vile, and at once ducked her head so that her hair all fell forward again. With a kind of violence she smoothed her skirt and straightened her suspenders.

Queenie, too, felt a rush of anger seeing the child pick up after herself like that. She had the trick from her father. If he could not run away, he would stand and pull down his jacket and grope through his pockets and pat the seat of his trousers. No-one should be so defenceless.

"So he's getting married." Why not? She wasn't the only fool — or perhaps she was, perhaps she was the only one with the sort of foolishness to make such hell of their wrong mix. "Then," she said, "you'll have a stepmother."

Almayer's face was invisible behind her hair. She had that advantage, she could hide behind her long hair. "She's very beautiful, really terribly beautiful. She looks just like Norma Shearer — well, they're related." Almayer lifted her head, composedly, and with a flourish, she put back her hair and looked at Queenie. "As a matter of fact, Norma Shearer and her are twins."

Queenie's nose prickled, she felt like putting her face down in her arms for a good cry. "Here's your sandwich."

Almayer said bleakly, "I always have the banana sliced."

"I'll do you another."

"I don't want a stepmother."

"Why not? Won't it be better than no mother at all?" The question was about to be asked, perhaps it was already being asked. Almayer, she noticed, did not bother much with answers. Perhaps she thought that Queenie's laughter was the only answer she would get. How to let her know, to make her understand, that asking was all she had to do, that there could be no refusal? "I wasn't laughing at you, you mustn't think that."

Philly put his head round the door and made a coaxing sound with his lips. He was nearly the last person she wanted to see: the only other with as little business there, whose presence could destroy her completely, was Sol.

"Go away, Philly!"

"I'm not intruding, am I?"

"Yes."

"Oh, my dear, I've had such wretched luck." He edged round

the door, stood woebegone before them. "Don't send me comfortless away."

"Go and have a bath or something."

"Solace for sore minds? You're thinking of sleep and it would take the big one to knit up my ravelled sleeve. I don't need ablutions, and as for the something, why that's here with you. Where else would it be?" From his pocket he took a red rose. "I brought you this, there should have been three dozen, but I could afford only one. Every other penny went on a little brown creature who betrayed me at Epsom."

Almayer was gazing at him, and he at her with an eager, devouring shyness. "It helps to talk. A trouble shared is a trouble halved."

"You still owe me five pounds."

"Ah Queenie, Queenie, there's no strength in being without a heart. I call it congenital weakness – "

"Call it what you like, I've got to pay the bills."

Philly said to Almayer, "The tortoise has a shell to protect his soft parts but is, nevertheless, all tortoise. Queenie has a ring of hard words. It's a defence mechanism. Soft parts and hard words, she is all woman."

"Her name's not Queenie."

"To me she is a queen." He squatted on his heels and looked into Almayer's face. "And you, little princess, what are you called?"

Queenie wondered if he knew. She didn't care, his malice couldn't change anything.

"Almayer? That's very pretty. You must be careful who you marry."

"I shan't marry."

"Why not?"

"Of course you will!" Queenie heard herself crying, "You mustn't think that everyone!" Could she stop her from thinking, or seeing, and believing? How could she stop her from anything? In desperation she appealed to Philly, "She's got her life to live, it won't be like anyone else's. It will all be different for her, it isn't bred in the bone – "

"Names do matter," said Philly. "Who'd want to see Greta Gustaffson when he could have Garbo? Or ask for a plate of buccinum undatum when he wants whelks?"

"If you think that —" Queenie made it her business to laugh — "if you think that children have to follow in their parents' footsteps, we may as well all give up."

"Names should make music together," Philly said to Almayer. "I take it yours do?"

"My name is Almayer Jenkin."

"It has a certain sound." He did not flicker an eyelid. "It will do to be going on with. Mine's Phillip Ingram. I don't think we've met."

"I haven't been here before." Her gaze, narrowing, went to Queenie. "Nobody asked me to come. It was my idea."

"What is more natural than to wish to be with someone you love? Never apologise for loving, it's a faculty, an art, and a form of genius. Few people can do it.

"Can you?"

"Oh, I'm capable of it. But unless one loves oneself—and a lot of people find that the most satisfactory arrangement—there are two sides to it. One must be able to love, and one must be allowed to love. And the older one gets, the harder it is to place one's love securely and allowably. Of course it's all right for you—" on his heels before her, he smiled and took her hands— "you have your parents. And one day—" as if he were coming to the end of a fairy-tale— "you'll have children of your own to love."

"No."

"No?"

"I shan't have children."

"Of course. You have said you don't intend to marry. What do you intend to do? Let's talk about you."

"You can't, you don't know me."

"I know Queenie."

Almayer's expression became wooden, she closed and tidied her lips as if she had spoken her last word.

Queenie could say that she hadn't changed, was still the woman who ran away, the same woman in the same panic. She ought to tell them that she would do it again, for they had the right to judge her. Everyone had the right to judge her. Almayer only had to say 'Come back', and she would go. Not for love: for something as independent of that as a gas-pipe of gas. Peter had wished her a streak of happiness. It was what he wished for himself because he thought it safe to ask. If he asked for more, he ran the risk of not getting it. He dared not think she might do better.

What kind of woman was she who could not love her own flesh and blood? But the flesh was not hers, it was his — she could see him sprouting out of the girl's movements, the way she held herself.

"Why are you wearing pyjamas?" Almayer said to Philly.

"Pyjamas are so cosy, why shouldn't I be cosy by day as well as by night?"

Almayer pulled her hands from his and thrust them behind her back. "Are you her lover?"

It was coolly spoken, as grown-up as you please: but it did not please, it pained. Queenie dropped into a chair. The best place for her, she felt, would be under the table, out of sight, and with a chance of dropping out of the child's mind.

"What gave you that idea?" said Philly.

"People run away to join their lovers."

"Queenie hasn't run away, she's been here all the time." Philly said sadly, "If you think that of us, we shall know what to think of you."

"I don't care." She held up her head, she had her father's useless courage. "And I don't think, I asked."

"Let's say you entertain the possibility."

"Are you?"

The answer to that had ceased to matter, if it ever did. The other question was answered already. All that mattered, Queenie thought confusedly, was that it should get asked.

"Queenie's lover?" Philly smiled. "I live here. So does Mr Solomon Spreckley and Mr George Kinsale and Mr Arthur West, and Joe Riceyman, and what I call the birds of passage, the cocks who roost for a few days or nights, whichever suits their line of business, and then move on. We all live here."

Something seemed to bother Almayer subliminally, like a hovering fly. She drew down her brows, then pushed them up in an effort to be free of it. She shook her head and threw back her hair. But the fly settled. "I must go. My father will wonder where I am."

"His little princess."

So she wasn't going to speak the words. They had been on her lips and Queenie had seen them — short certainly, sweet if she liked. She might have settled for a grain of sweetness and made it last the rest of her days. Or gone back to them without saving grace, in bitterness and despair. It would not have been to her credit: sweet or sour would not matter a jot. She knew—didn't she just!— what it was like to live alongside, not *with*.

The words had been bitten up and swallowed: wild horses wouldn't get Almayer to say 'Will you come back?' now. Queenie challenged her, she could do no less, it was not bravado. "Why did you come?"

"To see what you looked like."

"What does she look like?" said Philly.

"For God's sake!" cried Queenie.

"Shall you say she's beautiful?"

"I shan't say." Almayer stared hard at Queenie and Queenie watched the useless courage become a private and serviceable armament. "Goodbye, thank you for the banana sandwich. My father and I have condensed milk in it."

## IV

Passing the fountain in the Grand Avenue, Peter recalled his struggle that same morning with Mrs Frossey's ballcock. As he lay face down on the boards above the tank, a candle in his cap, his wallet had ridden up over his left breast and dropped into the water. He had been obliged to fish for it, and afterwards Mrs Frossey had dried his two pound notes over her gas-ring.

"What's this?" said the official at the turnstile. "Just made it?" He held up Peter's damp note and pretended to wring it.

"You can tell if it's genuine by the watermark," said someone.

"It's watermarked all over."

Peter, halfway through the turnstile, remembered his manners and turned back to let Miss Velva go first. The turnstile struck him cruelly in a personal place and the official shouted to him to make up his mind. Unable to comfort his pain by even a swift touch, he waited for her. By a delicate movement of her hips she avoided contact with the machinery as she came through.

He had been getting short of memories. While he was plastering a wall she might rise before him in her great hat, and once, as he clung to a chimney-stack. But she had eluded him when he was sitting alone and ready to think. All he could summon then was dismay at the strength of his feeling. He had hoped to have something to remember of this afternoon, but not the pain between his legs and the coldness of his damp wallet on his heart.

They entered the Palace to the sound of music: a stately band was playing one of the old tunes. She wore a mulberry-coloured coat with a fur collar although it was such a warm day that people were out in their summer clothes. He had noticed that she liked fur at her neck. He suggested they sit down and listen to the music.

"Those great coarse instruments?"

"It's the Metropolitan Tramways Band."

"Do you class Souza with Chopin and Mozart?"

"It's all music to me."

"Fortunate man to be so easily pleased." She paused before a marble group of men and boys fighting with a serpent. "Personally, I do not think so."

"I have my likes and dislikes. And I've got standards."

"I do not think you are fortunate. If it is all music to you, then none of it is music."

She stroked the coils of the serpent. The blow had made him painfully aware of himself, and the statues vexed him, for each had a little leaf between its straining thighs. How could men fighting for their lives and being slowly crushed to death keep on those absurd leaves which he estimated — though he himself was not extreme in that respect — were not big enough to hide anything?

Miss Velva pulled up her coat collar. "The light is so strong!" She went and sat on a bench under a tree. "I shall shelter here."

He had not known where to take her, it was so long since he had taken a woman anywhere. Remembering the shadowiness of her house and her spreading hats, he thought perhaps he should not have brought her to the Crystal Palace.

"This tree comes from equatorial Africa. I suppose it feels the cold." He touched the trunk which was lagged with strips of linen like an outside pipe. "There are so many sparrows here that they brought in sparrowhawks to keep them down. You wouldn't believe the damage the little beggars do. They will keep picking at the putty." He ventured to sit beside her. By pressing his knees together he managed almost to forget his pain. One day he would take off her hat, it would be like taking off another woman's dress. There was no other woman. "Left to themselves sparrows could bring this place down. They only have to make a few holes and the wind gets underneath and blows out the glass like piecrust."

"Why have we come here?"

"I thought it would be a change of air. It's high up and clean — there's a lot of sulphur in the atmosphere round the railway."

"Kind of you to think of it."

"There's a million and a half square feet of glass in the Crystal Palace. And more putty than I shall see in my lifetime."

"How is it that such a kind man is alone?"

"Are you alone?" He had intended to ask her later, when the answer could not spoil the day.

"I'm not kind."

"Almayer says there's someone living with you. A man." He could not hide his dismay.

"You believe her?"

"I'd rather she was a thief than a liar."

"Must she be either?"

"You can give back what you steal but you can't give back the truth. There's a time for it, and when the time's gone, the truth's gone."

"Do you know what the truth is, Mr Morcom?"

"Morcom's the man you're living with."

"I'm not living with any man. I am free as a bird." She pointed her toe at a sparrow pecking in the dust. "You see, you do not know what truth is."

A dwarf passed them. He was scarcely three feet tall and carried himself with dignity from the waist up: his bowed legs paddled in and out like a baby's. A little girl was following him, enthralled. He turned to her and shook his fist. When he paddled away into the tropical ferns she ran after him.

"Being different isn't easy." The afternoon sun turned to gold a pennyworth of flesh visible through the hole at the wrist of her glove. "As that poor creature knows."

Peter was puzzled, always having believed that being different was a superior and supreme condition.

And then she said, "What's the difference between me and your wife?"

He looked at the keyhole in her glove, unable to postpone his longing to put in his finger and find the softness of her palm. "I don't want to talk about her."

"I want you to." She moved along the bench towards him, her knees were little pinnacles under the soft stuff of her dress. "You should have beaten her."

"She was young, she didn't know what she wanted."

"I have always known." With her gloved fingers she struck his knee a light, skimming blow. From another woman it could have been interpreted as a flirtatious gesture. But it left him without any means of response.

"She was always laughing. When the baby was born, she had a bad time, but as soon as she could speak, she looked up and said, 'I thought I'd died and you were there repairing the Pearly Gates and of course they wouldn't open and I couldn't get through.'"

"She laughed at you?"

"She laughed at everything."

"You would not say she was like me, this Mrs Morcom?"

"You'd better ask Mr Morcom. I don't want his name, I don't want his wife, and I don't want him telling my daughter lies."

"Lies?"

"About you."

She stood up and said coldly that they must return.

"But we've only just come — "

"It isn't crystal, it's very dirty glass."

\*        \*        \*

She insisted on riding on top of the tram, bolt upright in the front seat, holding on to her hat, the fur on her coat all chopped in the draught. He did not know what it was she was enjoying.

"Why won't you tell me who he is?" A high reedy note accompanied the twittering of the trolley wires as they ran down Norwood Hill, and he was afraid she might be singing. "If you don't want me to know, why talk about him? Why keep bringing him into the conversation? It's Morcom, Morcom, Morcom — is his the only name in the world?"

He had to shout above the rush of the wind. It was doubtful if she heard, she was leaning over the rail like a figurehead on the prow of a ship. "If he's the only man in the world why don't you bring him out and use him?"

The tram reached the end of the gradient, on level ground the noise of their passage diminished. She *was* singing. "I'm not a child," he said, "I could understand."

She sat back in her seat and withdrew the pin from the crown of her hat. "Understand what?"

"I don't expect you never to have been with a man."

Smiling, she drove in the pin. "Here we are at St. John's church. It is St. Peter who keeps the keys of the Kingdom."

They got off and walked along Rosamund Road, past a house where once a snake's nest of old water pipes had burst all over the kitchen floor and took two days to put right. He had never been paid what was owed him for that job.

"If Stanley Morcom is the only man in the world, and I choose to call you by his name, what more do you want?"

"For you to call me by my own name. That for a start."

"A start?" Her hat brim swept up like a scythe. She did not steal glances, she took them.

"In that house Almey and I once paddled in the kitchen."

"Paddled?"

"There was a leak behind the range and the water came out over the floor. Of course it was warm as toast and Almey enjoyed herself." When he took her to Margate she declared the water had been better in Mrs Manchester's kitchen. "I thought she would take after her mother. When she was little, I could see her mother in her. Every day I saw something to remind me. She's grown out of it now."

"And the Heavens are to be praised?"

"Her mother had no respect. I never knew where she would take her fun." Almayer, taking hers in his disaster, stooping entranced over the blue water, had chilled him to the bone. "It will be better if she doesn't favour her mother."

The steam of a passing engine sank over them as they climbed the steps of the footbridge.

"Do you think she is a liar?" said Miss Velva.

"I don't know. Her mother wasn't. Nothing mattered that much to her."

"Pigs can see the wind and the child will tell you the colour of it."

"What does that mean?"

"A face at the window? A man watching? The colour of the wind!"

"Almey saw him. He lives in the house, in one of your back rooms. He talked to her about you."

Miss Velva sprang away from him and floated under the brim of her hat all the way down the steps of the footbridge. At her front gate he caught up with her. He was beside her on the doorstep as she put her key in the lock.

Inside the house it was pitch dark after the sunlight. She caught his hand and drew him after her along the passage. He felt himself on the brink of splendour, and gripped her fingers so violently that they cracked in his. She cried out, it was a high sound, as high as her singing, but between a warning and a threat, and then she flung open a door. There was a blaze of light. In the middle he saw a man, like a wick in a flame.

"This is he," said Miss Velva. Peter could not tell whether she was talking to him or to the man in the room.

An enormous fire was bolting up the chimney, liquefied tar ran out of the wood. Only old road blocks, thought Peter, would boil like that. The man had his back to it, the woolly fuzz all over his jersey, his head and the tops of his ears illumined as a kind of aureole.

"I didn't think you were real," he said to Peter.

"I knew you were."

"Ah, so she's been talking about me. I'm a subject and a half! Got to be seen to be believed. But you believed — so she's got you in her pocket."

"I can think of worse places to be."

"So can I. Sit down, Mr Morcom, you're very welcome."

"My name's Jenkin. You're Morcom. Don't let's start that again."

"I'm Scupham, Jack Scupham."

"Then who's Stanley Morcom?"

"He doesn't exist."

It was a load off Peter's mind. He had been afraid of having to compete with Morcom, of having to try to come up to him without knowing what or even where he was. He was rid of Morcom. Now there was Jack Scupham.

Peter judged him to be in his sixties, a man much reduced by something which had not yet finished with him, and would keep right on until he was halved, perhaps quartered. "Are you her husband?"

"You must be a bigger fool than you look to ask that. This is where I live and hope to die. If you're asking do I sleep with her — "

"I'm not asking."

Scupham pointed to a stretcher bed heaped with old wireless condensers. "The Marne runs under there. I'm no use to her or to any woman. You know what I mean?"

"The Marne is in France," Peter said stiffly.

Scupham turned to Miss Velva. "He doesn't know, he hasn't got a notion. What have you brought this time?"

She was watching Peter with what was, for her, a peculiarly steady gaze. He felt that he was being winkled out by a fierce and impartial probe.

"He thinks he's the only one, he thinks you've been waiting for him."

"I have."

"You'll let him think that?"

"It's true. I have waited."

"Not for him!" Tears welled in Scupham's yellow eyes, he wept openly with anger and hurt.

"I think we should like some refreshment," said Miss Velva. "We had no time for tea in the Crystal Palace."

"All these years — for him?"

"Why don't you remove your jacket?" she said to Peter.

Scupham wiped his wet muzzle on his sleeve. He brought out a bottle and glasses. His hand trembled and spilled the stuff he poured, but it was with cheerfulness that he pushed a glass into Peter's hand.

"Sit down, loosen your collar. Why do you wear such a stiff collar? Is it to keep your head on?" He grinned aimably.

The liquid in the glass was colourless and had no smell. Peter drank. Next moment the roof of his mouth had blown, his throat and chest were on fire, his eyes brimmed with tears. Through the blur he saw Miss Velva removing her left-hand glove, finger by finger.

"We were engaged to be married," said Scupham. "That's a picture of me in 1917. I weighed fourteen stone stripped, a young fellow, well proportioned. Army breeches showed off the shape of my leg and I had beautiful whiskers like a Cupid's bow. They were as good as a cat's. People said I felt more with my whiskers than with anything else. They were wrong. She knew that. You wouldn't believe, would you, that's what I looked like after we came out of Fricourt. At Fricourt we used the corpses for sandbags. That's me, crisp as a new fiver, and full of promise. I kept my promise to her. We had it all, barring the ceremony, which we couldn't spare the time for. The way we saw it, we had all our lives to get married in. That's how we saw it." He refilled his glass and drained it with the same movement. Peter was still trying to gather enough saliva to cool his throat. "Never doubted it. I came through Passchendaele and Bapaume: my name wasn't on anything. Not on a shell, nor a bullet, nor a bayonet, nor a grain of powder. I finished up with the Canadians in the Canal du Nord."

"I got trench-fever," said Peter.

"Everyone in the trenches got trench-fever."

"I got it before I went into the trenches."

Miss Velva was removing her right-hand glove. She pinched the tip of each finger and delicately withdrew it, allowing the glove to fall to the floor.

"Before?" said Scupham. "That's interesting. Time jumps like a buck rabbit. I was blown up, drowned, choked, burned and buried alive. Afterwards."

"Afterwards?"

"Something else time does, it goes backwards."

She had removed both gloves and they now lay on the floor, the fingers curled to the shape of her hands. They looked supplicating.

"It started in 1918."

Peter said stupidly, "What?" Miss Velva was slowly unbuttoning her coat.

"My war started in 1918. I've got to pay, I owe it. You can see how hard I'm being pushed, I'm being pushed right out of myself." He plucked at the folds of his empty jersey. "I'm no good to her any more."

Peter was afraid that time could also take a wrong turning. Perhaps everything that could be said and done, down to the last permutation, actually had to be said and done. Somewhere, sometime, what Scupham was saying and Miss Velva was doing — lifting first one shoulder, then the other, not checking or hurrying the passage of her sleeves slipping from her arms to her wrists — would have been all in order. The wrong thing, perhaps, was his being there to see it.

The coat clung to her hips. She moved, with scarcely a sigh, and it fell about her ankles. He was profoundly dismayed. An internal blush travelled through him faster than gas. He was hot all over in a winking. On his own behalf, not hers: stepping out of the encircling fur, she was as cool and pure as a lily.

"Look at her."

Peter had turned his face away.

"Look, you fool!"

"I'll look where I choose."

"Why do you wring your hands?"

Peter pressed his hands to his sides. His ankles, too, were pressed together, he was standing to attention.

"Tell me how you know what a woman wants. Don't be shy, I'm in a position to help you. I always gave her what she wanted, I anticipated her every wish. She's got some funny wishes — you don't want to be unprepared."

Peter, looking into Scupham's eyes, thought that they were the eyes of a wild animal — unreachable rather than savage. In the man's clouded yellow he saw a delight which repelled him.

"I swear I haven't laid a finger on her for years. I can't. Don't ask me why." Peter was obliged to witness a small pantomime wherein Scupham made his meaning clear. "The flesh is as willing as a wet straw and the spirit's gone. She's not vestal, but I can promise you'll be the first for a long time."

Miss Velva stretched out her foot and allowed her shoe to hang from her toes.

"Well?" Scupham put out a trembling hand to Peter.

Peter backed away. "Are you trying to make a fool of me?"

Miss Velva, balancing on one stockinged foot, took aim with the other, and a black patent slipper with a bow on the instep, one of a pair which Peter had admired on her small feet, flew across the room.

"I'm trying to make a man of you," said Scupham.

Peter thought he perceived the crux of the matter. If this wrong permutation was happening here, the right one must be going on somewhere else — perhaps at the Crystal Palace. Perhaps he and Miss Velva were having tea by the fountain and the band was playing on small, delicate instruments. He must remember that, and only that. Could he remember what had not happened? And what was she bound by?

She began, deliberately and lingeringly, to unbutton her dress. It was, it must be, the stuff he was drinking. After his very first sip — but not until then — she had started taking off her gloves.

"Hear that?" Scupham held up his finger. "That was the Jack Johnsons. They shake your balls off. Well, I've nothing to lose — and I like a bit of noise. It's the quiet I can't stand, I can hear too much when it's quiet. Of course I don't hear what you hear, I've only got one life, thank Christ. But there's no law about time. What's to stop it going up in a balloon?"

He was refilling their glasses. Peter determined not to touch any more of the stuff. It was responsible for what had happened — and for what had not happened.

"Nothing finishes, nothing stops. It's known as time immemorial — they can't get it all on their town-hall crosses. What's the matter with you? Why don't you help her?"

She did not need help. She had stepped out of her dress: that, too, had dropped round her ankles. So much of her was visible, so much that he had joyed to imagine — her slender arms, her delicate neck, and beneath it the adventuring curves, adventuring on and down, ever more bold and more beautiful.

Scupham emptied his glass and drank from the bottle. "He wrings his hands like a woman. I told her to find herself a man."

"You told her?"

"You'd better be good. You'd better be marvellous." Scupham was flourishing the bottle and something smelling of ferment splashed on Peter. "It took us seven days to fire a million and a half shells. That's as long as it took to make the world. A million and a half shells flying over is no worse than a seven-day rainstorm. But I've been counting the drops ever since."

To have an enemy was a new experience: it would have been as strange for Peter to have a friend. No-one had ever been well enough defined.

"Givenchy, Festubert, Charley Roy — remember the wooden shutters with the daisy holes? In the market square, Joan of Arc's lost her head, the Mairie's been shot up by German 105's and 201's, there's a burst main, it's never stopped raining for a week and the church is burning like merry hell in the wet. At night you can hear the Germans snoring in their trenches. We'll just wash over the town and go back the way we came. As they say, the situation's fluid."

Behind Peter and between him and the door was the camp bed. Facing him was Miss Velva in her silk directoire knickers.

"And then somebody walks out between you and the German line. A woman walks out. She shouldn't be alive, nothing should be alive here now. So what will you do? What can you do?"

If Peter shook like a jelly, it was because he felt as unsafe as a jelly. He had a positive dread of being shaken off the plate.

"You can, can't you, Sergeant Morcom?" Scupham stopped in the ready position, as if they were playing a game, and he was expecting Peter to make a run. "You must — this place isn't called La Raperie for nothing!"

Peter sighed, with expedience, not regret. By drawing a deep breath and releasing it, he thought to stop himself shaking.

Miss Velva was waiting. He went closer, and she withdrew the long pin from the crown of her hat. He lifted the hat from her head. Her hair sprang on her shoulders and uncoiled as if it were alive.

Peter threw the hat on the fire. Lusty flames seized and carried it up the chimney. He stepped on to the bed. Several of the condensers were trodden on and broken, but it was the quickest way to the door.

## V

When I was sixteen, my father caught his death of cold. His ladder blew down and marooned him on a roof during a rainstorm. He was soaked to the skin and frozen by the east wind. He told me that he could hear the ice creaking in his clothes. A week later he was dead.

My first experience was of being at a loss, not of him, of everything else. I felt no grief, shock or alarm. My dismay was at being undismayed. My reactions were practical ones. I should need to get my coat dyed; what should be put on his gravestone besides 'Peter Jenkin' and the dates of his birth and death? I did not know the date of his birth. Should he be buried with his shoes on? There was something derisory about his big toes and I felt that they should not deride him in death.

There were no surviving relatives that I knew, or wanted to know of. He used to say that he had had a termagant sister who brought him up. She had scrubbed his bare knees with the yard broom and he left her as soon as he could earn his living.

I had just started to earn mine. He had found me a job in the London office of a firm that manufactured wireless valves. It wasn't my choice, I had wanted to go to a firm that made cosmetics, but father said luxury goods were risky.

He chose wireless valves because he thought the firm would not go out of business and because wireless valves struck the right balance between technology and aesthetics. 'People will always want to listen to music and plays and hear what's going on in the world. The life of a valve is unpredictable and there are four at least to every set in the country. Whichever way you look at it, it's safe.'

The office was in Russell Square. I worked at filing and envelope-addressing in what had been the basement of one of the big houses, my desk was a board laid across the kitchen sink. The day after the funeral, Miss Hauptmann, the senior secretary, came and asked me what I was going to do.

"Fetch the post and make the tea."

"I mean hereafter. In the long term."

"I don't know. It's not much good making my mind up when things keep happening to unmake it."

"You must. There is no-one now to tell you what to do."

I did not say, for it would have been a betrayal, that father had not been able to tell me that.

"You are only a child. What will become of you?"

A woman would become of me I thought, but again did not say so.

"Have you none to turn to?"

I sensed an element of committal. If you gave your problems to someone you had to give yourself as well. I wished to be independent, I felt that the alternative would be panic.

"You should go to your mother."

"My mother is dead."

"That is not what your father told me. I talked to him when he came to see us about your job."

It had fallen to father, of all people, and I knew by then that he was not all people, to approve or disapprove the conditions in which I was to earn my living — the milieu, the human, social and intellectual context. To me it was an intimation of the power of circumstance and what creatures we are of it.

"I asked him," confessed Miss Hauptmann. "We like to know our employees' background, and he said that your mother was living."

"That was then. She is dead now."

"It was only a month ago! Are you saying you have sustained the loss of both father and mother within the month?"

"The truth is — " I bowed my head — "she is alive, but she keeps a house of ill-fame."

"What?"

"That's why I can't go to her."

Miss Hauptmann was Teutonic in build as well as name. To brush against her was to receive an immediate rebuff, to rebound, almost, from her solid flesh. She now drew herself up and, though I would not have thought it possible, solidified even further.

"I cannot tell if you are a liar, but I can see that you need help. You should go away."

"Go away?"

"Have you shed tears?"

"Where would I go?"

"Grief is corrosive in one so young." She was standing close beside me and from her formidable stomach came complicated stirrings, like a clock preparing to chime. "It must be leaked, the strings of the emotions loosed, the heart must be permitted to bleed."

"I don't want to bleed."

"If there is no-one else to arrange it, then I shall. Your father would wish it." Miss Hauptmann sighed and her bust rose up and cuffed my cheek.

\* \* \*

I was packed off to Miss Hauptmann's cousins in Sussex. She obviously felt a moral obligation towards me and could not think of another way to fulfil it. She was given a free hand by the directors of the valve company and it was prudent not to offend her. Had I refused to go, she would have found cause to sack me, and it wouldn't have taken her long.

Her cousins, the Ashmoles, appeared to me to be people of wealth and influence. They were neither, but the illusion served me as well as the truth would have done.

Their house, of ruby brick, in the style known as Victorian Gothic, overlooked the Downs which teemed, I was sure, with savage beasts and ghosts. I did not once set foot there. Great spaces horrify me and I thought it some proof of the Ashmoles' quality that they were able to live within sight of so much emptiness. They kept Nature in her place — as a picture on the windowpane.

The house belonged to Cedric's mother, and Cedric and his wife, Constance, lived with her: Mrs Ashmole the elder, she was sometimes called.

"So you're Gerda's friend," she said when I arrived.

"Gerda?"

"My mother's sister married Eberhard Hauptmann. I wonder why she sent you to us?"

It was not meant ungraciously, I sensed that she was questioning their fitness to cope with my situation, not the imposition of it. Cedric Ashmole saying, "It is for a few days, to recover from her bereavement," was an acceptance of the responsibility.

"One does not recover in a few days. In a few days one is still deciding who is dead. Unless of course it was a minor bereavement."

"She needs bucking up. She's here to be bucked up," said Cedric.

"One should be allowed to mourn. Mourning is natural, but of course not popular, for it leaves no-one else anything to do." Mrs Ashmole said to me, "You may mourn if you wish. We are not involved, for us nothing has stopped, so we shall not disturb you. This is perhaps what Gerda had in mind."

"I can't mourn." I could see myself being left discreetly alone, obliged to sit with my head draped, like one of Rossetti's figures, in a classic pose of despair. "I can't cry. My tear glands don't work. I tried to start them by sniffing up salt water and it all came out again."

"Great Scott!" cried Cedric. "Why shouldn't you weep through your nose? They could be real tears."

"No, it was the salt water I sniffed up coming back down."

"Well then, should you be weeping? Perhaps it was for the best. Death often is, you know. You could say it always is, at some point."

"Could you?" Constance said to him. "If it were me?"

"Right at the end — for to go back from there would be infinitely for the worst. Where to start weeping is what you have to decide." He was a burly young man, with some of Miss Hauptmann's solidity. And I thought I saw the edge of that same mettle which she was always on. Naturally enough, I supposed then that it was I who was at risk. "You must decide where, and what for. Cast your mind back, try to fix the point when it could have been reversed. The exact point. Events happen in sequence, you know, you come to the end of one, and start another. Grieving is a hundred-per-cent thing, and you want to make sure you're eligible for it."

"Miss Jenkin can have nothing to reproach herself with," said Mrs Ashmole.

"My father caught a cold."

"He must have had a delicate constitution to die of it," said Mrs Ashmole.

"One is always at risk using public transport," said Cedric. "Hanging about."

"He was on a roof."

"On a roof? What was he doing there?"

I hesitated. I did not want to say that my father had been mending somebody's chimney. Not to these people. I could hear Cedric asking, 'What was wrong with the chimney?'

"He was an architect, he climbed up to check the elevation."

"He checked that?"

"He was dedicated to his work. He said fine buildings express human ideals."

"I thought all art did that," said Constance.

Father had come home and put his feet into hot water. Only his feet, we had no bathroom and he sat in the kitchen and I was vexed at the shape of his toes, which I believed I had inherited. It was then that he told me about the ice in his clothes. 'It's the sort of thing that happened to Captain Scott in the Antarctic.' He had sounded quite pleased, and I had cried, 'Captain Scott froze to death!'

The Ashmoles were looking at me. Suddenly, and quite independently, my face began to organise itself for tears.

Constance said, "She is eligible for grieving."

\* \* \*

I stayed several weeks. Mrs Ashmole the elder was on the committees of all the local societies and institutes and found me useful as an unpaid secretary. I don't know what understanding she came to with Miss Hauptmann about keeping me so long away from my job, but I liked riding around in Mrs Ashmole's elderly Buick to meetings all over the county, taking minutes, writing letters, keeping her engagement book. It was good experience. My shorthand improved, so did my general knowledge, and my self-possession. Mrs Ashmole increased my proficiency by taking for granted that I was already proficient. She did not tell me how to do anything, she simply expected it to be done. I had to find out for myself and it was the best way of ensuring that I really knew. Later on, I was able to take a better-paid job than the one with the valve company.

Mrs Ashmole the elder was not kind so much as unobliged to be anything else — I expect if it had suited her, materially or morally, she would have had no compunction. Her charity could be ruthless. She disposed good, and where it was unacceptable she imposed it: if she had met with open resistance I think she would have inflicted it.

I did not resist, I needed her autocracy. From the first, she treated me as an adjunct of herself, party and privy to her thoughts and feelings. In telling me what she thought, she took for granted I thought the same, and as I got to know her, I took it for granted too. But sometimes I couldn't co-ordinate my immediate reactions with hers. If I laughed when she had started to frown, or acquiesced when she was indignant, she would deliver a look, her chin and eyebrows lifted as if to see over a high wall.

With father I had felt myself the superior being. *His* being had defects, unidentifiable, not even consistent. You couldn't say he had no sense, because he was sensible enough for his situation in life, and sometimes beyond it. You couldn't say he lacked knowhow; he had as much as he needed for his trade, and more than a great many people. You couldn't say he lacked courage – he would tackle anything and he did not recognise defeat. It was something he had, a knack of compounding events, of knitting up small mishaps, and it was a hurt pride with him to make sure that every bit stuck. I used to think that someone must be laughing, but oh, it wasn't me.

So now, to be the inferior, the only one who could – might even be expected to – step off on the wrong foot, was a bracing experience. I felt that I was learning and I accepted my failures as father had his, though without the hurt which he had taken full disadvantage of.

Mrs Ashmole assumed that I was fundamentally allright and that my lapses could be put down to youth. Cedric, on the other hand, kept trying to put me right. That I did resent, because I sensed that what he was really trying to do was manoeuvre me into a position in which he could feel happy. Happiness was something he was always working at. His ideas for me were not viable, I could never have gone away and put them into practice. Yet he was a practical man, his work as a quantity surveyor was essentially practical.

I think now that really he talked only to Constance, whether she was present to hear, or not. It was my first encounter with love between man and woman and I knew nothing of its manifestations. I did not dream that love, and the lack of it, could drive people right out of the other end of themselves.

About Constance I had no feeling whatsoever, though I was aware that there were grounds for very definite feelings indeed. She spoke little, perhaps because Cedric spoke so much. She was beautiful in a generous way, her white skin so thick as to be almost a rind: her plait of hair, she once told me, as round exactly as her own wrist. That was when she said she would cut it off.

"Why?" I didn't mind about her cutting off her hair, I was really asking why Cedric, who at that moment had been in the midst of explaining to me how I should conquer my aversion to the Downs, flushed brick-red and walked out of the room without another word.

"Why not?" said Constance. "It will grow again. It would be something to wait for."

I suppose she was bored. In that house on the edge of the empty Downs, with Cedric away at his office and Mrs Ashmole wrapped up in her committees, there was nothing for Constance to do. That was my first conclusion, but Nature, especially human nature, abhors a vacuum, and later, when the premise was offered, and with grounds displayed, as it were, before us all, I accepted that to waste the substance of a woman like Constance would be a crime — whereas its unauthorised use would rate no higher than a sin.

It was quite new to me, this experience of life in a family unit. When I had gone among the families of my schoolfriends the only difference had seemed to be that they were overlooked, which I would have resented anyway.

The Ashmoles did not overlook each other: in fact, they averted their gazes and practically had to be invited to take a personal look.

I don't remember exactly how the impression was transmitted to me that Constance had a lover. Sometimes I think it was by Mrs Ashmole: sometimes I think it came from Constance herself, sometimes I think it came from out of the ground. It was already in my mind when they first talked of building a pool.

Cedric said the garden 'lacked focus'. Mrs Ashmole said she found it quite sharp — because there were so many right angles in it. "I believe the criterion of a garden path is that it should seem to be going nowhere."

"A right angle can go nowhere."

"No," said Mrs Ashmole, "it is too determined."

"I wasn't thinking about the garden being in focus, but of its focal point. A pool," said Cedric, "would be just that."

Mrs Ashmole, who was working on her tapestry, glanced at him, the merest flicker of an eye, yet I fancied it was an instant summing up. I had seen that flicker before, and envied it. Hardly anything mattered more to me just then than the faculty of being able to keep one's mind made up.

"We could run a pipe from the mains," Cedric went on. "We might have a fountain with dolphins, or one of those pretty stone boys."

"Oh my dear," Constance said softly.

"We can have it big enough to swim in."

"I prefer the sea." Constance smiled. "The sea is alive."

"The sea is not convenient, and it's so very *open*. We'll dispense with the rockery and build a dry wall beneath the terrace. I'll calculate the area we could give it, we must have a surround so that we can take our chairs and a table there on hot days. It will be very pleasant. I think we should allow at least three feet."

Mrs Ashmole, frowning critically at her work, asked Constance when she had last swum in the sea.

"Oh, one day last week. Or was it two days? Or three? Tuesday, Wednesday, Thursday, I can't remember."

"On Tuesday, Almayer and I were at Rovington, on Thursday at Thrush Green, on Wednesday, the Farquhars came to lunch. I am not expecting you to remember my activities," said Mrs Ashmole, smiling, "but they might serve to indicate the availability of the car."

"I didn't take the car, I walked."

Mrs Ashmole's face tidied itself as if she were about to have her photograph taken.

"A pool," said Cedric, "would relieve you of that necessity."

"Nothing would relieve me of the necessity of walking, except the loss of my legs."

"It is many years since I swam in the sea." said Mrs Ashmole. "I used to have quite a penchant for it."

"Do you know, I would rather you didn't," Cedric said to Constance. "While I am away, working like billyo, I would rather not think of you in the sea."

"I never swam alone," said Mrs Ashmole. "I wasn't good enough."

"I'm not good."

"To enjoy it, I mean. I splashed about in the shallows and one cannot very agreeably do that by oneself." It was left to Mrs Ashmole and I, or rather only to me, for she kept her eyes on her tapestry, to observe Constance's face. "Of course there is no guarantee of safety, even in our own homes." Mrs Ashmole pressed out the stitches on her knees. "Perhaps least of all there. But I understand that there is a cold current under the cliffs. It can induce cramp and stop the heart."

Constance laughed. "If my heart is to be stopped, I would as soon the cold did it."

A rash pink stormed up under Cedric's tan, his face seemed to swell. "I don't want to think of you swimming alone in the sea."

"Then don't think it, my dear," said Mrs Ashmole, plunging her needle into her canvas.

\* \* \*

In those days, before coffee mornings were thought of, ladies met for afternoon tea, but from my experience it was no less of a bunfight. Mrs Ashmole had a host of dear friends and I truly admired her for not scrupling from whence they came. She would cry, 'She is one of my dearest!' just as warmly of a cowman's wife as of a colonel's lady. Here was real discrimination, I thought, nothing to do with class, and I gave the cowman's wife and the colonel's lady credit for whatever commended and endeared them, though I wasn't sure what it might be.

My suspicions about Constance were affirmed, and I found that it was not so much a secret, as privileged knowledge. Mrs Ashmole was promoting a theatre group and had taken me with her to record the preliminaries of their first meeting, which was held at Mrs George Farquhar's.

Although Mr Farquhar was not in the Army, his wife was at the colonel's lady end of the scale. Their house was as big as the Ashmoles', but not so pleasant. There was too little furniture in it for my taste. We were shown into a tall aqueous room set with a grand piano, a few occasional tables, and a potted palm which reached to the ceiling. I whispered to Mrs Ashmole that there surely would not be enough chairs for us all. She told me to notice the carpet. "It is real Kurdistan."

"I thought we would use the morning-room," said Mrs George. "The gardener is cutting the lawn at the front of the house and it might be distracting."

I was intrigued at the idea of a room being kept entirely for the morning. Did they get up and leave it at twelve noon? And what did the Farquhars do there, and nowhere else, in the morning, but at no other time of the day?

"Such a feeling of space, here you can really breathe!" One of the ladies held her ribs and swelled her bosom. "My late husband used to say that only small spirits need to be confined."

"It's a pretty carpet," I said. "We had one with a pattern like that but it was only stuck on, it wasn't woven."

Mrs George drew a chair up to one of the small tables and said to me, "You will need somewhere to rest your notepad."

Some of the ladies were put out when they realised the Mrs Ashmole intended their theatre-going to be an intellectual exercise.

"We will concentrate on the Bard. What an achievement to be able to say we have seen every one of the plays! Of course it is too much to hope. We shall have to see Shaw and Galsworthy, and we might take in a few musical productions."

"I should love to see 'The Merry Widow'."

"To some of us the idea could be anathema," warned Mrs George, and the lady who had breathed, and remembered her recent husband, touched her eyelids with a corner of her handkerchief.

"I was thinking rather of works such as 'Hiawatha' and Stainer's 'Crucifixion'," said Mrs Ashmole. "But first we must get down to the business of organising ourselves."

I used to amuse myself at those meetings trying to picture the various ladies in their night-dresses. It wasn't out of morbid interest, simply a feat of imagination. I had once seen Mrs Ashmole attired for bed, and the sight was a revelation. I had had no experience of ladies' nightly toilet — hair netted, face creamed, dentures removed and an unsuspected area of bosom and arms rising from a foam of tucking and frills. There was nothing coy about Mrs Ashmole, even in her night-dress, but that she should so array herself for her lonely bed gave me a hint of the tyranny of sex. I think I should have been less alarmed at discovering her naked.

I felt as if I now knew her public surface and her most secret depths without knowing any of her in between. I also felt that I was looking at the crux of the biggest matter of all. I felt so many things — dismay, fright, shame and physical glee.

I sat there while they argued about subscriptions and officers and whether they should meet to discuss the plays they went to — 'picking the bones', Mrs Ashmole called it — and where they should meet, and who should negotiate the theatre bookings and the transport, and I pictured them, one by one, getting into bed.

They were all past their first youth: whatever was revealed, necks, shoulders, bosoms, arms, would be blemished by time. I should not let it inhibit me, for it did not inhibit them.

Mrs George was sandy-haired and freckled to match. Freckles went all the way down and gathered in the hollow at the base of her neck. The backs of her hands were covered with them. They disappeared into her sleeves and would surely emerge again out of the frills, hundreds and hundreds of sandy spots plunging past knots of ribbon into unthinkable depths. But Mrs George had some excuse — there was a Mr George.

"Almayer," Mrs Ashmole said, "Please read back the last resolution."

"We need more members," said Mrs George, "a quorum of at least twelve if we are to get worthwhile discounts."

"We should each undertake to bring a friend."

"My daughter will join us. What about yours?"

"Constance is Mrs Ashmole's daughter-*in-law*."

"Constance is not gregarious."

"What does that mean?" said someone.

Someone else replied, "She prefers to be alone."

Mrs Ashmole laughed lightly. "Constance has her own interests. She does not care for the theatre."

"She is fond of music, I suppose. I saw her on the pier listening to the band. She was not alone then."

"Ah," said Mrs Ashmole, and I wondered at the swiftness with which she turned to the speaker.

"Of course it would be difficult to be alone on the pier at this time of year."

"Who was specifically accompanying her?"

"There was a man next to her."

Mrs Ashmole raised her eyebrows at Mrs George. "Who was he? I ask merely to identify the occasion."

"I don't know. He was quite elderly and his wife was sharing their programme with Constance."

There was a sigh, or was it a rustle, as Mrs Ashmole sat back in her chair.

"My dear," Mrs George leaned towards her, whispering. "You will never find out like that."

Mrs Ashmole replied, just as softly, "If a stone offers, I do not leave it unturned. What more can I do?"

"Have her followed."

\*   \*   \*

As we drove home, Mrs Ashmole closed the panel between the chauffeur and ourselves and asked me if I had been for a walk with Constance.

"No."

"On one of her expeditions across the Downs?"

"No."

She spoke with amusement, as if she did not believe me, "Such a strange whim for a naturally indolent person."

"I would never go on the Downs."

"Why not?"

"I don't like them."

"Does Constance go on to the Downs?"

"Of course."

"So you know?"

"Well she would, wouldn't she? It's the quickest way to the sea."

"Ah yes, the sea." Opening the panel, she said to the chauffeur, "You had better go straight to the station if you are to be in time to meet Mr Cedric's train."

I was often left to my own company when she was resting, or reading, or writing personal letters. I was still unable to mourn for my father. What I felt was not grief, it was guilt and alarm. Guilt at being alive when he was dead, alarm at being flesh of his flesh. I would have liked to put off my body like an unsuitable dress.

I asked myself what grief was. Was it a pain which would suddenly arrive? Where would I feel it? Was it wishing him alive again? I had not done that, I never would. Was it losing my appetite and wanting to die? The Ashmoles ate well, far better than I had been accustomed to, and I was growing fast. I hungrily anticipated and enjoyed every meal. Far from wanting to die, I was aware of the importance of life, and, guilty or not, I was going to hang on to it.

"You are not pining, are you?" Mrs Ashmole said to me. The question worried me. I bowed my head, I did not ask her about the nature of grief. Something told me that it would be imprudent.

I spent a lot of time sketching. I thought I was rather good. I was good enough, anyway, to enjoy doing it. I liked best to draw people. I still have some drawings I made of Constance. I think I managed to catch on paper her rather professional unhappiness — or something which reminds me of it. It was a finished state, and vastly became her. Had she been happy, or even not unhappy, she would not have been memorable. She would have been just a wholesome young woman to be passed in a crowd.

Disillusion, dissatisfaction, discontent — Constance had none of these. Her unhappiness was a positive asset. To me she seemed wonderfully endowed, for had she not a lover as well as a husband, and a secret life of which not a moment was overlooked? I had seen enough of Mrs Ashmole's friends to know that that was an achievement.

It had become clear to me that Constance's heart was elsewhere. She was, as Mrs Ashmole said, of an indolent nature. How impressed I was by her indolence! One would think, one could swear, day in, day out, there was nothing. So when did she come alive? Where did she keep that life until she could come to it? I used to look at her and marvel how well, and how badly, she kept her secret. Once you knew, it was all you saw: until you knew, it was all you saw.

She always got up late and came down for the cup of coffee which she took alone for breakfast. I remember her smoking her coloured cigarettes with the gold tips. One sketch I have, it is only a few lines, but there is the mixture of effrontery and despair in her pose which I found so unsettling. I think other people did too, even Mrs Ashmole and Cedric. Especially Mrs Ashmole, especially Cedric.

She did not talk to me about myself and try to arrange my future. She wasn't concerned about my future, she told me that thinking for other people was like trying to drive a bus from the top of a tram.

I was very naive, passion was only a word. Something told me that Constance had it, but not what she did with it. I imagined her and some person unknown entwined together like the calyx of a flower. The idea of her double life stirred and shocked me. My sympathies were with Cedric. He tried so hard, and had so much success. None of it was what he wanted, but he had to have it, he had to make everything a challenge – professional, practical, human – and meet every one. He would battle with an uncalled-for pause in the conversation and take arms against his own face. I have seen him tucking down his jaw at his reflection in a mirror. Once Constance brought a bunch of creamy May-blossom into the house. He took a deep breath of its sweetness and cried 'What nonsense!' I don't think even Mrs Ashmole was sure what he meant. She said, 'Nothing so beautiful could be unlucky.'

He tried to teach me to play what he called a 'useful set' of tennis. "It's a social asset, like playing the piano used to be, and before that, bezique. Lay your thumb along the haft of the racket – why do you hold it like a frying pan?"

"I'd rather you taught me to swim."

He said he never went to the beach.

"I'll ask Constance to teach me."

"She can't swim."

"Then why does she go to the beach?"

I had asked him that on the tennis court, and he shouted as he threw up the ball. "For lots of reasons. The waves, the pebbles, the shells!"

"The seagulls!"

He heard the note of derision in my voice, and lowered his racket.

"Seagulls?"

"They are the souls of drowned sailors."

"What would she want with them?"

"To talk to."

He said, lobbing the ball hard at me, "She does better than that!"

\*     \*     \*

Cedric was good-looking, kind, cheerful, rich, and I couldn't think what more Constance wanted in a husband. But there *was* more, and she had found it somewhere. In what sort of man? He would have to be all that Cedric was, and a great deal that Cedric was not. For instance, I couldn't call Cedric romantic: he was too solid, too healthy, and he gargled. And the other man might be a peer, a prince stooping to conquer. But Constance was not impressed by titles. I had heard her teasing Cedric, who was.

I began to think about her lover and found that there was nothing to think about, no facts that I could be sure of. It didn't stop me, I was free to dwell, to dream, to covet. In a very little while I was looking at the place where he had just been, the room he had just left, the corner he had just turned. He became so real a ghost that I could sense the air coming together after he had passed by. I envisaged him as slender, wild, cold, intense. A merman. I was half in love. It was weird, sixteen is a weird age.

Every day he grew more important to me. I did not think about the ultimate reality of having a lover. A kiss, the purest touch of the lips, was the ultimate for me. Over the rest I drew a veil and did not think of lifting it.

I became bitterly, absurdly, jealous of Constance who had found him and was keeping him, and one day I followed her. It was mid-August and very hot. Mrs Ashmole was resting, Cedric had gone out, and Constance was off to meet her lover.

I could tell by the way she moved, with a half-swimming motion — she infuriated me! — that she was already entering his embrace. She went down through the garden and into the meadow, trailing her hands through the long grass. I watched it part and sink back behind her. She left a darkish track. Like a great snail! I said spitefully. When only her head showed in the middle of the field, I stepped in her wake.

I felt entirely justified. Mrs George had said 'Have her followed.' Other people were as interested as I was to know the identity of her lover. Whether I should tell them would be my eventual choice.

Constance paused and I at once lay down out of sight in the grass. The feathered and speckled heads leaned gently over me. I seized a handful at the roots and wrung them.

I might tell Mrs Ashmole. It would teach *him* a lesson. I imagined him, the lover, bowed with shame, hiding his face in his hands. But he would be hiding only from me. For although I was prepared for Mrs Ashmole knowing, I was not prepared for what her knowing would entail.

Constance moved on. She came to the edge of the meadow where it gave way to a bean field. She began to walk over the bean rows. I went as far as I dared, then crouched in the grass and watched.

After the bean field came some scrub land, hawthorn and gorse and short turf – the beginning of the long sheepish shanks of those seahills I so disliked. Constance, in an orange linen dress, was moving very slowly now that the ground was rising – she did not enjoy physical exertion – and suddenly she did not move at all. I crept along the edge of the meadow, and under cover of a hedge which bounded the bean field, drew level with Constance. She was some twenty yards away, lying on her back with her legs bent and her skirt tenting over her knees.

My father had seldom cautioned me: when he did, I remembered it. Once, as I was sitting in a deck-chair, I had drawn up my legs and hung my heels on the edge of the seat. He gave me a shove and said I was getting too old to sit like an Arab. 'This is the first time I've done it,' I said, indignant at a privilege withdrawn before I had enjoyed it. 'One day I'll tell you why you shouldn't,' he said.

Constance was not sitting like an Arab. She was lying with her face to the sky, her palms upturned, looking at once plundered and replete. I found the posture offensive, even threatening, like the upholding of a fist. But she was alone.

I knelt behind the hedge to wait. Now that I was about to see him, I felt no curiosity. I expected anything, a demon lover would not have surprised me. It did not for an instant occur to me that he might be an ordinary unknown man, with no damning or redeeming feature by which I could identify him to someone else. A lover was not ordinary, and I did not think about identifying him to someone else. I just wanted to see him, I was waiting for a visitation.

Minutes passed. There were things – plants, earth, insects – which I could smell, individually or mixed together: a bitter whiff of beetles, a sharp breath of sap from trodden stalks, even the personal odour of a spider's web. The heat was pretty intimate under that hedge. I moved so that I was closer to Constance. I had never hated and despaired more.

Because I was so low down, with a worm's, or at any rate a

rabbit's eye view, I did not at once see someone approaching across the meadow. He came by the track through the grass which Constance had made and which I had followed. The first I saw of him was the top of his head as he was about to break cover and cross the bean field. Another moment and I must have been discovered, for he was on my side of the hedge.

I rolled into the dry ditch, hoping that the sprays of cow-parsley would hide me. He was coming, making for the gap in the bushes through which I had been watching Constance. My heart began to race. There was violence in the way he walked, treading the caked earth, kicking through the furrows. He was already angry. Perhaps he knew I was there to spy.

I dared not look, I huddled in the ditch and put my face on my knees. He came on, I heard the stones scraping against his shoes, he was breathing through his nostrils like a horse. I was terrified, and when he came to a stop scarcely two feet away I waited for the blow to fall. Gone were my tender visions of a merman or demon lover. I was frightened stiff of what I now knew was an uncommonly angry man. Next minute he had passed me by, and I understood how an animal feels when the eye of the predator is turned aside and the hunt is off.

Feet trampled through the scrub, so near that twigs broke into my hair. Only a man possessed could have missed seeing me. Followed the fierce sipping sound of feet moving across dry turf, then a silence that made my head sing.

I uncurled, a finger at a time. The scrape of a leaf sounded like a gunshot and I didn't even know whether he was still standing, watching me.

It wasn't me he was watching, it was Constance. I saw them through the gap in the hedge. She hadn't moved, she was capable of not having moved since she had first lain down. The man stood beside her, with his back to me, but I knew who he was. I was so surprised, and chagrined, I sat up with an exclamation.

Evidently they did not hear. Cedric dropped to his knees and leaned over her. I thought perhaps she was asleep. I could tell that he was going to do something, and it made me shudder — I don't know to this day whether with fear or pleasure.

Then Constance moved. She lowered her knees and spread out her arms, opened them to the sky. There was nothing personal in it, and nothing generous either. It was not meant for Cedric, nor for the whole wide world. She was not offering her body, simply staking it out and leaving it.

At sixteen, although I hadn't acquired any morals, I was straight-laced right down the middle, and it shocked me. I knew I was right to be shocked and I didn't have to work it out.

Cedric got to his feet and walked away. He climbed the first slope of the Downs, his silhouette hung briefly against the sky before he disappeared over the hill.

\*   \*   \*

Mrs Ashmole, who had been talking about Shakespeare's Globe, asked if I would like to go to the theatre. I supposed she meant to the Globe, wherever that might be, to poke around an old empty place among tipped-up seats. I said guardedly that I wouldn't mind seeing what it was like.

"Have you not seen any Barrie before?"

"No."

"Then it will be a good introduction. What plays have you seen?"

"I have never been to the theatre."

"Never?"

"Not even to a pantomine?" said Constance.

"Did your father object?"

"He didn't think about it."

"How extraordinary. What were his reactions?"

What indeed? He read the paper, but he used to say it was an obligation: 'I don't like what goes on in the world but that's no excuse for shutting my eyes.' Perhaps he had never been recreated.

"He thought a lot."

"What about?"

"About everything."

"Except the theatre."

"Perhaps he thought about leg shows," said Cedric.

"*Mary Rose* is not a leg show. The most conscientious parent could not object."

"Isn't there a hint of incest in it somewhere?"

"My father had lots of friends."

"Ah, so he was gregarious?"

"He was universally admired."

"I'm sure he was," said Mrs Ashmole kindly. "And if he disapproved of the theatre but did not tell you so, we may presume it was a personal prejudice and has died with him. I do not think you need feel that it should influence your attitude to a major art form."

"After he lost my mother he had a tragic love affair with a famous musician. She was very beautiful and rich, and unhappy. I never knew what happened, I think she was married to a cripple. My father could not come between husband and wife."

"How terrible," said Constance.

"From then on he dedicated his life to me. But he never got over it." The Bible says 'Honour thy father', and that's what I was doing."

"I shall be happy to take you to the theatre." Mrs Ashmole turned to Cedric. "As it is the guild's inaugural outing, perhaps you and Constance will join us as my guests?"

"Thank you, mother. I shall be away all that day at Tangley Mere."

"Tangley Mere? Where's that?" said Constance.

"In the depths of Horridshire. I shan't be home till late. It would be nice if you went to the play."

Constance lit a bright green cigarette. "Is that the play about a girl who went to an island, and when she came back everyone was twenty years older, but she was still the same age?"

"She lost her place in time. A terrible thing to happen."

"It rather depends on what she was doing in those twenty years," said Constance.

Mrs Ashmole was laughing lightly. "Of course it couldn't happen."

"I don't think I shall come, it would be such an effort."

"Hardly that. The coach is picking us up here."

"Of the imagination, I meant," said Constance.

There was a pause. Cedric said that scientists were working on a method of suspending life. Mrs Ashmole said she must go and telephone the coach company because some of the ladies had a superstition about riding in a green vehicle.

When she had gone out of the room, Cedric said to Constance, "It would be nicer if you went."

"Nicer of me?"

"Nicer than if you didn't."

"That rather depends on what I plan to do that evening."

"What do you plan to do?"

"Nothing." Constance blew a smoke ring. "I always enjoy that."

"If that's what it is to you, I don't know which of us comes off worst. I think it must be you. Don't you remember anything? There was a bit about forsaking all others —"

"We both promised that."

"I kept my promise!"

Constance raised her eyebrows, which cost her less effort than a shrug, but expressed the same disassociation.

"Does *he* know that it means nothing to you?"

"He?"

"The poor devil sees you coming to him, meetings, secret assignations — naturally he thinks — he hopes — he believes — my God!" Cedric threw up his hands. "It's so inconsistent!"

Constance hadn't forgotten me, she looked over and smiled.

Cedric began to walk up and down. He was wearing rubber-soled shoes, his step was energetic, as if he was about to break into a run, or into a leap and a shout as he was fond of doing on the tennis court. His energy embarrassed me. I was aware — as I had not been before, even on the hillside — that I had no business to be there.

"I want you to tell me — yes, I actually ask you to speak out. Why not? You don't lie with conviction, you don't do me the courtesy, you don't take even a little trouble to make it credible. I'm not a fool, how can I believe you?" He flung himself to his knees beside her chair. "Tell me about him! I won't be angry — I promise."

"In that case — " She leaned forward and whispered in his ear, then lay back in her chair, smiling. Cedric's face went brick-red and gathered, as if he was about to burst into tears.

\* \* \*

I was looking forward to the theatre. I asked Mrs Ashmole to tell me the story of the play and then I stopped her because I preferred it to come as a surprise. I asked if there would be music and she said there would be a little singing. She said it was a sad play and rather eerie. I thought that when I had been to the theatre my education would be complete.

We were to have an early supper and the coach was to call for us at six o'clock. I spent the morning looking through a pair of opera glasses which Constance was lending to me. Then I found that I had torn my skirt, the only one fit to wear to a theatre. I mended it carefully, taking trouble to match the colour of the thread to the material and sewing it with small stitches so that it wouldn't show. When it was done, I pressed the skirt and hung it over the rail of my bed. I put out my jacket and gloves and a clean handkerchief. Then I went to Mrs Ashmole and told her I had a sick headache and could not go.

"My dear, you must take a powder and lie down. It will soon pass."

"No. It will last for hours."

"You must not give way to a headache. I have never done so and I am four times your age."

At a quick reckoning I made her sixty-four years old and I saw that I should need to be more explicit. "It isn't just a headache, it's nervous debility."

"Nonsense! You are neither nervous nor debilitated, you are a strong, healthy girl. Do as I say and you will be perfectly well by the time we are ready to go."

"I'm going to be sick – "

She steered me upstairs and made me lie flat on my bed with my eyes closed. Nausea, she said, was a symptom of vertigo, and obliged me to swallow a Seidlitz powder. Then she drew the curtains and rustled away to her early supper.

I was hungry, and sorely tempted to stage a quick recovery which would enable me to eat and to go to the theatre. Flesh and spirit were tempted, and probity too. It would have been nice to give up lying. Sheer stubbornness kept me on my bed in the darkened room for the next hour. When Mrs Ashmole looked in, I lay with a handkerchief over my eyes.

"How are you feeling?"

I groaned and she touched my forehead with her finger-tips. "You are quite cool."

"It will pass," I said faintly.

"Perhaps we should call the doctor."

"He'll say I'm growing too fast."

"He will not say anything so stupid. If you are not quite well by the morning I shall send for him."

"I'll get better if I stay here quietly. But I shall miss the theatre —"

"Don't fret, there will be other times. Constance shall come and sit with you."

"Please — " I snatched the handkerchief to my mouth — "I couldn't be sick in comfort with anyone here."

She looked at me compassionately. At the door she said, "Try to sleep, poor child," and finally she went. The coach came soon afterwards.

I had prepared a chink in the curtains. 'One could call you a martyr to your principles,' I said to myself as I watched it drive away.

There was not long to wait. Constance came to look at me, and when she saw that I was, apparently, sleeping, she quietly crept away. Under the blankets I was dressed and ready. As soon as I heard her leave the house, I ran downstairs.

I was sure she would not look back, and I did not trouble to keep out of sight. Her footsteps crunched on the gravel, mine on the grass verge were silent.

\*     \*     \*

The next morning I was put through an inquisition. Mrs Ashmole not only asked questions she satisfied herself by examining my tongue, the lids of my eyes, and taking my temperature.

I assured her I was fully recovered: after a sick headache, I said, I always felt better than before. "It clears the system."

"No doubt," she said dryly, and asked if I had trouble every month.

"No, only now and then."

"I was referring to your periods. I consider myself responsible for you. Never ignore Nature's warnings. The system does not require cleansing unless it has been poisoned or overloaded. Certainly not at your age. Have you had a bowel movement this morning?"

Mercifully, Cedric came in and she could not ask me any more intimate questions.

"You may have three rashers if you like," she told him.

"Almayer will not be having any."

"I could eat a little bacon." I said.

"It would be wiser not to. Dry toast and China tea for you this morning."

"I'm not hungry either," said Cedric. "It's a barbarous habit, eating meat at this time of day."

"This is the best time to eat it, when the digestion has rested overnight. Who was it said that the British gave up their Empire when they gave up their four-course breakfast?" While she was helping herself to bacon I managed to hide a slice of bread and butter in my lap. "Almayer has been rather unwell and could not come to the theatre with us last evening."

"What a shame." Cedric looked at me kindly, but briefly, "Did you enjoy the play, Mother?"

"Tolerably. The Mary Rose was too coy for my taste. Her performance would have been more appropriate to Gilbert and Sullivan." Cedric was using the end of his knife to spring crumbs off the tablecloth, Mrs Ashmole said sharply, "You remember the three little girls tittering behind their fans in *The Mikado*?"

"It would depend."

"What would?"

"The degree of coyness would depend on what she had to hide."

"You will make a hole in the tablecloth."

"What was she doing?"

"Mary Rose?"

"Constance. Last night."

Mrs Ashmole, who was always quite content, managed to isolate herself completely by drawing a long, faintly whistling breath. "Why don't you ask her?"

"She'd say she did nothing."

"And why not? I have never known anyone so relaxed as Constance is able to be. She will age very slowly."

"Like a cabbage?"

"You know I do not mean that. Constance has a lively mind, I have the highest regard for her intelligence. She is also blessed with a rare quality of repose."

"I'll find out — you see if I don't!" He sounded, and looked, like a mutinous schoolboy.

"My dear, it will pass—"

"And if it does, will she become a loving wife?" Mrs Ashmole glanced at me. He looked too, but unseeingly. "I shouldn't be surprised. I'd say quite certainly — no doubt at all!"

I said, "I can tell you what she did."

"Loving who?" cried Cedric. "That's the point!"

"What did you say, Almayer?"

"I know what Constance did yesterday evening."

"How do you know?"

"I followed her. I saw what she did. Everything."

"That's not possible."

"It is," I said eagerly. "You'd only just gone, when I suddenly felt better. If it had happened a few minutes earlier I could have come with you. It must have been the Seidlitz powder. I shall know what to take next time."

"Wait a minute," said Cedric. "If you saw what she did, why didn't you tell me?"

"I was going to."

"Everyone knows except me? Is that about the size of it?"

"I haven't told anyone."

"I should hope not," Mrs Ashmole said sharply. "It is no one else's concern. It is certainly not yours."

"There's nothing much to tell, anyway. She took the bus outside the Post Office, she went inside the bus and I went on top. She didn't see me but I saw her get off at the Pier gardens —"

"It is quite immaterial what you saw," said Mrs Ashmole. "We do not wish to hear it."

"I do," said Cedric.

"Don't encourage her to engage in idle gossip —"

"Go on!" he said and pointed the knife at me.

"Well, she went into the gardens and walked round and looked at the lily pool, and then she went into a café called the Roserie and had a cup of tea. Or it might have been coffee."

"Who with?"

"No one. She was the only person there. They put up the closed sign and she came out. She looked in shop windows. Then she got on the eight o'clock bus and sat with old Mrs Merchant. She didn't meet anyone."

"Are we to understand," said Mrs Ashmole, "that you spent last night spying on Constance?"

"Not spying —"

"I should like to know what else it can be called."

"Mrs George said at the meeting that you ought to have Constance followed."

"The meeting?" said Cedric.

"The theatre-guild meeting – "

"Good God! Did they discuss it in detail? Was it on the agenda? Did they vote on it?"

"It is a complete fabrication. Of course it was not discussed at the guild meeting – "

"I didn't say it was. I said that Mrs George – "

"Almayer! You have said enough!"

"It doesn't prove anything," said Cedric. "Except that she didn't meet him last night."

"There isn't anyone," I said.

"For some reason he couldn't come, so she went to the places they usually go together. Women do that, they wallow!"

"She wasn't doing anything – "

"I know where, and I know when. Any place, any time, that's the size of it. That's a clue. It means he's not known locally and he isn't tied to an office. He's a commercial traveller, or he runs a one-man business. He's an actor and puts on a different disguise every time. What the devil does it matter who or what he is, so long as I find him!" Cedric sprang to his feet. "When I do, I'll break his neck!" His chair crashed over backwards as he strode out of the room.

"I shall not ask if you know what you have done," Mrs Ashmole said. "Obviously you do not. It would be beyond your comprehension."

"I can't help it if he won't believe me – "

"I have only myself to blame for not being omniscient, or at any rate hyper-cautious. For not holding my tongue – whatever other people did with theirs – and my emotions." She said bitterly, "Those I should have denied."

I didn't know what she was talking about. I could see she wasn't pleased, and pleased was what I had expected her and Cedric to be.

"I was afraid of this," she said, picking up his chair.

"He'll get over it, he didn't mean what he said."

"On what do you base that assumption?" she spoke so icily that the words dried in my throat. "We shall not be able to continue living together in this house."

I cried — thinking that here was the light, and glad to see it — "If you're angry because I told a lie about being sick, it was only so that I could stay behind. You wanted to know who she was meeting and I wanted to find out for you. That's why I did it. Of course I wanted to go to the theatre, right up to the last I let myself think I was going — I don't enjoy lying and pretending — "

"What you enjoy is unimportant."

"But it's important not to have to think the worst of her! It's very important to Cedric. He must believe me —"

"Thinking the worst of someone can be the same as thinking the best of oneself. Of course you would not understand the importance of that." What a lot of cracks there were in her face, fine but rigid, like the little networks under porcelain glaze. It occurred to me, with a quake of alarm, that I had not noticed them before because they had not been there. "Have you succeeded in finding yourself another situation?"

"I haven't been looking for one."

"You should do so at once."

"You want me to go?"

Evidently my astonishment and dismay reached her, for she smiled faintly. "I will write to Gerda Hauptmann."

"Why?"

"She will help you."

"Why do you want me to go?"

She lifted her chin and looked at me over the high wall. "If I catch the midday post she can meet you at Victoria tomorrow afternoon."

"I don't need Miss Hauptmann." I did, of course. I had no money and no home and no prospects. I needed all the help I could get. "I thought you'd be *pleased*!"

"About what?"

"About Constance not having a lover."

"A lover?"

I have never been able to rid the word of her distaste. Even now I still get a wryness at the back of my tongue whenever I hear it. "I believe you're sorry."

"It would be better for us all if there was someone," she said.

# VI

Humbert Vine, having moved, with a definite purpose in view, from one frowzy bed-sitter to another no less frowzy, went at once to look at himself in the mirror. The irreversible process could be said to have started: his arteries had half a millimetre less bore, a million cells had died, his mean blood temperature had fallen, and 150 hairs had dropped out of the crown of his head. One day it must begin to show.

But he still looked like somebody's dream boy, strong yet wistful. If he sucked in his cheeks he could deepen the hollows under his eyes. A face to be worn in a locket. He didn't fancy being between some woman's mammary glands, he would rather be on a knitting pattern. Perhaps if he sent his photograph to Paton and Baldwin he could become a model and make some extra money. A dreamboy in Fair Isle — with all the imperfect garments given as a bonus he would be set up for life.

Something caught his eye, a screw of paper pushed into the awful barbola frame of the mirror. He prised it out and unrolled it and found written a number, with crossed sevens, and a telephone exchange, in a Continental hand.

Clissold. He tucked the paper in his pocket and looked round the room. Now he felt he had unpacked and was at home. The parcel with his clothes in he pushed out of sight under the bed. Clissold was a lovely name. Almayer Clissold he could have loved. Jenkins had had an ear, and started a Spanish war with it.

From the window there was an interrupted view of tabby houses, and immediately behind them the incinerator chimney of the local hospital from whence he might expect the smell of burning babies. At intervals along the street the leaves of the trees were turning the colour of fried bread because it was late August. Their roots came up through the pavement like bunions. Maple Road — someone had scrawled 'Kosher' on the wall opposite.

How odd if this should be the abode of love! Love of all things, could not afford to live here. Love had appearances to keep up. What David saw, persuaded himself that he saw, kept the small ball rolling, rolling. This place would not only bear heavily on his powers of persuasion, it would chaw them to bits.

The meat-safe proved to contain half a jar of jam which had gone mouldy. He tossed the jar out of the window and it landed in a holly-bush in the next-door garden. Too late he noticed the lady of the house emerging. She looked up, her startled expression changing to anger when she saw him leaning on the sill.

"It's those Jew-baiters!" he said before she could open her mouth. "They were aiming at me because they think I wear a phylactery. It's only my eye-shade. I have to shade my right eye, you see, because it gets over-active and runs rings round the left one — which leaves me with disturbed vision. So I wear this black patch which, when I push it into the middle of my forehead, looks like one of those little boxes with Hebrew texts in, and they think I'm a son of Abraham and throw things at me. The other day, believe it or not, it was a pig's trotter and it hit me in the face. They thought they'd defiled me for life. Are you going to complain to the police? I'll testify if you do." The woman put up her umbrella. "Or perhaps you'll sign the petition I'm drawing up to have them evicted? Anti-Semitism is paranoiac."

She went down her garden path and away along the street and it was indeed starting to rain. He left the window open so that he could listen to it, and lay down on the bed.

He had not eaten since six o'clock that morning when he had had three hamburgers, two helpings of spaghetti bolognese and two rounds of toast. By staying in bed he usually managed to make his late supper last until his early one, but this afternoon the move into the new place had taxed his resources. He was as hollow as a drum.

David had once told him that there were thirty million glands in the stomach wall, manufacturing the gastric juices to break down and convert food into bodily energy. He worried what his glands could be doing now with nothing to convert. They might start on his stomach wall, or on each other. How could they know the difference? He pulled up his shirt and tapped for resonance. Some places sounded thinner than others.

To make matters worse, he was aware of sausages cooking, not a smell so much as a consciousness. Of all food he probably liked sausages least, but he thought now of the firm little body between his teeth, the skin expolding to release hot savoury sawdust, and his tongue watered. Perhaps he should go and ask the landlady to lend him a sausage. She would certainly refuse, she was a female spider.

'It's most awfully good of you to let me come in on a Thursday,' he had said, using his ardent boy approach as she looked out of her crevice. She told him that the fortnight's rent in advance was payable from the previous Monday. So he was three days out of pocket and all he had until he was paid on Saturday was four and eightpence.

'Mrs Phelan dear – ' some ugly leprechaun had had to wed her in fulfilment of a curse laid on him by the chief witch – 'I'm so confused, what with changing my apartment and everything, I quite forgot to replenish my larder. Could I beg a spoonful of bread and a slice of tea?' He would enjoy the sheer absurdity of trying to milk human kindness out of the old spider.

He stood up to the chiming of the bed springs, a sound new and virginal enough for him to want to hear it again. He bounced around, trying to vary the pitch, and was about to attempt a major chord by jumping hard, when there was a rap at the door. As he stepped off, the springs throbbed with a deep organ note.

Opening the door he cried, "Did you hear that?"

"Hear what?"

"My bed," he said proudly. "I shall write music for it – a Symphony for Unaccompanied Bed Springs."

"Please will you help me?"

"If it's a symphony it can't be unaccompanied. I shall write a fugue. Help you? Of course I will." Almayer Jenkin wasn't even pretty, she had put on eyeshadow in blue rings. He thought, I shall call her Bonzo. "What do you want me to do?"

"Are you good with birds?"

"Which sort? I'm average with both."

"Can you touch them? Handle them, I mean?" She shuddered, pulling her right shoulder up to her ear and pressing her chin down into it. "I can't. I'm actually terrified of them, and there's a pigeon stuck in the chimney."

"Oh the poor thing!"

"Please will you come and get it out? My room's across the landing – "

"Have you thought how terrified the pigeon must be? It must

feel like death in the dark, its wings fixed down, the smoke rising all round — "

"I haven't got a fire."

More than anything he wanted to see what her room was like, more than he wanted to see her. Clues might be found in her face, but the answer would be there. It would tell him what David felt when he went into that room, and when he knew, he would understand, and if he understood he could take it apart.

The first thing he saw was that it was the same as his in reverse. Mrs Spider Phelan had bought up the stock of a rundown hotel: a dozen overworked beds, twelve fumed oak wardrobes, sundry basket chairs unknitted at the edges, and bedside cupboards with double doors opening on the jerry. It was all represented here, and there were other things — chintz curtains, rag rugs, china kittens, velvet cushions, two wine-glasses, a sink-tidy and pink sponge splash-rings on the taps. 'Oh David, David,' he said under his breath, and laughed. He had been expecting something really formidable.

"I'll put newspaper down, it's bound to make a mess," and she spread, as he knew she would, sheets of the *Ashburn Examiner* on the hearthrug.

"You know what they say? If you want dirt, read the *Trashbin Examiner*."

"It's a very good paper!" she said sharply.

He dropped to his knees. "Oh I don't believe what people say, I believe what they do." He thrust his arm into the chimney. "I hope the poor thing isn't too far up."

"Could we push it out with a broom?"

"It would get hurt." He looked at her curiously while he was groping in the chimney. Her nose prevented her from being pretty. It was a good nose, well-shaped, but it didn't fit her face. She had nice hair and a queenly curve of neck and bosom. Her eyes were like currants in a Chelsea bun.

"I think I've — yes — can you hear him scuffling, trying to get away from my hand? Its allright, pidgewudge, keep still and I shan't hurt you."

"They sit on the chimney-pot billing and cooing. It's enough to drive you crazy."

"May I call you Bonzo?"

"My name's Almayer Jenkin."

"I know."

"How do you know?"

"I've got him. Here he comes!"

"Oh be careful — "

"I wouldn't hurt him for the world."

"You're making such a mess!"

The bird's heart was pumping in his hand. "Poor Wudgie, he's terrified — much more than you are." He held out the bird to her. She backed away with a scream. "It's allright," he said to the bird, "you're safe," and laid it against his cheek.

"Do you always give people and things nicknames?"

"Always." But not David. "What else could you call a silly fat old pigeon that gets itself stuck in a chimney but Wudgie? Now let's see if he's allright. Yes, his wings are undamaged — what a span they are! He'll fly as well as ever."

"Oh, do put it out!"

"Look at his pink feet. I wish mine were that colour."

"Please — "

"Coral pink feet would go beautifully with a pale blue suit, but I haven't got that, either."

"What are you doing now?"

"He can't go home all sooted up like this. His friends will think he's a crow and ostracise him. Birds are conformists, you know. A thrush won't sit on an egg that hasn't exactly the same number of speckles as all the others. There, I've dusted off the worst. If we let him flutter about in here he'll shake off the rest of the soot."

"No! No, no, no!"

He said interestedly, "Do you often do that?"

"Do what?"

"Stamp your foot."

"Will you please put that horrible bird out!"

From her window he could see the garden, rampant with grass and Old Man's Beard. "Look Wudgie, there's your tree, just a few little flap-flaps and you're home. Off you go, and keep away from Bonzo's chimney in future."

He threw the bird into the air. It fell like a stone, then, recovering, beat clumsily up and back on to the roof. Immediately there was an outbreak of cooing.

"I don't think I want to be called Bonzo."

"You can call me Georgie. Everyone does."

"Georgie's not a nickname."

"It's short for Humbert Cloudesley Vine. After the admiral, Sir Cloudesley Shovel, one of my ancestors. I've always been glad we're Vines and not Shovels. Imagine being Humbert Shovel!"

"How did you know my name?"

"Spider Phelan told me. I've just moved in. She said, 'Come along, poor beetle, there's a place in my web for you, with a pretty young Almayer fly right opposite.'"

"Spider? Fly? You do fabricate, don't you!"

"Listen to Wudgie telling his mates what a time he had."

"I'm ever so grateful to you for getting it out."

He smiled his shy smile, remarking what he had glimpsed at the moment of entry: there was food on the table. "I must go and buy something to eat. I left my tea at the other place, you can't pack butter and kippers with your pyjamas, can you?"

"The corner shop closes Thursday afternoon. I haven't any kippers but there's ham. Won't you have some?"

That's how he got to know David's girl.

He could not forget, or forgive, the way he had got to know *about* her. He bore a grudge against the time, the place (Wednesday evening in the Cressy Arms), the Man Who Told him, everyone in the bar, the smell of Guinness, the maps on the marble table-tops of 'perilous seas and faerylands forlorn' David had said, and those beastly white china beerpulls which never until then had reminded him of women's breasts.

It should have been done, if it had to be done, at a pure time and in a pure place. He might have been able to bear it if they had been on the Heath in the depths of winter with every grassblade a glassblade, and every twig furred with frost. Or in the park at the height of summer, pacing in green cathedrals, the two of them bleeding but dignified.

He had been waiting in the Cressy Arms. Wednesday was still their evening, or he thought it still was, and the world was a merry-go-round with music. On Wednesdays everything looked better than life to him. If he had been asked how it was, he would have said it was like being carried on someone's shoulder, and if he had been told to put it in a word, he would have said 'safe'.

The bar of the Cressy was well-primed with David, it was David's favourite pub. Even the beer rings were his.

The Man Who Told him paused on his way to the bar to ask how he was.

"I'm fine, thank you."

"I've seen you look better. I said so to Desiree."

"I couldn't possibly feel better."

"She said, 'He's putting a brave face on.' "

"A brave face on what?"

"Desiree gets to know everything. 'Shame about those two,' she said, 'it's a crying shame. I'm sorry for Georgie.' "

"Tell her to mind her own business."

"It was well meant. Never turn away a kindly word."

The barmaid, blue-powdered, strawberry-haired, had given them some laughs. At least, he had laughed, and David had dropped a smile into his beer. David had a superstition that to laugh in someone's face was to expose your own rear.

"What did she mean – a shame?"

"He's not coming, your Davey. Didn't come last night either, did he?"

"He was working."

"And the night before? And Sunday? Who works Sundays?"

"David does, he's a reporter. News breaks on Sundays too, you know."

"Not round here." The Man Who Told him put his beer on Georgie's table and sat down. "Nothing happens here on Sundays."

"I expect he's gone to report one of the world's trouble-spots – Wimbledon or Penge."

"You'll have to find another playmate. Your Davey's got a girl."

"Do you think I don't know?" Quick, quick, quick was the thing to be, for there was no false alarm, there was only alarm, which, true or false, held the same degree of fright. "When hasn't he had a girl? He's a womaniser." If you don't stand still, you can't be hit.

The man, having told him, took his beer to another table.

Georgie stayed in the Cressy Arms until it was time to go to work, but David did not come. That night he whipped his spirits up so high, aping about and cheeking everyone, he nearly was given the sack.

The next evening he went round to David's digs. David was out and he persuaded the landlady to let him wait in David's room.

"He's expecting me, we always spend Wednesday evenings together."

"Today's Thursday."

"I know, he couldn't make it yesterday."

He made a quick search but found no traces of the girl. In the pocket of one of David's jackets were the stubs of two tickets for the Haymarket the previous night. There was also a significant omission: the photograph of David's wife was gone from the mantel-shelf. On the table was his typewriter, surrounded by balls of screwed-up paper.

It was some comfort to be there among his things. Georgie had never thought what he would do without the prospect of David. Of course he could remember what it was like before they met, but it was not worth remembering, and he didn't bother about the future. Being in David's room was like being in the warm, knowing he would have to go out into the cold.

David's wife's picture was in the bottom drawer of the chest. He took it out and studied it. He knew little about David's past. He wasn't very interested: David's past was a stalk and the flower on the end of it was now. But this woman had fulfilled, or had promised to, a need of David's which, apparently, still existed. Georgie wasn't so green as to be surprised; he was curious, ravenously curious. And a bit edgy.

She had a little, wishy face, this fulfiller. Or she had had. His impression was that she was dead. Once, and once only, he had ventured to ask about her. He had been feeling assured enough to cope with her ghost, enough to lay it, enough to shoot it to shreds. David smiled, not in the least haunted — 'Old, unhappy, far-off things are best forgotton.' Forgotten they were, and would have been still, but for David's need.

Look as he might at the photograph, he could not see what need this woman could have fulfilled, except as a picture on a chocolate box. She was pouting, as if life had not offered her what she wanted. *Her* need, whatever it was, had swallowed David's up, and there they were, a pair of gaping birds, unable to help each other.

Now David was trying again. Let him try. Let him succeed, if he could. It was going to be unimportant, even to David. Especially to David.

Georgie laid the poor-baby face in the drawer and covered it with David's pants.

Did David lie in bed on Sunday mornings and talk to the new girl on the telephone? Saying what? On occasions Georgie had stood by while David looked at girls, his eyes narrowed as if against sun or smoke, or as if he were taking aim. But he could not now remember what David has said or, more importantly, how he had said it.

He picked up the receiver. "Trunks? I want to call Appleaston in Wiltshire. I have the number."

While he waited, he went through David's telephone list. There was one number newly written in pencil, and beside it the initials 'A.J.' Sweet Annie Jaundice, the new girl.

"Yes — Lady Vine, please. Hello, mummy, it's me. How are you? Are you well? Oh, I'm in rude health ... No, no particular reason, I just wondered how you are ... Money? That's not why I rang. I'm using a friend's phone — David Pollock, he's a reporter on a local paper. Shall I bring him down? I've told him you look like Pola Negri and he's dying to meet you. I can't, though — bring him, I mean. I haven't the fare. Did I tell you I've got a new job? At the Hotspur, a sort of all-night beer cellar just off Leicester Square. I'm a kitchen boy, I start at nine and finish at six ... No, nine at night, six in the morning. I have the lovely long day to myself. And they give me as much food as I can eat. You know how much I can eat! It's stuff nobody else wants, the rest of the staff have first choice. I'm way down the social scale ... Yes, I know what you said, you said I must try to keep myself in the manner to which I've become accustomed, and that's what I'm doing, and it gets easier all the time because my standards are getting lower ... I'm not asking, I don't want money, it only complicates. I'm blissfully, beatically, blazingly happy, so please don't be angry, you'll make your nose red ... Darling, whether you like it or not, your little Humbert's a bumbert ..."

Hearing David's key in the lock he hung up. He reached the other side of the room with one bound and was in the armchair, nursing his knees, when David came in.

David stopped on the threshold, the process of thought evident in his face, David always showed that he was thinking, but not what.

There was time enough, while he stood and looked, for a

conclusion to be reached. But as if deciding to take it from there, he raised his hand and twitched the first fingers in greeting. He had done that the first time they met. They had not actually spoken, David had just signalled his whereabouts. There was no need to make themselves known. David had always been more than a possibility and rather less than an ideal. When he finally took substance, the substance had the patina of use. Of course it was a recognised fact that — just as the grass was greener on someone else's patch — if you did not expect to get to thirty-five, people of that age seemed rather special.

David was neither good-looking nor ugly. His features were even and his mouth well-shaped, but he had a mottled complexion which deepened to liver colour when he was cold or angry. His hair was getting thin on top. He dressed in tweed jackets and baggy flannels.

What made him special? Perhaps the conviction, which need not be widely held, that besides having left its mark on him, experience had left grace as well.

David sat on the bed and filled his meerschaum. It had a lid and an elaborately carved bowl. He could take as long or as little time as he liked getting it primed and drawing, and he claimed that it was better than psychology for loosing people's tongues.

Georgie said, "Aren't you going to ask what I'm doing here?"

"I know what you're doing." He dropped tobacco shred by shred into the bowl and pressed it down.

"Why didn't you ring?"

"I've been expecting you to come."

"I'd have come ages ago if I'd known that. It's been ages. I went to the Cressy and sat around waiting. Whenever I rang your office they said you were out."

"On a job."

"Not morning, noon and night! You told me not to come here. If I'd known you wanted me to come —"

"To expect isn't necessarily to want."

"You've had a bad day. I can always tell, you start chopping me. I don't mind, chop away, chop me up, a finger and a toe at a time, like Chinese torture, if it makes you feel better."

David dropped the meerschaum and stretched himself on the bed. Two entrenched lines between his eyes met in a cleft aiming down the middle of his nose.

"People are such fools," said Georgie. "It does help to chop me, doesn't it?"

"People are sick."

Georgie went and stood beside the bed and with the tips of his fingers lifted the cleft from between David's closed eyes and smoothed it away over his temples. "I'm not sick, I'm fit as a flea and pure as a pearl."

"I've been expecting you, Georgie, and it has to happen, but the last thing I need is for it to happen tonight."

"Then let it happen tomorrow. Or next week. Or next year."

David sat up. "Keep your hands off! How many times do I have to tell you not to touch me? People will think we're catamites."

"There are no people here to think anything, and no one could think it of me, for I've had dozens of girls. Women too. I told you about that friend of my mother's, didn't I? And you've been married. Otherwise —" he thrust his hands into his pockets and shrugged — "well, I'd have been more careful. People don't forget that sort of thing, they think you're born without, or with not enough, or you're not all there, or you're back to front —"

"Shut up."

"I wouldn't want anyone to think about me for the rest of my life. I could never prove them wrong, not without giving a public demonstration. So I wouldn't, I certainly wouldn't, have come to your room like this if I hadn't genuinely believed you were married."

David picked up the meerschaum and cursed because the tobacco had fallen out.

"It was the first thing my mother asked when I told her about you. I said you had a lovely wife. You did tell me she was lovely, and so long as you've been a husband, you're identified. Like having a hole punched in your ear — everyone knows where you belong."

"My wife died. In a hospital for the criminally insane."

"Oh God. Why?"

"She killed our son."

"How was I to know?" He burst into tears. "It isn't fair to keep a thing like that up your sleeve. Making a fool of me!"

"A fool of you?"

"I should have been told!"

David smiled. "Would you prefer not to have associated with me?"

"You took advantage of my not knowing. You wouldn't let me share, you went around cuddling that awful thing, saying 'Ah, if he only knew! He'd be so nice to me and oh, what a worm he'd feel about the times he hasn't been!' "

"Nice?"

"You loved thinking how wormy I'd feel. It means you aren't sure of yourself."

"Who is?"

"Contrary to what most people think, martyrdom is the easy way out."

"I believe you're sure of yourself."

"Well, it's over now. I know. And you've got a girl. I know that too. Why the great stone face? I'm glad! It's what I wanted for you. I always thought you should have a feminine influence in your life, to smooth those rough male edges. You can be very rough and male. Every man needs a woman. Like hell needs snow."

But he knew better than to twinkle at that moment. He was serious, even weighty. "Tell me about her. Have I seen her? Is she pretty? Is she clever? Is it Dolores in the Back Number Department?"

David might be dismissed as slow-witted by those who did not suspect how far his mind went into a question, and how thoroughly, between the time of asking, and his reply. He might be feared, because of the purely mechanistic face he put on his thought, good or bad, and on his impulses. It was possible not to know what he was thinking until he acted on it, and if he did not choose to act, it was possible not to know at all.

"It's no one you're acquainted with. Or ever will be."

"Why not?"

"For Christ's sake." He spoke equably, as if he were saying grace. "It's over, Georgie. I'm going to marry her."

"Oh how marvellous!" Quick, quick, quick was the thing to be. "Are you engaged? Oh thrilling! Am I the first to know? Say I'm the first! I couldn't stand it if I wasn't. After all we've — " But of course he knew when to stop. "We've had such good times together, it would be a breach of privilege if you told anyone before you told me."

David finished packing the meerschaum and hung it in his

mouth — perhaps the cruellest thing he could have done, it made the heart ache with loss. He said, "You're not to come here and we're not going to meet again."

"What an old-fashioned thing you are! She won't mind you having a boy friend, women like to think of men as boys. She'll want to make a pet of me —"

"Sit down, Georgie. You look ready to fall down."

"Don't be kind — I can't bear it if you're kind."

David gave him a shove which unbalanced and dropped him on the bed. "I'm to blame for letting it go on. We've nothing in common, we're completely alien. Background, age, interests. I don't know what you see in me."

"What do you see in me?"

"Wetness."

"Wetness!"

David smiled. "Behind the ears."

"Then what I see in you is dryness behind the ears."

"The cure's in the malady. You're immature, therefore you can afford not to be fussy and to take what you want from wherever you please." Smoke was wreathing round his head. It came out grey with his breath. His thoughts, too, were half smoke. Lit up just in time, hadn't he, to get the mixture. But which came first, the thoughts or the pipe? "For you, it's part of growing up. If you choose the wrong people you can grow out of them. I've got to be careful, time's against me. I'm slower to adjust, to make up my mind. And there's something else. The question of committal. It isn't easy come, easy go, at my age. I have to commit myself."

"You don't want me any more. Is that what you're saying?"

"I'm saying I may never find another girl like her."

\*       \*       \*

The first time David saw them together he saw them both at once. There they were, one in each eye: then he looked at Almayer only, then only at Georgie. He stood reviewing the whole thing. Everything Georgie had done, he went back and turned it up. He had always had a way of getting to the gist of whatever it was Georgie had done. He reviewed Georgie's actions and analysed his motives, and Georgie watched him do it. The girl, of course, did not know what she was watching.

It had been easy to find out where she lived. Georgie simply followed David to the house and into it. He was quite brassfaced. He stood in the hall and watched David climb the stairs. He even went up a few steps to get a glimpse when she opened her door on the first-floor landing. He was unlucky that time, there was only a murmur of voices as the door closed on David.

So then he knocked up the landlady and asked if she had a room to let. She said the first floor front might be, and it might not. He wanted to see it but she said there was someone in residence. It would have been fun to go and look over it, only a few paces away from David.

Georgie asked were they quiet, the people across the landing, and Spider Phelan said there was a young lady who was no trouble to anyone. He was such a light sleeper, Georgie said, and he thought the husband had stomped as he went upstairs. Miss Jenkin was unmarried, and gentlemen friends had to be out of the house by ten o'clock. The same, she said looking sideways at him — which was when he decided to call her Spider — went for lady friends.

"This is Mr Pollock," said the girl, introducing them. "David, this is Mr Vine — "

Georgie advanced solemnly. "How do you do?" David did not take his hand.

The girl said, "He has the room across the landing."

"Has he, by God."

Georgie cried, "I swear to you this is the way it happened. I'm absolutely transfixed, though not as transfixed as you are, because Bonzo has been talking about you — naming no names — and I was beginning to have a faint suspicion. But when I moved in, I had no idea, I didn't dream. How could I, when you hadn't told me anything? Not one single clue."

"Clue?" said Almayer.

"Well, hint, for it never occurred to me to try to find out. How could I? By snooping around, following you? I should find that thoroughly distasteful."

"Don't overdo it," said David.

Almayer looked at them. "Do you know each other?"

"We're old friends. Isn't it marvellous?" Georgie cried, "I believe in Fate. David doesn't, he says it would kill his self-respect."

"Bonzo?" said David.

"I call her that, just between ourselves." He turned to the girl. "Shall we let him call you that?"

*"Bonzo?"*

"It's a pet name. You mustn't mind, David, I'm quite catholic. I mean, Mrs Spider Spelan isn't my sort of pet."

"How well do you know him?" David asked the girl.

"We only met yesterday."

"I feel I've known her for years! There's such a lot to say and such a lot we don't need to say. That's how it was with David and me when we first met."

David told the girl, "He's the son of Sir Frederick and Lady Vine of Old Hall, Wiltshire. His brother is a Junior Minister in the Government and his sister is married to a Q.C. Georgie's the baby of the family. He works as a kitchen-boy and chucker-out at the Hotspur Club."

She looked wide-eyed. "But — why?"

"They're frightfully discreet at the Hotspur," said Georgie. "They don't like anything noisy or vulgar to happen. So, when people are silly, I'm sent to escort them off the premises. I do it nicely, I put on a dinner-jacket and go upstairs and pretend we're old friends and put my arm around their necks and jolly them along. But most of the time I help wash up."

"Why do you do it?"

"Well, I'm no good at anything else. I'm not political like my brother, nor marriageable like my sister. I'm the sort of black baby of the family."

"But can't you do better than that?" Ah yes, he thought, there it was, a note of authority, and moral pique. "Washing-up and policing drunks — don't your parents mind?"

"Oh, strenuously! But I'm of age, and they can't stop me. What would you say if I told you I was happy? Not a care in the world?" Except one. But he didn't give a damn what she said, or thought, or was. "I earn enough to pay for my room. I work all night and I try to sleep all day, because when I get up I get hungry. I can have all I want to eat at the Hotspur. And I love drunks, they're sweet people. I love greasy dishes and the puddles of Chambertin and Beaune. I sweat like a horse and I feel pure as a lily."

"He doesn't have to think," said David. "That's best of all."

"Haven't you any ambition? Don't you want to make something of yourself?"

"Oh listen, listen to the voice of the turtle! I shall make a marvellous husband, with all my washing-up expertise."

He laughed at David with his thought-mills grinding, and the girl with eyes like prunes in blue saucers. "My dears, I'll have to go or I shall miss my supper. Chef's special tonight is lobster mornay. And there's frequently some beef stroganoff left over."

David was wrong in saying that he did not think. He thought a lot, and he did not put on a special face to do it. He could work, at the sort of work he was required to do, and be deep in thought at the same time. He didn't go as deep as David and he wasn't as exhaustive, but he went in fifty other directions as well. He liked to speculate.

\*     \*     \*

He ran, feeling the need of action. Knees up, and chin, elbows in, moving in time with his chest or his feet. He glimpsed himself in a shop window and was reminded of when, as children, they had played at trains, arms for pistons, and white steam dropping all over the nursery floor.

No-one knew how he hated the food at the Hotspur. Sometimes his empty stomach revolted at the nameless gobbets blanketed in grey or brown sauce. Sometimes he asked whether it was fish or meat, and was told that if he cared to take his plate upstairs he could pay for it and tip the waiter too.

"Poop, poop!" He stamped up the Fish Street gradient like a little class four engine. A woman called to him and a policeman held up his hand as if to a flood of traffic.

"Now then, why the hurry?"

"I'm going to work."

"Why the hurry?"

"I'm late, and I'm running because it's better than riding on the bus."

"Is it now?"

"For the old liver it is. Mine can do with a shake-up. Besides, it saves the fare. Killing two birds with one gallstone."

"Killing?" said the policeman, and hung his thumbs in his top pockets. "Where do you work?"

"At the Hotspur in Ryder Street. I'm sure you know it."

"I've got my eye on it."

"I'll tell Mr Balestri, he's the manager. He'll be so glad you're looking after us."

"Walk the rest of the way, mind — no running." He unhooked one thumb and touched Georgie's cheek. "Or I'll run you in."

There wasn't much farther to go. He had had his exercise and was proud to find that his heart-beat, though pronounced, was still deep in his chest. But he was hot from running, and when he went into the kitchen felt the heat of the place meeting the heat of his blood. As if a circuit had closed.

He threw off his jacket and shirt and was stripped to the waist before the doors had ceased to swing behind him. Delville looked up from his newspaper. Pose, the cook, stopped trimming steak and put his bloody fingers over his mouth.

"Does anyone mind if I take my trousers off? It must be two hundred in the shade in here."

"It is barely chambré."

"Don't you do anything natural?" said Pose. "When you open your eyes, what's the first thing you do?"

"Shut them tighter and dream about you, Pose."

"Put your shirt on." said Delville. "Mr Balestri can't bear the sight of navels."

"You're the one who can't bear it," said Pose.

"Mine's nice and neat," said Georgie. "I was well finished."

"Even shell-fish remind you of navels."

"I'm going upstairs." Delville folded his newspaper into certain individual creases. "I advise you, Vine, and you, Cook, to prepare yourselves for Mr Balestri."

Georgie dipped his fingers in a bowl of egg-white and sprinkled it over Pose and himself. "With a ceremony of purification."

"It's true about the shell-fish," said Pose. "He raves when I bring them in."

"The holes and the whorls? I suppose they might remind him. Perhaps it's the continuity he objects to. There's no doubt where you come from, and how, when you look at a navel. I expect he'd rather think he was a single strike."

"He does it to disparage me. Shell-fish is a gift, a calling, I put my best work in shell-fish. He knows that, so he keeps them off the menu. Another thing he does, he waters my soup before he serves it."

"He wouldn't dare!"

"He puts sugar on my pommes duchesse and when the customers complain he says it's a culinary refinement I picked up at cookery school in Sydenham."

Georgie was in the act of helping himself to a bread roll when Pose speared it with his steak-knife and wagged it in his face. "First you scrub this table, then you take up the bins, then you mop this floor, *then* you eat."

"But Pose, I'm starving!"

"If you don't work you don't eat."

"If I don't eat I can't work." He whipped the roll off the point of Pose's knife and thrust it between his teeth.

He referred to Delville as 'the Maitre'. He didn't know whether it pleased Delville, but if it didn't, he must be equally split between the fear of being mocked and the wish to keep an unsolicited testimonial and a tacit acknowledgement. The title fitted him more than it did Balestri, who would have been regarded as but a figurehead were it not for Delville's attention to protocol. It was 'Yes, Mr Balestri', 'No, Mr Balestri, as you wish —' when Balestri patently wished for nothing except not to have to make his mind up. It suited Delville to act as if he were escorting visiting royalty when Balestri came to the kitchen — partly to manifest the injustice of a man like him deferring to a man like Balestri, partly so that he did not have to line up with Pose and Georgie.

By tearing the roll to pieces, Georgie managed to stuff it all into his mouth, leaving his hands free to fill the bucket at the sink. "You're wrong about the Maitre, he thinks the world of you, he told me so. 'Where would the Hotspur be without Pose's cooking?' Those were his words."

"Where does he think it would be?"

"It was a rhetorical question."

Pose had thick lips, and to curl them he was obliged to push up one side of his face. "The master's voice, are you?"

Georgie brought his brimming bucket to the table. "He meant nowhere, Pose. I'm sure he did."

"Keep your baby-blue thoughts to yourself. That man's mind is another colour entirely. And remember what I told you. Never scrub this table with anything but salt. There's no purifier like salt. I imbibed that with my mother's milk. I never had expensive training, I'm not cordon bleu. I grew up with the basic facts bred in me. You start to know, not from books and classes and cooking dollies' dinners, but from here." Pose thumped his stomach. "I don't rate the seat of intelligence any higher."

"The way I feel now I could eat a horse." Georgie was drawing arabesques in salt on the table, and stood back to survey his handiwork. He was pleasantly surprised at how pretty it looked, quite Victorian. "Hoofs and all. I shouldn't fuss how it was served." He started to write David's name, but Pose seized the jar from him.

"I could serve my saddle of lamb or my grilled oxtail or my ham custard or my apricot soufflé on a rhubarb leaf, and every scrap would get eaten. See how they'd like it if all they got was that ape Delville whisking his napkin and shooting his bracelets."

"Pose, that's unkind." Some of the salt had spilled and Georgie threw a pinch over his left shoulder. "The Maitre puts his whole soul into everything he does." So saying, he sprang up on his toes, bowing and smiling, the tail of his shirt draped over his arm.

Pose threw him another roll. "Baby, you've earned your supper."

The roll fell into Georgie's pail. Pose laughed, not seeing, as Georgie did, that Delville was with them again, one well-manicured hand, with the fine gold chain at his wrist, on the knob of the half-open door.

"Chef's special" said Georgie. "Bucket brioche, a crisp alternative to the enervating bath bun." Snatching the roll out of the water he tossed it towards the door. "Oh, I do beg your pardon, Maitre, I didn't know you were there."

Delville said acidly, "When you have nothing better to do, perhaps you will fetch me some lager from the cellar."

"Of course. Do you mind if I just scrub this table? Not that it's a better thing to do, or worse, than fetching the beer. But Pose did ask first."

"If you'd done it when you were asked, you'd be finished now." Pose's thick lips rolled back as he looked at Delville. "Get a move on, scrub it clean, Mr Balestri can't stand the sight of blood."

"He is not coming." said Delville. "He has a migraine and has left me in charge."

"Oh what a shame!" cried Georgie. "I have a message for him. From the police."

"The police?"

"Yes, I met a nice constable this evening and when I said I worked at the Hotspur he said he was keeping his eye on us."

"Is he, by God," said Pose. He and Delville exchanged glances. A message passed and was understood.

"Come upstairs, Vine, I want a word with you," said Delville. Pose took the brush from Georgie's hand. "I'll finish this."

He followed Delville, stuffing his shirt into his trousers as he went. At the door, behind Delville's back, he waved his hand in imitation of Delville's imperious floor summons to staff. Pose watched, unsmiling.

The receptionist had not yet arrived. Delville sat himself behind the desk and arranged his wrists to the advantage of glossy cuffs and gold chain. "Now, Vine, tell me exactly what happened."

"Well, I was running because I didn't want to be late for work, and a policeman asked what my hurry was, and I told him. 'I'm sure you know the Hotspur Club,' I said — policemen know everything, don't they? — and he said he did. 'I've got my eye on it,' he said."

"What else?"

"I said Mr Balestri would be glad the police were looking after us. Then the constable cautioned me."

"Cautioned you?"

"He told me to walk the rest of the way or he'd run me in. He was very droll."

"You're not a fool, are you, Vine?" Delville seemed to be actually asking. He stared at Georgie, pressing his fingers on the desk, the blood ran a little way down under his pink nails. "No." Evidently the answer dissatisfied him. He frowned. "Do you discuss this with anyone outside?"

"Discuss what?"

"This place, anything that happens here."

"Only what happens in the kitchen. Things like Pose's profiteroles or his tartare sauce and his curried chicken and his strawberry mousse — "

"What else?"

Georgie blinked. "I might tell my friend about Pose throwing his knife at me. He does it in fun, of course, he says he used to do a knife-throwing act on the stage. I don't believe it, I don't think he's good enough."

"What else, besides the kitchen, do you find to talk about?"

113

"I don't see anything else, do I ? I don't know anything else. When I come up here —" Georgie looked wonderingly about him, "It's another world. So polished and civilised."

"This friend of yours, the one you talk to, what sort of boy is he?"

Georgie smiled. "He's no boy, he's old enough to be my father."

"What sort of man is he?"

"He comes here sometimes. He's a journalist."

Delville's milk-white face became a wild-rose pink, merging to lilac where his beard would be if he did not shave so scrupulously. Colours beautifully blended, Georgie thought.

"Don't try me too far, Vine." In his rich crimson lips, to Georgie's admiration, there appeared a touch of purple. "I am not amused by your brand of humour."

"Oh, Maitre! My friend's a sports writer, he only reports things like football matches and racing events."

\* \* \*

By three a.m. the club was half full. It was drinking, not eating time. It would be another hour before anyone wanted breakfast. Pose was asleep at the kitchen table and Georgie was making coffee when he heard someone blunder against the dustbins in the area yard. He knew who it would be: his joy was ready and unconfined, he did not have time or heart to conceal it.

At the same time he marvelled at himself, sad at this man's power to redeem. Not a chink of glory showed, he was just a man with black hair on his fingers, wearing a multi-million tweed jacket and grey flannels hung at the knees. At first sight there was nothing to choose between him and half the male population of the country. At second sight, there was the meaning of existence. David, oh David.

"Why, it's you," Georgie said. "I thought it was the dustbin tribe. They come every morning to look for titbits."

"Tribe?"

"Whiskers twitching, claws unsheathed, they hang from the edge of the bins by their tails, like furry jugs. Cold bacon fat they adore, and they sit up and eat the chicken feet as daintily as if they were asparagus tips." David's face darkened. His jacket collar was turned up and his hands thrust into his pockets. "Are you cold? You shall have piping hot coffee."

"I want to talk to you."

"I'd love that. I am so glad to see you!"

"Is he — ?" David nodded towards Pose.

"Asleep, yes. He's drunk two bottles of that awful red wine he gets in the market. He calls it Parrish's Food for his anaemia." Pose's head dropped forward and the middle of his forehead rested on the mouth of the empty bottle which stood on the table before him. Georgie giggled. "Doesn't he look penitential!"

"How did you find out where she lives?"

"She?"

"Almayer." He spoke her name with an air of privilege which Georgie found both painful and funny. Funny that the vision should be so ridiculously bossed in one direction, painful that the vision was David's. It was a victory of the reproductive glands over the intelligence, one of Nature's little jokes. "What are you grinning at?"

"You ask such funny things."

"I want to know how you found out where she lives. It will go a long way towards telling me why."

"Where *I* live is what I found out. I heard there was a room to let, I went and saw it, I liked it and I moved in. It was just happen-chance that Almayer lived in the same house."

"You're a liar, Georgie."

"My dear, do you think I followed you? And accosted Spider Phelan? 'Have you a pretty little Almayer-fly in your web? well, I want the strand next to hers.' How could I? I didn't even know her name."

David sat down at the table beside Pose. He looked tired: Almayer didn't exactly revitalize him, or if she did, it was localised in the old repro system. Georgie's smile gagged as he turned away to get the coffee.

"You mix truth and lies so you don't know which is which."

Georgie set the coffee on the table — "Be nice to me —" longing, but not daring, to touch him. There were grains of salt in the cracks of the wood. He went after them with his finger-nail. "I never want to be anything but nice to you."

"I don't want you to see her again."

"How can I not, when she's just across the passage?"

"I don't want you to talk to her." He snatched up Georgie's fingers as if to break them. "Not the way you talk."

"You're hurting! What way do I talk?"

"She'll think Christ knows what. I think it myself when I listen to you, I think is there anything to choose between me and the men who pay a fiver to get into your trousers pocket."

"You're such a prude, David. I don't think you'd forgive me even if I did it all for love. Which is all I would do it for. But I haven't — we haven't. You and I haven't. So far as I'm concerned you're technically a virgin. Do I have to tell you that the lingering touch, the odd caress and the tiny kiss won't rob you of your maidenhood?" David's face suffused and blotched, his lip drew back to show his long eye-teeth. He looked really homely. "Are you as innocent, my darling, as the little girl who thought that because a man touched her bosom she was bound to have a baby?"

Georgie felt his stomach crawling, but he laughed. David threw coffee in his face.

Georgie had time slightly to turn his head and most of the hot liquid hit him on one cheek. By a miracle it missed his eyes. He sat down at the table and allowed the coffee to run off his lashes. The front of his shirt clung, scalding, to his chest. David sat there too; he could not see how David was looking because the coffee blurred his vision.

After a long moment, when it began to cool on his skin, David got up and went to the sink. He brought a cloth soaked in water and wiped Georgie's cheek.

Georgie held up his face like a child being washed. When David had finished and was gingerly lifting the wet shirt off his chest he said, "But I *like* her, you're depriving me of a friend." His lip trembled. "I haven't got so many friends."

\* \* \*

It was quite easy to avoid Almayer, and he did so for a few days. When she went out in the mornings he was in bed, and when he got up in the afternoon she wasn't at home. In the evenings he had to be careful and he peeped about before venturing on the landing. Spider Phelan caught him once. Hearing footsteps outside, he had opened his door a crack and put his eye to it. Another eye, glittery and black, was applied to the other side.

"Why, Mrs P., what a delightful surprise! Do come in – " He flung wide his door and pulled her bodily into the room. "Let's shut the door tight. It's wiser."

"Wiser?"

"I think the less we see one another the better. She is very susceptible, isn't she?" Mrs Spider Phelan, who was herself susceptible to certain things, waited with a stillness which Georgie felt would see him out. " Miss Jenkin, I mean, Almayer Jenkin. It's odd, isn't it, about likes and dislikes? One takes naturally to some people – I'm sure everyone takes to you – but others, they're like blood and jelly, they don't mix. You know what I mean?" He needed, if not her understanding, her comprehension. She must at least twig. "I call her Bonzo. Perhaps even that – perhaps I shouldn't have ventured so far as to give her a pet name."

"Miss Jenkin," said Mrs Phelan, with approval, "has taken a dislike to you?"

Georgie summoned the blush to his cheek. "It's the other way round."

"She has a gentleman friend."

"And I should never forgive myself if I came between them. They are to be married, you know." Mrs Phelan applied her inimical energy to the information. It was chilling to watch, like seeing an insect being sucked dry. "Congratulations are in order. They'll make a lovely couple. Of course he's a wee bit older, not enough to be her father, but enough to give her a cosy feeling. Young girls prefer older men – at least, they ought to." Georgie said earnestly, "Bonzo and I have a great deal in common. The attraction is mutual and it will be easier for both of us if we don't come face to face. Life can be so awfully difficult – I do think experience is important, don't you?"

Mrs Spider Phelan, who probably relied a lot on instinct, said nothing. And did nothing. She hung, motionless, and Georgie felt himself beginning to evaporate. He concentrated on her right eyeball. "I've been wanting to ask you something. Who had this room before me? What sort of a person?"

"Why?"

"Sometimes I feel there's a presence waiting to be recognised. Not a ghost or anything like that. Don't be alarmed." He smiled warmly into her black eyeball which reflected him as little more than a pinpoint. "But I do think people rub off wherever they've

117

been happy or sad. Places get hearts. This room has, It's got a lovely heart, so there must have been a lovely person here. I know it was a woman, I found her hairpin in the sink."

"It was a man."

"A Mr Clissold?"

"No."

Of course not. Clissold was the name of the telephone exchange the lovely man had rung. Or meant to ring. But Mrs Phelan, turning to the door, would not tell Georgie anything more. Imagine moving into *her* place after she had gone, feeling that bloated presence hanging in the corner. . . .

"Miss Jenkin must give a fortnight's notice or a fortnight's rent. No doubt," said Mrs Phelan dryly, "she will inform me when she intends to go."

"It won't be yet. But when she does, her room will have a happy heart."

That same evening, Almayer knocked at his door. She was angry, there was colour in her cheeks and sparkle in her eyes.

"Why Bonzo, how pretty you look."

"I want a word with you." She came in, slamming the door behind her.

"Yes, do come in. I'm afraid the room's in rather a mess, I haven't made my bed."

"Mrs Phelan has just told me that I'm getting married." Almayer pressed her hands together and drew herself up to her not inconsiderable height. "It seems she had the information from you."

"The old dear was so excited by the news."

"What news? This is the first I've heard of it."

"Hasn't David asked you? He will. I expect he thinks it's understood. It is understood, isn't it?"

"Not by me."

"But I took it for granted!" He looked at her in bewilderment, "And I know that David —"

"Takes it for granted? Does he indeed? Let me tell you something. When I decide to get married — if I do — I shall be the first to know. And I shall be the first to give out the news."

"Bonzo, I've upset you! I'd rather die than do that — "

"Obviously it has escaped David Pollock's notice that he is not the only man in the world."

"Is there someone else?"

"There are millions else."

"Oh dear," he said miserably. "What have I done?"

"It's not your fault."

"I've been such a fool, rushing in where angels — you'll never forgive me!"

"There's nothing to forgive."

"David won't, David will never, never forgive me."

"It's David Pollock who will have to ask forgiveness."

"He's angry already." His eyes brimmed. "He threw his coffee at me."

"For Heaven's sake, why?"

"I don't know. It was something I said. I was joking, trying to make him smile. It's marvellous when he smiles!" Almayer lifted her eyebrows. It was noticeably not marvellous when she smiled, but he struggled on. "I can't remember what I said. Oh God, it's awful to think we are so out of touch. I was only teasing and he took it seriously."

"David Pollock —" he wished she wouldn't keep saying that — "takes himself seriously."

"Please don't tell him!"

"Don't tell him what?"

"That I told you he was going to marry you. He'll be livid —"

"What about me? I'm not going to let him get away with it. I'm not a chattel to be picked up without asking."

"Oh I'm sure he'll ask you. He's waiting for the right moment, he likes everything cut and dried."

"That's not all he likes." They stared at each other, Georgie with distaste, she with a triumph which hardly recognised his presence. "Unfortunately for him."

"Bonzo, don't tell him, please don't tell him."

"You're crying — you silly child."

"David's friendship means more to me than anything in the world. If I lost it, I'd kill myself."

"What nonsense."

"I would, I swear!"

"Why should you lose his friendship?"

"Because he wants you more than he wants me."

It was the very thing to say, it gave her thought, which she had not been disposed to. He watched through his lashes, he could practically watch the thought she gave it. A few hairs stirred on

119

his neck as she looked hard at him, then frowned at her fingers as if working out a sum.

"We'll see," she said. "I don't promise, it will depend."

"What on?"

"On Mr David Pollock." At the door she turned and said more gently, "I won't let him be unkind to you."

When she had gone he did a dance of rage on his unmade bed. It would be perfect justice to leave David to her. There was a side of David which she brought to the fore. It had become so much in evidence that Georgie found himself asking what he was bleeding about. The loss of this superseded, adulterated David? The reason was there, but it had to be looked for and some of it had to be remembered. Those two in a few years time — Georgie could remember as clearly as if he had already seen it — she, the young matron, all passion spent, except for the jealousy with which she maintained her status: David, the incumbent, his identity shrunk to a pea.

The soiled and trampled bedclothes brought to his mind the woman who had died in a criminal lunatic asylum, who had not been able to keep her status or her sanity. Did Almayer Jenkin know about the first Mrs Pollock? Would it deter her from becoming the second? Hardly. She would think, 'I am I and altogether different.' It might however, inhibit her. Again. How many inhibitions did it take to make a cast-iron rejection?

Georgie did not trust her. She pretended to be affronted so that David would have to placate her. It was a tender trap which David would gladly run into. They would kiss and make up, and kiss and kiss and kiss.

He knelt on his bed and put his face into the pillow. He didn't have to think about the sicky softness of a woman's mouth — who would want it, except in a moment of disease? There was a time for everything, everything had its time. Some time had to be killed. He stood up and stamped his pillow flat.

Then he went downstairs. The telephone was on a table in the hall outside Spider Phelan's door. While waiting for his number he might hear her scuttling about. He lifted the receiver and at the faint echo of the bell he laid his ear to her door. There was a sort of ticking sound on the other side.

"Clissold —" Smiling, he read the number from the screw of paper which he had found on the mirror. A woman's voice answered.

He said softly, "I've been waiting for you to ring."

"Who is that?"

"You could have put me out of my misery. You only had to lift the thing of its hook, like you've just done, and ask for this number."

"Who are you?"

"It isn't pride, is it? No, you were never stiff-necked, your neck is like a swan's."

"You have the wrong number."

"They used to say you had a neck like a swan's and a smile like a tiger's. Remember?"

"They?"

"If you forget your friends," he said sadly, "you forget yourself, my darling."

"Unless you tell me who you are I shall hang up."

"I never needed to tell you that. Right from the start you were the only person who knew who I was."

"Who do you think *I* am?"

" 'A garden inclosed is my sister, my spouse; a spring shut up, a fountain sealed.' " He said into the silence at the other end, "Doesn't that strike a chord?"

"I am not your sister or your spouse."

"Let me see if I can remember more. 'Thy two breasts are like two young roes that are twins, which feed among the lilies –' No, don't hang up, it's the Song of Solomon, the most beautiful thing ever written to a woman. Or a man. It's the only bit of the Bible I have by heart. I'll tell you my telephone number –" the hinge of the door groaned as he gave Mrs Spider Phelan's number. "Those four figures used to be written on your heart." He could hear a tiny rasping sound over the wire and guessed that the mouthpiece of the instrument was being held against her shoulder. Was she afraid that someone else might hear? Or of what she herself might say? "Are you alone?" She had said very little and he couldn't be sure, but thought she must be into her thirties or even her forties. An older woman, there was maturity in her voice. "Don't hang up, please."

"You're not –" she finished gingerly – "anyone I know."

She wasn't going to give him a clue. But she was alone.

"Does my voice sound so different? So does yours. It's a bad line. But I know it's you. You have a special way of asking. You

121

don't demand to be told, you ask so nicely it's already a little thank-you." That at least was true. He wished to be truthful, and tried to think if he had been, so far. Perhaps in the spirit, if not the letter. Only Spider Phelan, all her legs crooked at the ready on the other side of the door, cared about the letter.

"Don't frown. That lovely space between your eyes —" How odd, he was in no doubt what she looked like. He would recognise her anywhere. "I must see you, my darling." That also was true, though looking at her would be but a formality. "When can we meet?"

"I think you must be very young and very foolish."

"Nobody's young and wise!"

"If you do this again I shall inform the police."

"Shall you? Shall you tell the police you were threatened with words of love, insulted with the Bible?"

"What if I call my husband to the phone?"

"Oh my dear." He had to smile, he almost laughed aloud. " 'My beloved is white and ruddy, his locks are bushy and black as a raven, his legs are as pillars of marble' —"

"I don't want to listen."

"There's no-one else I can talk to." The truth of that caused him to go cold all over. He was quite alone, he could see himself clinging to the end of a telephone wire, like a fly on one of Mrs Spider Phelan's threads.

"Goodbye," she said.

"No! Please — please don't go. There's something I've got to say. He made me promise."

"He?"

He was promising himself at that moment that he would think of something, something binding, to bind her, at least until he had finished on the telephone. "It's about him. You see, I'm living where he lived, I've got his room. He left things when he went, things of yours. That was careless of him. I'm talking as if he's dead — but he *was* careless. Sometimes I wake up and it's as if someone has just gone out and shut the door. I call out, 'Don't go!' Waking up is the loneliest thing. I'm by myself and I don't know whether there's anyone else alive, I don't even know whether I'm alive. I can't bear waking up alone!"

"What things of mine?"

"Hairpins, little brown ones, the colour of your hair.

I gathered them up for you."

"I don't use hairpins."

"Your telephone number was tucked away in a secret place. Not so secret that I couldn't find it."

"The number you're ringing from belongs to the man who re-upholstered my drawing-room chairs a month ago."

"What?"

"I shall give the number to the police."

Tears sprang to his eyes. He shouted into the phone, "I am not the man with the beastly horsehair and mouldy jam! I am beautiful and strong, leaping upon the mountains, skipping upon the hills like a roe or a young hart, I am the chiefest among ten thousand!"

The click as she hung up was followed by such silence that he thought she had cut him off from the whole world and he would never be able to make contact with anyone. He pumped the receiver rest up and down. "Hallo! Hallo! Hal — bloody — oh!" The line was dead. "You've killed it! I hope you know that killing a line is murder in the third degree! They won't hang you for it, they'll cut out your tongue!"

Mrs Spider Phelan opened her door.

"Yes, my darling," he said into the phone. "I'll be there, at our usual place. I promise I won't forget. I didn't forget last time, I was sent out on a story, yes, a big one, it was all over the front page. You mustn't cry, my beautiful Clissolda, I love you."

\*     \*     \*

On the nights Georgie did not have to go to the Hotspur, David had been used to staying awake with him, stretched on the bed, smoking his meerschaum. When it began to grow light he would roll off and go to an all-night coffee stall, leaving Georgie among the tobacco-ash to sleep like a baby.

Saturday afternoon and evening they always spent together, and Sunday was joy-day. Now there was no joy, only the long, long time to kill. Waking at midday his stomach, too, cried out with emptiness. What did it matter if the joy had stemmed from doubts as well as certainties, had sometimes come from nothing — from minus nothing? Now that the months of Sundays were over, the question could be answered.

One cold grey dawn he had suggested, as David pulled aside the curtains, 'Stay here, I'll make you coffee,' and David had said, 'Christ, don't you think I've had enough?' It could have been the worst thing in his life, but David had made it right. The coffee at the coffee stall was so awful, he said, it shocked him alive for the rest of the day, he really needed that awful coffee, and gently smiling, he had caught Georgie by the nape of the neck and held him. A little had had to go a long way. All the blazing way.

He did not wash or shave, he put on his dirtiest shirt, feeling that he was entitled to sackcloth and ashes. The shirt was blue and shone up his blondness and the golden glints in his jaw. It was at once a consolation and a shame that he should still look as fresh as a daisy. A shame, because while he had looks they were being wasted, and when he had them no longer he would need them most. Sometimes the face he saw in the mirror was not his; it responded to feelings he was not aware of, and reflected thoughts he did not know about. As soon as it realised that he was watching, it put on a performance, sucking in its cheeks, prissing up its mouth and smiling with its eyes. Sometimes, as he was turning away, he glimpsed an altogether other face, and when he looked again it had gone. In colour it was grey, like the negative of a spoiled snapshot. He knew that one day it would wait in the mirror and tell him, this is all you have left, you will have to make do with this.

In lieu of a brush he clasped his hands and drew them hard across his head from forehead to nape, and the bright hair sprang from under his fingers.

From the window he saw a man in shirtsleeves and a dog with its tongue hanging like a pink ribbon. The street was full of sun, the tabby houses had turned tawny, and in the road new tar shone like diamonds. Two boys were playing dibstones on the pavement outside Spider Phelan's gate.

Georgie went down to them and sat on the gate with his feet hooked under the bars. The boys glanced up. He said, "How many can you catch?"

"He can't catch any."

"Liar."

"Let's see you."

"Let's see *you*." The boy who had the stones threw them up, turned his wrist and caught three on the back of his hand. "Go on, beat that."

The other boy scorned. "You and your stinking stones!"

"I'd like to try." said Georgie. He caught three, but one rolled off. "I bet you can do better." He held them out and the other boy took the stones, tossed them, but made no attempt to catch them. They scattered in the road. "You and your stinking stones," he said again, and walked away.

"Oh dear, did I upset him?"

"He's no good." The boy gathered his stones out of the dust and polished them on his sleeve. "It's not you, it's me he doesn't like."

"Why not?"

The boy eyed him. "Does everyone like you?"

"No, just one or two who matter."

"Everyone's going to like me." He was a bat-eared child and wore steel-framed glasses. His eyes swam behind the thick lenses. "I'll bash them over the head if they don't."

"Let me have another try. If I only catch three it means I'll come to a sticky end, four means I'll get my heart's desire." He was fond of trying his luck, finding out the future. He had had encouragement from paving-stones, and iron bars might not make a cage, but they made a sooth-say — 'I will, I won't, this year, next year, sometime, never —' and he bore malice towards those same railings, that stretch of pavement, when events disproved what he had been led to expect.

He threw up the stones and the boy cried gleefully, "It's two — you'll get bashed!"

"My hand wasn't steady, I'll have another try."

This time all five landed on the back of his hand, but one stone hit his knuckle and fell.

"I bet your heart's desire is cuddling and kissing girls."

Georgie felt a full measure of revulsion. First lust, and then every mortal sin, came down with a bump. He felt as if he had suddenly come upon the heart, or rather the grisly green bud of the matter.

It was in something he had done, was doing. The stones? No, they were ordinary enough: held in the palm they were rather pleasant. The pavement, the act of squatting in the gutter? The child's knees, covered with old scars and scabs like crusted stained glass — or the child's gums which were as naked as a baby's and topped with brown stubs like an old man's?

"Georgie!" He turned. David and the girl were coming out of Mrs Spider Phelan's gate. The girl had called his name. David's hand was on her shoulder as if to march her away. "Georgie, what are you doing?"

David did not want to know what he was doing. He needed *not* to know much more than he needed to stop her. He was ready to break into a run.

"Is she your girl?" said the boy.

Georgie got up from his heels. He was already entirely happy, if David had run, he would have sung out loud.

"Dibstones? We used to play with beans," said Almayer.

"Isn't it a lovely day? A day for living!" Georgie took a flying leap over the boy still sitting on the kerb, causing him to crouch down with a startled snarl. "I think I'll go to the river and get a boat and row all the way to the sea."

"David's just back from Edinburgh on the night train."

"He'll sleep like an ancient log all the afternoon."

"I hope he won't."

"I've seen him go to sleep for a hundred years. I had to wake him for his own good." He smiled at her. "You can do it with a kiss."

She said stiffly, "I should let him sleep if he needed to."

"Perhaps it was for *my* good. I was afraid I shouldn't last a hundred years."

"Is that her?" The boy pushed like a puppy under Georgie's arm.

"Are you coming?" David said to Almayer.

"We're going to a film," she told Georgie. "Kermesse Héroique. It's French."

"I'd rather go to a real one."

"Real what?"

"Fair. There's one on the common. Roundabouts and swing-boats and coconut-shies and china-shies and all the fun."

"I'll come with you," the boy said.

"Riding a dragon, walking the cake, shooting the Big Apple. On a day like this, that's where I'd rather be."

"So would I! David, let's go to the fair —"

David walked away. They all followed; first Almayer, then Georgie, then the boy. "Go back," Georgie said to him. "You can't come."

At the corner of the street David turned right, away from the common. Almayer, Georgie, and the boy, stopped. They stood looking after David's retreating figure, then Almayer shrugged and moved to the left. Georgie hesitated.

"Come on!" The boy ran forward, putting himself between Almayer and Georgie. "This way!"

"Buzz off, I don't want you." The boy's mouth shut like a trap, but his eyes, which had been swimming behind his glasses, began to drown. "Look," Georgie said "it's no use your coming. I haven't any money."

"I have." He dragged out the lining of his trousers pocket and picked sixpence out of the corner.

Almayer called to Georgie and he went reluctantly to her side. "Do come on! It was your idea to go to the fair."

"What about David?"

David was going along the street, striding out of sunlight into shadow. As they watched, he reached a block of shade and almost vanished.

"David knows where we'll be. We know where he'll be." Georgie detected resentment being stacked, and when she sang out, "He'll be in a stuffy cinema!" he understood that its reflex was the expropriation of himself.

"He'll be angry."

"I don't care if he is. I'm going to enjoy myself."

She would have her way of doing that and it would not be a way Georgie could share or understand.

The three of them, struggling up the hill to the common, did not look as if they were together. Almayer, dressed for the cinema foyer, with hat, suit and handbag all of the same strangled pink, led the way, rocking on her high heels: he followed in his grubby shirt and satin-kneed flannels. But she turned and waited and caught and held his arm with a gaiety which he could see she expected him to maintain. It was to be a victory: colours flying, bands playing, marching away from David.

He giggled. "We look like a family outing."

She saw the dibstones boy, his face tight as a fist, following on behind. "Send him away."

"He wants to come to the fair."

She called out, "You'd better go home, you're not with us." The boy stopped to pull up his socks. They watched him fold and refold them over his garters.

"He's taken a fancy to us."

"Oh well, let him alone. He's doing no harm." They went on up the hill, the boy following.

It was a big fair. Georgie had seen it arrive one morning early as he walked home from the Hotspur: the Alpine Racer and the Helter-Skelter swaying along the street in the half-light, the painted boards promising Thrills of a Lifetime; Death Divers and a Snake Princess, Fire Eaters, the Mighty Whirligig, Murder Mansion, the Butterfly on the Wheel. A man driving one of the lorries had leaned out of his cab and doffed his bushwhacker's hat in a friendly way.

They heard before they saw it. The common was throbbing, Georgie imagined it being felt all over the country. People putting their ear to the ground at Land's End would undoubtedly hear it, throbbing like a great boil.

"I'll race you!" He escaped from Almayer's arm. She called something as he sprang away up the hill, and the boy cried to him to wait. He felt released: if he felt that after two minutes, he thought, how about two weeks, two months, two years? Oh David, David! He ran for them both.

When he reached the common he was out of breath. He dropped on the grass and lay flat on his back. Tilting his head he could see the lights of the fair upside down. They were all on, pricking at the sun which reduced them to rows of glass beads.

How did it feel to be David, going away as fast as his legs could carry him but not faster, because it did not really matter — Georgie, and even the girl, did not matter enough. How did it feel to allow people to give and take while it suited, and to leave when it did not, simply to walk away from them. That was sufficiency and he coveted it, but would it go with the rest of himself? Or would it be like the Roman nose which he had always wanted and which would be wrong in his face? David was a mixture, there was something which qualified and sometimes discounted his sufficiency. Georgie had sensed his panic and known it to be groundless, and how odd that was — like seeing someone in mortal dread of a shadow — odd and endearing. Georgie rolled on his stomach and buried his face in his arms.

The boy was first to arrive. He slogged up the hill, the blakeys on his boots striking sparks. His socks were over his ankles, his chest heaved, he ran across the grass to Georgie's side.

"Come on – run! She'll never find us!"

Just as he had gone away from David against his every grain and without reason, Georgie now waited, face down in the grass, for Almayer to catch up with him. There was no reason for that, either, only the disinclination to take any of it into his own hands.

The boy's boots, which were close to Georgie's nose, smelled of urine. His general unattractiveness almost certainly included slack personal habits.

"Is she your heart's desire?"

"Buzz off."

"I can win more money. I was here yesterday and I won half a crown, rolling pennies. It's a knack, like with dibstones. I bet you could too, I bet we could win a fortune."

"Yes," said Georgie, sitting up, "she is," and as Almayer came across the grass he sprang to meet her. Catching her by the waist he whirled her round and round crying, "As I was going to Strawberry Fair, singing, singing, 'Buttercups and Daisies'!"

"What animal spirits!" She was breathless. "A puppy's"

She meant to use the afternoon, and him, against David. She knew how miserable it would make David to think that she had enjoyed herself while he could not.

"A tiger's!" Georgie pulled her after him across the common towards the crowd. She rocked on her stupid heels.

"Whoops!" She actually said it and he wanted to fling her own hand right into her face. It was not disinclination that stopped him, it was lack of co-ordination. The moment for action passed while he was being made aware of the need for it.

"She cried, "Oh, why did I wear these shoes!"

He turned and laughed at her, not disguising anything. "Because you're a fool of a woman!" Being occupied watching where she put her feet, only the boy, still following, saw his expression.

\*   \*   \*

She said she did not believe in fortune-tellers. "Of course not – she brushed aside all mysteries – "it's nonsense really, they make educated guesses. Anyone can do it with practice. It's character-reading that's all. You can tell a lot just by looking at people."

"I'm always looking at people and I tell myself this and that.

But is it true?" She was the person to tell him what he saw in her. If she said there was a doubt he would give her the benefit of it. "My own character gets in the way, I'm thinking what I want to think, aren't I?"

" ' The Great Mahal, prophet, palmist, seer.' " She was reading from the board outside the booth. "This man does it for a living, he's a professional. Personal feelings don't come into it."

"Is it like never being able to see your own face? I wonder, can you really trust your own eyes?"

"You have to. 'Diviner of the Future, Adviser of Princes, Confidant of Kings.' What nonsense!" She laughed. "I think I'll have a look at him."

"Do you think he'll look into your face and see David?"

"I don't carry David in my face."

He hated the softness of her voice. "Then where?"

"You're such a baby."

He sat on the edge of the roundabout to wait for her. Brass and paint and people flew past in a molten mass. The great organ steamed out a rhythm, clambered laboriously up and down the scale, engulfed them. She had not answered his question, any of his questions. He was free to think what he liked or, if not what he liked, what came. He should think, too, from whence it came. Not all from him because of David: he should try to be fair and think would he have liked her anyway?

The roundabout began to hurry him — 'Be fair, be fair', insisting first on impartiality and then on any old meaning of the word. She was much too young for one thing, and as far as he was concerned that was the only thing. She had the drawbacks, deficiencies and gross over-provisions of all young girls. The very same that David, God help him, saw as innocence, tenderness and purity — a massive alkaline dose to break down the acid in his soul.

The roundabout was slowing, the tune was changing to 'Singing, singing, Buttercups and Daisies'. Fair was beautiful as well as just: not so good, as well as legitimate; and now it was blazing away all over the common.

Before the turntable stopped, the dibstone boy slid off one of the horses and came to sit beside him. "I won two shillings rolling the pennies."

"Good for you."

"I'll win more. Coming?" Georgie shook his head. "I'm going

to aim for the half-crown spot. You've to roll right across the board, and if the penny goes too far it drops into a slot at the back."

"Is half a crown the highest stake?"

"There's five-shilling spots and ten-shilling spots. They're on the edge where the man stands with a wooden rake and rakes in the money. You've got to be good to stop a penny there." He prised up a scab on his knee. "I reckon you have to be tall for the big money."

"No, it's better to be short."

"I could show you how to roll them."

"Let me have another try with the dibstones."

The boy hauled himself on the turntable which was still moving, though not fast. He lay on his stomach, shouting as he was borne away, "You got your heart's desire, didn't you?"

Almayer came out of the Great Mahal's booth dabbing at the skirt of her dress. "I'm sure that grubby mark wasn't there before. Do you know, he was a black man, but not really, only made up. Wouldn't you think he'd be the real thing?"

"What did he say?"

"A lot of nonsense. He was polite and very gentle, but he'd forgotten to colour his eyelids. They were white, he looked like a statue."

"Tell me the nonsense."

"It was routine stuff. I'll be going on a journey, there's some money coming, I'll meet a stranger and lose a friend."

"That's me."

"You?"

"What you lose upon the roundabouts you make up on the swings."

"He said I shall marry someone tall and fair, of noble lineage. I asked him do you mean with a title, like a duke or an earl?"

He took her hand as the roundabout lurched into the *Merry Widow*. "How high will you go on the swings to make up for losing me?"

Up came her chin and with it the colour from some point deep in her neck. He felt an absolutely detached curiosity as to where the point might be. She said, "What you've never had you never miss."

"You've had more than anyone of me." It was true. She, of

the anyones, had had the most. She had had David. "You still do."
Wasn't it reasonable to suppose that the pink in her throat and
face had its source in the two buttons on her breasts? "Pink-
wells."

"What?"

He tried to pull her with him into the crowd, but she held
back, crying out something of which he caught only the one word.
"David?"

"I have to think of him."

"Do you suppose I don't?" They stared at each other. Georgie
almost burst out laughing, thinking what she thought he thought,
and knowing that she would never know. "Come on!"

"Where to?"

He felt wild and reckless, he had come to the end of consecu-
tive thought and relevant action. There was nothing to be let in
for now, certainly not to undertake. The reasonless acts were all
accomplished, the disinclination had run out. There was only a
spree or a frenzy or sleep till tomorrow. He was holding her hand
as he would a piece of rope to pull on or twist, and on the end of
this rope was the end of the world. "To break a window in the
sky!"

But the world, which had never stopped, suddenly appeared
behind her, turning like the merry-go-round, not merry, but solid
with unnameable joy. *She* could not end it.

"David?" he said. It was the mother and father of all questions,
but what scared him was the magnitude of his dread of the
answer.

She said, "Oh, it's you," speaking as if to her second self. In
three words she annulled everyone else under the sun. "We're going on the roundabouts."

David was looking at their clasped hands.

"No, the swings." said Georgie.

"You were right," said David. "It is too good an afternoon to
spend in the cinema."

"I'm glad you came." Of course she was, but why? Did David
ask himself, or was any gladness, on any score, enough for him?
"I've been wanting you."

Of course she had, in her own way, as much as she was able.
Poor David, Georgie thought, with a treacherous rising of the
heart — wanted like that, as much as that, and glad of it!

"Come —" She took David's hand, linking the three of them — "we'll all go on the swings."

"No," said David, "We'll go on the roundabout."

Georgie drew her arm through his like a loving husband. "Which would you rather? To be stirred like a pudding or fly like a bird?"

"Like a bird on a string, only allowed to go so high. But yes, that's better than pudding."

"You're going to make fools of us, aren't you?" David said to him.

They were pushing through the crowd and Georgie cried, "There's no need!" But he had heard pity in David's voice. It was like a needle in a haystack, and it pierced him.

"I always felt a fool with you —"

"You talk as if I'm dead!"

"— and that's death to any relationship. Don't you know that?"

Almayer, who was ahead of them in the crush of people looked round and laughed.

"You want to say the worst thing you can think of —"

"The worst thing would be to say that you make everyone feel a fool."

"What do you care?"

"There'd be no hope for you Georgie."

They had broken through the crowds and come to the swing-boats. Georgie climbed into an empty boat and held out his hand to Almayer. She turned to David. "I want you to come with me."

"I hate the things. They make me sick."

Georgie seized the rope. "Bonzo — we'll go higher than anyone, we'll stand on our heads!"

"Shall we be able to see St Paul's?" She used David's shoulder to help her climb in.

"We'll go over the top, over the sun, over the moon! Lie back and pull — pull for your life!"

"Don't be a fool." David gripped the side of the boat.

"Oh David, don't be stuffy!"

"Sixpence each and fasten your belts." A man hooked a pole on one end of the boat and swung it to get them started. David, losing hold, was sent sprawling. Georgie laughed.

"Oh dear, he looks angry," said Almayer.

"He looks frightened."

"These swing boats are perfectly safe, they wouldn't be allowed otherwise —"

"Of course. Nothing's allowed that isn't safe. Pull on your rope, pull us up to the sky!"

Almayer twined the rope round her arms and hung on it like a sailor. To and fro they went, with a deepening pendulum stroke.

Georgie lay back, face to the sky, and hauled. "Do you know what my heart's desire is? To turn one complete beautiful circle — to stand the world on my head!"

Almayer laughed. She swung now above, now below him, her hair swooping off her head, her breasts rigid, her legs braced against the sides of the boat.

"Look," he said, "Look down — you can see how David is losing his hair."

Almayer began to scream. As she flew up, she screamed. As she plunged, she closed her eyes in ecstasy and pulled on the rope.

The sky burst out round Georgie's feet and the ground was held up like a mirror. It flashed like a mirror and in it he glimpsed a painfully upturned face with black gaps for eyes, and an open mouth.

"Oh my dear," he said.

# VII

How pure the world was when I was first married. Such universal purity was unknown to me even in my childhood, and I'm sure I felt younger than I did as a child. I certainly felt virginal from the moment I ceased to be Almayer Jenkin, spinster, and became Mrs Clarence Burgoyne.

We had a little house in Brunswick Park. It had only just been built and the workmen's cigarette ends peeped up between the floorboards. Everything was brand new, furniture, linen, china, gas-cooker, brooms. I could confirm the purity of the world by looking at our unblemished dustbin which shone like silver in the raw garden.

It was summer when we moved in, the furniture smelled of bananas, the house of new paint and new putty and damp cement: such scrupulous newness — even the dirt was organically incomplete, waiting on us for its history.

Clarry himself was not pristine, but it was a novelty to him having a place of his own. He had been married before, and he and his first wife had lived in a hotel.

"Isa was a bird of passage. Not like you."

"What sort of bird am I?"

"You're my goose."

I would sooner he had called me his dove, or a bird of paradise, or even his chickadee. "I stayed in a hotel at Ramsgate once. It was lovely." Gracious living it had seemed to me.

"Ours wasn't, ours was crummy. We heard everything they did in the next room, especially after they went to bed. They gave us some good ideas. Don't button your mouth, you've had the benefit too."

"It sounds so cold-blooded."

"It was anything but." He drew me down to his lap and that always amused us because I'm much taller than he is. It was like mother sitting on baby, he said. He was not bothered about the difference in our heights. Clarry didn't care how he looked to other people. I suppose that's why he never looked vulnerable. "Isa never had anything that you didn't, or that you won't get in due time."

"I'm not worried about that."

He always came out, straight out, with the little hang-ups that people are afraid to mention. I thought then that if I could acquire the kind of honesty he was showing me we would move into each other's skins. I wanted — how I wanted! — to be under his.

"What are you worried about?"

"Nothing."

The truth, which I decided was not worth mentioning — I thought that one could choose one's truth and failed to see that that would be twisting it — was that I believed the intimacies of love ought to be inspired, by spontaneous combustion, not a working demonstration.

Clarry was only entertained up to a point by my passion for the house. When, in the street I turned back to look at it, he said, "We'll get something better one day."

"I don't want anything better."

"You will. You'll grow out of it."

"I never shall."

"These are early days. We have to have them." He kissed my hand quite seriously. "God bless our early days."

I lived to see Brunswick Park settle into a mature little enclave of lawns and laburnum, its brash yellow bricks discreetly grained with soot and I never lost my affection for it.

Clarry was freight-manager for an air line. In those days it was a small company and carried more freight than passengers. Later it became big enough to be known by its initials, and Clarry moved from freight to personnel. Clarry didn't change. He was born very much all there, with everything he needed and was going to need. Life didn't surprise him, and once he had passed childhood he settled into a shape which was his own self manifest. He was implicit in his barrel-chested, purpose-built body, with no concession to style, his bright ruddy skin, the practical way his hair thatched his head and his brows bushed to take the edge off the rain. He was all ready, and he pleased himself — in sweet minor things as well as predictable pleasures. I have seen him, coming away from a Cup Final, pick up a prickly horse-chestnut and break out the kernel with the same relish he had shown all afternoon shouting and groaning at the game.

Because he had no secrets from me, I had none from him. He knew my doubts and reservations, often he brushed them aside or shot them to pieces for our mutual amusement. I had no mind of my own, I shared his, and what is freedom but a feeling? So I felt free, in a skin cage, tied hand and foot, head, heart and nerve-endings.

When Clarry liked people, he used them. The more he liked them, the more he used them. It wasn't opportunism of the rank material sort: it was the need to involve. He trusted in strings, and it followed that he expected and wanted to be used. The more strings — both ways — the more secure he felt. When he said, to promise or console me, 'We'll get it all tied up,' I saw the knots and the dashing bows and a right, tight parcel. He used me all the time, I was all-purpose, all his one purpose.

One day he said we must go and visit Uncle Jim. He spoke of him as his only surviving relative and I had been surprised that we did not hear from him at the time of our marriage. Clarry said he would have forgotten. 'He's old, my grandfather's big brother, my great-uncle really.' We were on the train, actually taking down our luggage from the rack at Stoke Prior when he admitted that he had not told Uncle Jim about his second marriage.

"So?" I said, feeling as if I had missed something, a whole chain of logic.

"So," he smiled, "you mustn't mind if he calls you Isa. He doesn't know about the divorce, either."

"But I shall mind!" I was ready to weep. "Oh why didn't you tell him?"

"He doesn't approve of divorce. He's been a reprobate all his life but now he takes a high moral tone, just to be on the safe side."

"He'll know I'm not Isa."

"I don't think so. He only saw her once and his sight's not good, nor his hearing. Just play along, there's a darling, and keep him happy."

"Other people will know I'm not Isa!"

"Well, of course you and Isa are chalk and cheese. But the old devil sacks his housekeeper every six months. The one who was here when I brought Isa went long ago and the only other person who saw us then was the jobbing gardener. Nobody's going to talk family to him."

Anyone else, I would have said it of anyone but Clarry, must have had it all worked out. But the thought, if it entered my head, was turned back on the threshold.

"Why must your Uncle Jim be kept happy at my expense?"

"Dear girl, what will it cost you?"

"My identity. I'm me and I don't want to be anyone else. I particularly don't want to be your first wife."

He was on the platform and I in the carriage doorway. He lifted me out, suitcase and all, and held me. "You are my first true wife."

"I don't want to be Isa — you divorced her!"

"The guard blew his whistle and Clarry put me down on the platform. "Uncle Jim's going to love you."

That was the general idea, that Uncle Jim should love me, and I made up my mind to endear myself, for Clarry's sake.

The house was a surprise. It was shut away in a yard behind tall wooden gates. The walls were dark stone slabs picked out with yellow lichen, and at the side, high up, a door opened on midair. Over it hung the rusty remnant of a pulley.

"Why is it called the Salt House?"

"Salt used to be stored here. Not in Jim's time, he bought it cheap because it was a warehouse, and blocked off a few rooms to live in. There's brine in the walls to pickle him in when he dies. He's getting on for ninety, so you must be prepared for some give and take." Clarry grinned. "You take what he dishes out."

We had walked from the station and he was in the act of closing the yard gates behind us when a motorbike came round the back of the house. It was ridden by a man in a brown velvet suit and a round hat like a bummaree's. He also wore pince-nez. He held up one hand to stop Clarry from shutting the gate and slipped neatly through the gap into the road. As he rode away he lifted the round hat an inch or so in salutation. Then he began to wobble so wildly he was obliged to grab the handlebars. We watched him weave to and fro across the road which, fortunately, was empty, until he regained control and the machine puttered steadily away.

"Who on earth was that?" said Clarry. "He looked like a piano-tuner, but Jim hasn't got a piano."

Uncle Jim had reached a stage where he didn't have to like people or care if they liked him. It was a strength which he could be confident would never desert him.

"You remember her?" Clarry said, taking my hand but not taking me too close.

The old man's face had lost its identity and now relied solely on bone structure for its shape. The skin was stretched like the webbing on the wings of a bat. And was something of the same colour. I could not see his eyes. But something moved, alerted, between his puffy lids.

"You've changed," he said. "How long is it since you were here? Two years, three? That's nothing at your time of life."

I hissed at Clarry, "He knows!"

Clarry picked up a card from a pack on the mantelshelf and held it before the old man's face. "Here's her picture — isn't she a Queen of Hearts?"

"That's a bad photograph. Makes her look tall and skinny. I like a plump woman, though it's not relative any more." He leaned out of his chair with the intention of digging Clarry in the ribs. Clarry was out of his reach but he seemed neither to know nor to care that his fingers were encountering only air. "Chance would be a fine thing!"

Clarry held his wavering hand. "You had your chances, and took them."

It seemed harmless enough to say, but while Clarry was smiling into his face I saw the old man's hackles rise. He gave Clarry a purely mean look. Then he turned to me, baring big brown teeth in a lipless grin. "Did you bring the negro head?"

"I beg your pardon?"

"You always bring a quarter pound of negro head."

"Tobacco." Clarry said to me. To the old man he said loudly, "It's in our suitcase. But Mrs Dover tells me you're not allowed it any more."

"She's the doctor's creature. They creep over me, those two, finger by finger. 'Doctor, will you look at his neck, look at the vein, doctor, feel his legs, doctor, here where my hand is.' Pah! They dover me together, her and the doctor. Fetch me the baccy, Clarry child, I can do with a plug."

He pointed his stick at the chair opposite him and I sat down, trying to make myself Isa's size.

"Well," he said, "what do you make of it?"

I thought of asking him what, exactly I was expected to make something of, but it would only have saved me for a few seconds. "I haven't changed my mind."

"And I haven't forgotten you. We used to have such talks, you and I, when we could get Clarry to leave us alone."

Isa, I thought, must have been ready to work at it. She had found a way of coping single-handed with Uncle Jim and had even made it appear that she was engineering their tête-à-têtes. Perhaps she did in fact engineer them. For what purpose? The same, no doubt, that I was committed to. Endearment. But I had been badly briefed, she must have had more to go on.

"We talked about life and death, your death. I didn't want to talk about mine. But I told you about my life. There's more to tell — " he had a curious rapacity, curious because I was not sure where it was directed — "I can tell you plenty more."

"We won't talk about my death. Or anyone's."

"If I don't tell my story for money I'll tell it for love." An eyelid trembled. He was winking. How much money, I wondered, and how much love, did he think it was worth? I was sorry for him. To be old was to have nothing to sell. And then he said, coaxing, "Won't you do what you always did? I get so tired, so very tired. Oh not bodily —" He abandoned his cry for sympathy and giggled, and patted his shrunken loins. "Nowadays it's all in the mind. I have a very busy mind and I get a terrible ache in my sinciput. I wish you'd do what you used to, Clarry's wife."

"I don't know that word — sinciput?"

"It's the front of the skull, where the action is. That's what I'm reduced to. I'm like a dog on a sinking log." His chest crackled with laughter. "But it won't be me that dies, it'll be everyone else. Have you forgotten what you used to do?"

"Of course not."

"Then stroke my head."

I looked at the dome of his skull, the dragged skin with the old bone under it. Here and there clung grey fuzz, almost a mould. I could imagine it coming off on my fingers.

"Your touch was soft as a bird's wing, but vibrant. 'Isa has healing hands,' Clarry says." Does he indeed, or was the old man laughing? That lipless gape tended to get left behind, either as a camouflage or because his mood was quicker than his jaws. "I'd know your touch anywhere."

Then Clarry came back, bringing the tobacco. "Here you are,

Jim, chew it or burn it, but don't let Mrs D. see it. What happens if you want to spit?"

"I spit."

Clarry laughed. "With a jet like sperm-whale. By the way, who was the queer fish we saw as we came in?"

"Mrs Dover Sole."

"Before we saw her. He was riding a motorbike, he wore a velvet suit and pinchnose glasses."

"I don't want to talk about him."

"No talk, no tobacco."

Uncle Jim lunged with his stick to knock the parcel out of Clarry's hand.

Clarry sat on his heels and teased him. "A bailiff, was he? Mrs Dover's weakness? Or does he come to get a pinch of salt for his egg?"

"He's a typewriter. You'll hear him tap-tapping in the room next to yours."

"You mean he's staying here?"

"Sounds like tin rain."

"What's he doing?"

"Writing about me. I told him, 'You'll lose me on that little piano. Take a pen or pencil and you might catch something — if you're any good as a journalist.' "

"You mean he's —" Clarry rose from his haunches — "actually writing for a newspaper?"

"I told him, 'You've come to the wrong place. There's nothing at Salt House except salt. I warrant you don't offer your readers a grain of that.' "

"About you?" said Clarry. "What's he writing about you?"

"What do you think?"

Clarry's face darkened. "Not after all these years!"

" 'Salt's a preservative,' he said. 'My readers would like to see your story out of pickle.' He's got a turn of phrase, I'll say that for him. Edelstein the Jew I call him. That's not a term of opprobrium, it's what he is." His eyelids turned towards me without a glimmer between them. "Like you are Clarry's wife."

"How did he get on to you?"

"Newspaper men can smell out a story."

"Story! You call it a story?" The old man got up with a firing of bones like muted pistol shots and Clarry let him have the tobacco. He stood gingerly, his knees trembling in the hollow pouches of his trousers, and tore at the wrapping. "Jim, it's as dead as mutton!"

"A good story never dies, Edelstein says. I shouldn't mind seeing my name in the papers again. It would be a bit of a laugh for Isa."

"It's nothing whatever to do with her."

"She's married into the family." Sniffing at his tobacco, he did not look at me.

\* \* \*

"What was all that about?" I said when we were alone.

"It's the old man's seamy past. He thinks it's livelier than anyone else's present."

"Is it?"

Clarry grimaced. "I daresay it was a lot livelier than some people's past, present and future."

I waited for him to tell me, but he started to wash himself and to call out between puffing and groaning at the coldness of the water, "I warned you, didn't I, that he wouldn't have a bathroom put in. So far as he's concerned, water's for fish to swim in. You'll only be able to wash your goosepimples, my love."

"He knows I'm not Isa."

"He's perfectly happy with you, you're doing fine."

"What am I supposed to be doing?"

He raised his wet face and smiled at me as the drops ran out of his hair. "Just keep it up till Monday night."

"I'll have to hear the story first."

"I'd have told you if it mattered." His face emerged from the towel with the bright blood summoned and almost bursting from under his skin. "The whole wretched business is dead and buried."

"But Isa knew."

"What's that got to do with it?"

"If she knew, so should I."

"She knew too much!" He threw aside the towel. His vexation was not with me. "All right, here it is. Fifty or sixty years ago, there was a family living at a place called Ampthill in Wiltshire or Hampshire or somewhere. I can't remember and it doesn't matter. There was the mother, a widow in her late thirties, her daughter, who was about eighteen years old, and a son of fourteen. He was subnormal. They were well-to-do, they had servants and kept a carriage —"

"Subnormal?"

"Mentally. And he had a lump on his back like a camel."

"Poor boy."

"He was a freak. Uncle Jim was engaged as a sort of male nurse-cum-tutor."

I was surprised at his tone, for he was fundamentally kind and I supposed that kindness, like virtue, was consistent.

"What about the daughter?"

"There was nothing wrong with her."

"Was she pretty?"

"By all accounts."

"Whose accounts?"

"Witnesses. Jim had been with them for about a year when the boy drowned in the fishpond in the garden. He had some sort of a fit and fell face down in the water. Of course the coroner found it was death from 'natural causes'. But a little while after, the woman and her daughter were murdered. Jim was arrested and tried, but of course there was no case against him."

"Of course?"

Clarry said sharply, "He may not be all sweetness and light, but he was never a murderer. Besides, it was an impossibility he couldn't have done it. He was in the local hospital at the time, having a boil lanced. It was a bad one and they kept him overnight. The case went on record as 'murder by a person or persons unknown'." Clarry pulled his shirt over his head. "That's the story."

"It is quite a story."

"It was a squalid little business."

"Squalid? Little? Those people losing their lives?"

Clarry, in his undervest, put his hands on his hips and gazed at me. "Are you going to drop on everything I say? Whatever it was then, it's squalid and unimportant now."

"How did they die? The mother and daughter? It is relevant," I said earnestly.

"To what?"

"To how I see Uncle Jim, how I talk to him."

"It'll be enough if you just listen to Uncle Jim. I've told

you as much as is good for you."

"You've only given me the bare bones."

"What more do you think there is, after fifty years?"

\* \* \*

I wasn't satisfied, though I was quite satisfied with his reasons for not telling me any more. He was old-fashioned about women. He would not repeat a bawdy joke in my hearing, nor would he allow anyone else to. I supposed he thought me unequipped to plumb the ugly depths of life. I did not see the other side of the coin: that in his estimation, women had a limited range short of the uttermost depths, and of the supreme heights as well.

The way he had told Uncle Jim's story fretted me. He had bundled it out, thrown it away. He had not even mentioned those people's names and for two pins — less — I knew that he would not have told me anything.

"Who were they? What was the family's name?"

"I forget. Something like Felix."

"Felix?"

"You know, the cat."

"What was the girl called?"

"Ethel or Amy — girls were all called Ethel or Amy in those days."

It was unlike him. He respected facts and had no difficulty retaining them. I reminded myself that even he, my solid Clarry, had a subconscious working for him and I believed that if he honestly preferred to forget the details of Uncle Jim's past, it was for me to respect his reasons.

Later that night I was awakened by the sound of a motorbike turning into the yard, and it struck me, though not so forcibly as to keep me long awake, that the reporter might be persuaded to tell me the rest of the story.

Clarry said next morning, "The old man liked Isa the first time he saw her and he likes her better still now. He told me so. 'She's filled out nicely,' he said, 'married life agrees with her.' "

"I haven't fooled him. He knows I'm not Isa."

Clarry blithely lathered his chin. "If he thought that, he'd have one of his Old Testament scenes. He fancies himself as Moses."

"You're the only one who's fooled and you're trying to be. I wish I knew why."

"I told you, to keep the old chap sweet."

"Happy, you said."

"Happy and sweet. It's a good thing to be both at his age."

But I saw a difference and it occurred to me that Clarry might be hoping for something more substantial from Uncle Jim than goodwill. Not that I minded what his expectations were. I knew that he made no distinction between happiness for the old man's sake and sweetness for his own. But I felt stupid at not having thought of it before.

Clarry swept the razor through the foam on his jaw. "I'm going to talk to that reporter. I won't have Jim being dished up with the breakfast bacon all over England."

"He doesn't seem to mind."

Clarry held his nose and drew the razor down his upper lip. "He minds, but not about the same things as I do."

As it happened, I was not present when he met Edelstein, which was just as well, for my presence would have been inhibiting later on. Edelstein might have refused to answer my questions and I shouldn't have found it easy to ask if I had been there listening to Clarry damning the subject, and Edelstein too.

"Mr Burgoyne wants to see you," said Mrs Dover as Clarry and I were finishing breakfast.

"We'll be with him directly."

"Only the lady. 'My great-niece,' he said, 'or whatever she chooses to call herself.'" Mrs Dover stared at me, openly reserving her opinion.

Clarry grinned. "You go, darling. I promise to come and rescue you."

"That won't be necessary." I was determined to keep my end up. 'Whatever she chooses to call herself' had decided me. I had chosen, because Clarry had chosen, to call myself Isa Burgoyne. "I'll come as soon as I've finished breakfast."

"He's still in bed. He never rises up till after lunch." Mrs Dover folded her arms and looked grimly at Clarry. "You'd do well to warn her."

"She's seen it before."

"It's not my fault he kennels like a dog."

"What have I seen?" I said, as she went out.

"Uncle Jim in his bed." Clarry got up and closed the door after her. "Isa went up there and got a surprise. It's a bit of a pickle, he likes to have everything to hand."

"I wish I knew what Isa said to him."

"She just listened. That's what he wants."

It seemed to me that Isa was always a success. Even her ultimate failure, the divorce, could not console me. Suppose the failure had been Clarry's, Clarry's loss, and he knew and accepted it, and that was why, when he talked about her, she came over so well?

Uncle Jim's bedroom was almost filled, wall to wall, with a great iron bedstead which was loaded like a ship to the gunwales. Above it hung a stuffed eagle, wings outstretched, in the act of swooping on the old man's cranium immediately beneath. There were no sheets, just dark grey blankets and a libidinously swelling satin pink eiderdown.

"Come in. Hand me the tray, there's some raspberry jam on it. Edelstein the Jew brought it."

"Jam?"

"Old people like sweet things, he said. I told him, I'm not old, I'm past that. I've come to the point of return, and I'm going backwards, getting young again. See, my gums are like a baby's. And up here —" he tapped his skull — "is the fontanelle."

I looked into the black hole of his mouth and tried to smile.

"You're welcome to sit on the bed, Clarry's wife. Push that biscuit tin aside, and the magnifying glass — I use it to examine the food that forced virgin brings me. I don't mind dust, dust's impersonal, and mould's a natural growth, but one of her hairs would strangle my heart." He took a spoonful of jam, tenderly putting out his tongue to receive it. But when he sucked it in, he winced. "Stuff's not sweet, it's sour."

"How is Edelstein getting on with his article?"

"What article?"

"The one he's writing about you."

"My story is what he's writing, and he writes what I tell him. He can get no farther than I'm prepared to let him go."

"How far it that?"

"I'm giving him the background, my background, my formative years. The first time round." Jam dribbled out of the side of his mouth. "I intend to live twice."

At that moment I really thought he could.

"He came here with his little tin piano and I told him he couldn't play anything on it I wanted to hear. He rang a bell at the side of it and said, 'What about the pound notes?' He's got a turn of phrase. 'Tell me about yourself,' he said. So I started with my grandfather who was at Quatre Bras. He wanted to know, what's Waterloo got to do with the Ampthill case?" Uncle Jim giggled. "Begin at the beginning, I told him, or you shan't begin at all."

I wondered if Edelstein knew what he was up against. Perhaps he had already decided that the game as Uncle Jim played it was not worth the candle. Clarry's warning him off might be the deciding factor, he might leave before I had a chance to question him. I very much wanted to hear more. I wanted to know about the three people who had died violently and mysteriously all those years ago — how, and why.

"Clarry's wife, do you think you're going to be happy?"

It was a shock to be asked at that moment, to be asked by him, with a look compounded of malice and ribaldry and yet with a hint of pity. "Do you remember that row you had?" He creaked with joy. "Oh it was an up and a downer! Remember what I said to you?"

"You said a lot of things."

"I told you you must learn to look through glass. Don't make the mistake of thinking that what isn't complicated is easy."

"I don't find anything easy."

"Clarry will make it so. You must be careful what you take from him."

I said coldly, "I am his wife."

"The onlooker sees most."

"You haven't looked on us. At least, not much."

"I've looked enough on him."

Was he talking to me or to Isa? If to me, then he must at once have found me lacking. If to Isa, I needn't worry.

He lay back on his pillows and shut his eyes. "I don't sleep much now. I don't like letting go, never know if I'll be able to catch hold again."

In those days, only black, white and carnal red existed for me. I did not suspect that there were permissible gradations, I had never wondered what the material difference was between fallen angel and risen beast.

"There'll be plenty of time for sleep soon," he said, and I thought he's afraid, and prayed that he wouldn't be, for my own sake, for I didn't know how to comfort him. And then he winked open both eyes and I swear he contrived a dimple in his hollow cheek. "Babies sleep a lot."

\* \* \*

Clarry seemed quite satisfied. He thought he had dealt with Edelstein because he had got the man to admit that he got nowhere with Jim.

"He's found it a dead loss in every sense of the word. The old man's stringing him along, making out he has beans to spill."

"And hasn't he?"

"Of course not. I don't doubt he could talk about it once, he was always a gossip. But he wasn't there at the material time."

"Perhaps the immaterial time's important now. To Edelstein's readers. They want to know about before and after."

"What could be left in that old, old barbarism to titillate a couple of million newspaper readers?"

"Barbarism?"

"Murder is, isn't it? I told Edelstein that his idea was pathetic and nasty."

"What did he say?"

"He agreed. He's freelancing, financing himself, he can't afford to waste his time. It's his living, when he can make it. He'll pack up and go now."

"He's staying here in the house?"

"Yes." Clarry shrugged. "The old chap obviously expected to have a little fun with him."

Later that same morning the clink of a spanner alerted me as I was passing the landing window. I looked out and saw the journalist bent over his motorbike in the yard. I went down at once.

"Mr Edelstein." He straightened and removed his hat. "Are you leaving?"

He was a slender young man with an olive skin and a strong, well-fleshed nose on which his gold pince-nez perched like a butterfly.

"I don't think I was intended to stay more than a day or two." He held his hat against his chest. "To whom have I the pleasure of speaking?"

"Mrs Clarence Burgoyne." He bent his head. His hair was black, curling, unEnglish. "You didn't get your story."

"I always get something."

"But not what you came for?"

"That would hardly be possible." He smiled. "I have a too-fruitful imagination."

"Then you don't really need Uncle Jim."

"I am a journalist, not a novelist." He waited, regarding me, one hand on the saddle of his machine. I sensed repression in those splayed fingers.

"Could we go inside? It's so cold —" And I was thinking that Clarry might see us in the yard and interrupt at any moment.

If he was surprised he did not show it. I began to realise his scrupulosity. With a little Mediterranean gesture, he indicated that I should precede him into the house. "Perhaps the kitchen? Where there is a fire?"

The last thing I wanted was Mrs Dover's presence. "No, in here —" I pushed open a door which proved to give on to a stone room scarcely bigger than a cupboard. The window was stuffed with sacking and there was a row of brass taps above a series of shallow gullies in the floor. The walls were covered with stains, ragged contours like the tracing of a map. But what map, what continent, had shore after shore after shore? "This will do."

"There is nowhere for you to sit."

"It will do." I felt silly, standing in the middle of the floor with this young man who, with an almost mocking modesty, covered his chest with his hard round hat. "What was this room used for?"

"Some sort of sluice, I imagine. The walls retain the crustation of brine."

Clarry would not interrupt us here, but aside from that, there was nothing to be said for the place. It was cold, colder than outside. Edelstein looked calmly and incuriously into my face.

"Please tell me the story," I said.

"The one I came for?"

"Uncle Jim's story. The facts."

"You don't know them?"

"Never mind what I know."

"There are some reports of the case, Mrs Burgoyne. And it has been written up in a book of unsolved murder trials."

"I want to hear it from you."

"Why?" The light skinned the lenses of his glasses and I could not see his eyes. "May I recommend that you verify such facts as I can give you with the official sources? I cannot guarantee that there will not be a degree of imaginative bias."

"It doesn't matter."

"Very well. In the summer of 1886 a boy aged fourteen was drowned in an ornamental pond, thirty feet in diameter and nowhere more than two feet deep. He was the son of a Mrs Belle Felice, widow of a manufacturer of cattle-cake. The tragedy occurred on the family estate in Berkshire and attracted little notice at the time because the boy, Lovatt, was delicate and subject to fainting fits. With the onset of puberty these had become frequent and it was accepted, without much question, that he must have fallen, unconscious, face down into the pond."

It wasn't such a bad way to go, I thought, to dissolve in a little water.

"His life, while it lasted, had had compensations. He was a musician, a violinist, and quite accomplished for his age. Mrs Felice and her daughter, Marianne, led a full social life. They had good looks and money, they were in great demand. Lovatt was not. Except, possibly, by your husband's great-uncle, Mr Burgoyne. Lovatt was the raison d'etre for his presence in the house. Mr Burgoyne was the boy's tutor."

"I know."

"Perhaps you would tell me what you do not know."

"I want to hear it all from you."

He nodded, like a waiter taking a small order. "The inquest was a formality, the verdict, accidental death. There the matter rested until, three months later, Mrs Felice and Marianne were thoroughly murdered in their drawing-room."

"Thoroughly?"

"By someone with the haziest knowledge of human anatomy or who was in a super — or rather, sub-human passion. Or was simply indulging himself. The *Times* reported that the Felice drawing-room resembled a butcher's shop. The analogy was imprecise, for a butcher knows what he is doing."

It struck me that Edelstein was without conscience. His smile arrived in his face as a social refinement, and remained as such.

"The case presented contradictory elements which have never

been resolved. To name but three: there was no apparent motive, nothing was stolen and the Felice fortune passed to an elderly relative in America who was already more than comfortably off. There had been great violence, but servants in the house heard and saw nothing unusual and, perhaps the most inexplicable, evidently mother and daughter were in the room together when the crime occurred. Therefore one of them must have stood by, abetting, if not actually aiding, the killer."

"Perhaps there was more than one killer?"

"A hypothesis not favoured by the investigators. As you would expect, the crime aroused horror and anger among the social set to which the Felices were considered an ornament, and there was widespread interest throughout the country. The police were under strong pressure to apprehend the murderer. Two suspects were speedily found — procured, one might say. A vagrant who had been in the neighbourhood at the time — and James Burgoyne."

Edelstein looked at me athwart his long nose. "The vagrant was not brought to trial. He was old and frail and it was obvious, even to the intelligence of the country constabulary, that he had not the strength for the deed. In fact, he died while in detention. Scotland Yard was called in, but with no more success. Burgoyne remained under suspicion. It was suggested that a motive might be looked for in the death of Lovatt, that it might not have been accidental, and that James was a triple murderer. However, he maintained that he was in the public ward of the County hospital thirty miles away while the ladies were hacked to death. The Crown could not break his alibi and he was acquitted. The case remains unsolved to this day."

"And this day?"

"A figure of speech."

"But you came here because you know something more?"

"I have given you the essential points."

"What about Uncle Jim?"

"At the time he was thirty years old, very personable, judging by the photographs, and with considerable charm, judging by the evidence of female witnesses."

No wonder, I thought, that Clarry had not wished to dwell on it. "The idea's preposterous! You came here to rake it all up and trick that old man into saying something which could be twisted into a bit of cheap sensationalism."

"The idea of the series is to present a new angle on some famous unsolved crimes."

"And the truth is irrelevant!"

"Indeed I think it may be, if you mean the whole truth and nothing but. As an abstract truth does not exist, it is but private persuasion. You have yours, I have mine, and your uncle has his. Bits of broken mirror, and if they could all be put together we should still not have a true picture, for each fragment would distort the next."

"How very convenient for you!" I cried. "I don't admit the difference!"

"I'm not sure I know what the difference is myself. I have established a few facts which individually are not significant. If I could relate them, a credible answer might emerge."

"Credible — perhaps insupportable."

"Perhaps." We stared at each other. His smile ran out at the corners of his mouth.

I said, "He's playing with you."

"Mr Burgoyne is an old man who doesn't have much fun."

"You tried to buy him."

"I made a down payment —"

"The more fool you. He won't, he can't, tell you anything."

"It was towards my bed and board. The daily rate, he suggested, should be the same as they charge at the Bull Inn in the village."

"That's not funny."

"I think the joke has been on me. At the inn, for the same price, I would have had morning and afternoon tea and my shoes cleaned."

"If we had known we would have improved the service at the Salt House." I heard my scorn and it humiliated me.

He opened the door. "It has been worth it to be here."

"Do you expect to interest your readers when all you can offer them is conjecture?"

"And wild surmise. Every story is new to someone. Many people, more than enough in my editor's opinion, have never heard about the Ampthill murders."

"It can do nothing but harm."

"To you, Mrs Burgoyne?"

"My husband is his only living relative."

"Does your husband know that his uncle is penurious?"

"I beg your pardon?"

"Old Mr Burgoyne has no money."

"What nonsense!" He shrugged and I cried, "What business is it of yours? Or perhaps it is, perhaps it's not his past you're interested in. I don't believe you're a reporter, I never saw anyone less like a reporter!"

He smiled his smile of accommodation. "Should I take that as a compliment? Your uncle has told me, 'I shall go out with nothing and come back with the same.' I am wondering what he means."

\* \* \*

I had accepted unquestioningly the plain statement that Clarry's uncle had lived in a house where a murder had been committed and, sixty years later, a hack journalist was trying to stir up the old man's memories of the events. I had wanted a little more to it: now I suspected that I might get too much. I began to feel a complicated unease. I tried to be rational, I asked how much was I prepared to learn about life. That, I said to myself, was the question. Could I accept, and use, the knowledge, or was I to be Bluebell in Fairyland for the rest of my days?

I asked Clarry, "Is Uncle Jim destitute?"

"Destitute? Of course not!"

"Are you sure?"

"Of course I'm sure! Where on earth did you get that idea?"

"From Edelstein."

"What the blazes does he know about it?"

"He says Uncle Jim told him."

Clarry burst out laughing. "Dear girl, why not? Jim's a joker, of course he'll spin a yarn to the gutter press."

"I think it's true."

"You think!" His anger flared up so quickly and so violently I flinched with shock. His cheek turned dark, the colour of old wine, his eyes glittered. He pushed past me and out of the room.

I ran after him. He was taking the stairs two at a time. "Clarry!" I had never seen him in such a rage, such a single passion, excluding all else, excluding me. I was afraid for him and for the old man.

But he did not frighten Jim. When I got to his room he was sitting up in bed with all the signs of his own brand of pleasure. Clarry's rage pleased him. When one is old it must be rare to feel the adrenalin rise: when one is too old, the only remaining joy is to watch it in someone else.

"So you heard," he was saying. "The word's gone round. I guessed it wouldn't take long to get to you."

"The word's a lie!"

"The word 'money' travels fastest of all."

"No doubt you've got your reasons for spreading a lie. You can spread lies like butter for all I care — but not touching the family."

"Is that girl family?" he said, peering at me under his lids.

"We're all the family you've got."

"I wanted you to be the first to know, Clarry, but I couldn't bring myself to tell you."

"Tell me what?"

"Clarry, child, I don't want to be a burden to you. It can't be for long though, can it? Six months, a year, five years? I don't fancy being a centenarian."

"A burden?"

"You're young, hard-up. I forget a lot of things, but not what it is to be poor."

"You've got the house and the land —"

"Mortgaged. There's nothing left to keep me, but I must possess my soul and what's left of my body in patience until it pleases God to call me."

"Listen —"

"I'm ready to go. Every night I ask, Why not now? Oh Lord, make it tonight, take me back into the womb."

"Into the womb?" I said.

He twinkled at me over Clarry's shoulder. "Of time, where we all go."

"Listen to me!" Ungently, Clarry seized the old man's face between his hands. "I don't believe you! You're codding, you love to cod, but you shan't cod me. I rate the truth from you."

"Dear child, I don't want to convince you, I don't even want to try. I'm so tired. Let me go, let me rest."

"Not until you admit you're lying."

"Ask the woman downstairs. She's had no money for months,

the reason she stays is for fear she won't get anything if she leaves." He closed his eyes. Then it was all working for him: lantern jaw, pallor, the ominous brown patches on his temple, the delicate fuzz on his skull, and his poor, knotted neck.

"Stop that!" cried Clarry. "Stop it!"

"Dear children." A tear crept from under his eyelid. I don't say it wasn't shed with weariness or defeat, but I swear he delayed it on his cheek to get a maximum effect. "Let me starve, it doesn't matter. I'm so tired."

Clarry straightened and stood looking down at him. I could not see his face, but his thumbs were twitching, a sign of extreme provocation.

I shared it. Not at the prospect of supporting Uncle Jim, though it would be a serious strain on our resources, but at the way the situation had evolved. There was a precision, a tidiness about it which I associated with Edelstein. It was Edelstein's style, and with him I was provoked. I see now that he was only an instrument in the necessary process of living and learning.

He also provided me with my first real intimation of my mortality, for Clarry turned to me and did the thing that destroyed us.

He cried, as if we were all against him, "I don't care!"

I knew that it was a lie and I knew why he said it. I would have been happy — how happy! — to have been denied that knowledge.

"You mustn't," said the dreadful old man, opening his eyes. "You mustn't care whether I starve or whether I'm tired to death. Clarry, Clarry, be sensible I beg of you. Go away and forget about me."

"I don't care about the money," Clarry said between his teeth. "I don't give a cuss whether you've got it or whether you haven't."

"Is he angry?" quavered Uncle Jim, lifting his head from his pillow and putting out a tremulous hand to me. "Don't let him be angry. I'll slip away quietly. It won't take long, a little pang, a little tremor, and it will all be over."

"Shut up!" Clarry was looking at me.

"I don't want to be a trouble to *you*, Clarry's wife. You're not liable, you only married into the family. Go away, lock the door and leave me to die. I promise not to hang on, there's no reason, nothing to live for."

"I thought you were going to be born again," I said.

He gave me a fleeting glance from under his lids. "Non omnis moriar."

I heard a sound behind me and turned to see Edelstein in the doorway.

"I beg your pardon, I thought Mr Burgoyne was alone." He made as if to go, but I stopped him.

"What was that he just said?"

" 'I shall not wholly die.' "

Clarry said to him, "You're not wanted here."

"I am leaving. I came to say goodbye and to thank your uncle for his hospitality."

Uncle Jim sat up. "You didn't get what you came for."

"I have an impression."

"What are you going to do with it?" said Clarry. Edelstein spread his hands and lifted his shoulders. "We'll sue you for libel if you print it."

"You didn't come for impressions, you came for a story," said Uncle Jim.

"I hardly expected to turn up anything new."

"Why not? I remember it as if it was yesterday."

Edelstein smiled. "The farther the consequence of an act has to travel through time and emotion the more it is subject to mutation."

"In here — " Uncle Jim tapped his forehead — "is the day of my life. It doesn't fade and it doesn't alter, it's not yesterday, it's today. And always will be. When yours comes, if it ever does, you'll know what I'm talking about."

"Mine?" said Edelstein.

"The day you were born for. It might only last a minute, so take care you don't miss it."

"What act?" Clarry said to Edelstein. "What are you getting at?"

"I said 'the consequence of an act', I did not stipulate whose."

"After that day, or that minute," said Uncle Jim, "you're as good as dead, and you might as well be buried."

"What about knowledge — apperception and philosophy?" said Edelstein.

"Pshaw! I never found out anything I didn't already know about anyone."

"And about yourself?"

Uncle Jim turned to us. "You see what he's after? The inside story of Jimmy Burgoyne and the Felice ladies."

"It would only be supposition," said Edelstein gently.

"Supposition is what you've got, it's all you've got. The facts are with me. Don't you forget it." Uncle Jim grinned. "That makes me worth something to somebody."

"He's fooling," said Clarry. "There's nothing to tell."

"That's what the boy said."

"The boy? Lovatt?" Edelstein said quickly, "Why did he say that?"

For the first time I saw the old man unsure of himself. He looked from one to the other of us like a wary monkey.

"Through his music, he meant. They tried to make him play at their parties so they could have a bit of fun with him."

"They?"

"The women. They weren't musical. Nor was I, for that matter."

"If not them, and not you," I said, "who was there to tell?"

"Why, the wide world. Given the time, he'd have been famous. He wasn't, though. The Lord giveth and the Lord taketh away. He put his face into the water and when we turned him over a goldfish swam out of his mouth." I shivered and Uncle Jim looked pleased. "He had a peaceful end. Requiescat in pace — I gave him that."

"*You* did?"

"Well, he never gave anyone any peace, he had none to give. He was always in pain, and you know what hurt him most? Music. It actually hurt him to play. How's that for a joke? His backbone was so twisted he could hardly get the fiddle under his chin, but when he did, he played it like an archangel. I knew it was peace he wanted."

"And so you gave it to him?" said Edelstein.

Clarry cried, "What the hell's that supposed to mean?"

Uncle Jim grinned his lipless grin. "I carved it on his cross. What did you think?"

"The merest supposition," said Edelstein.

"Keep your supposition to yourself," said Clarry, "Or you'll be in deep trouble!"

"Indeed, a journalist unable to differentiate between licence and libel would not last long."

"A little boxwood cross. It sank into the ground up to its armpits. Years after, when I went to look, all that was showing was 'Requiescat'. No peace."

"He could not rest in anything else," Edelstein said softly.

"I didn't like him. He was an evil-minded brat. He talked about things I never dreamed of, and I was no prude. Things I wouldn't want to dream of. I asked him how he knew about them. He said from Marianne."

"His sister!" I said.

"Mind you, a dog shouldn't suffer as he did." Jim looked at us with canniness. "Marianne and I — "

I thought, can one so old be shy?

"You were in love," said Edelstein. "And I now quote — 'with a beautiful ebullient girl who had no thought in her head beyond parties, clothes, and the conquest of men'. Barwell's pamphlet, *Some Unfinished Business*, a study of the Ampthill murders, published in 1900."

"Marianne had another thought!" Uncle Jim dry-spat with disgust. "Barwell's piece was rubbish. He described Ampthill as a grey stone mansion in the middle of a park. It was red brick, and right on the road. He said Belle was dark, her hair was yellow as a guinea."

" 'Mrs Belle Felice, a woman of mature attractions, commanding presence and southern complexion.' You called her Belle. Was she, I wonder," said Edelstein, "Marianne's other thought?"

"They called me Tara."

"Why?"

"After the tonic wine, Burgoyne's Tintara." Jim chuckled. "As if those two needed a tonic!"

"And Lovatt?" said Edelstein.

"Lovatt called me Mister Burgoyne. I had to fight his devils for him."

"Devils?"

"He used to beg me to kill them. 'Mr Burgoyne, they're all over me!' He used to tell me some were no bigger than bugs, others the size of cats, and every one with a ring of blue fire round it. 'They can't hurt you,' he'd say, 'because they're not yours, they can't even blister you, they've got no power over you. Step on them, crush them, or they'll kill me.' " Uncle Jim winked at

Edelstein. "No, I didn't stamp on them, I didn't crush them. I just picked him up in my arms and walked about with him like a babe. I could feel them dropping off him one by one, big as bugs and small as cats."

"You were good to him, everyone knew," Clarry said furiously.

"It was 'Mister Burgoyne, Mister Burgoyne' all day long. Night too, he'd come to my room and wake me up. If he couldn't sleep he didn't intend I should."

"The boy was constantly at your elbow. A disadvantage perhaps: a consideration certainly." Edelstein, I noticed, had stopped asking and was stating. Clarry was biting his knuckles.

"Marianne," said Uncle Jim. The name, as it emerged, was neither question, answer, nor statement: even at this distance of time it was food for more than thought. He lay back and closed his eyes and we watched him smile. We were not party or privy to anything that went on under his eyelids. His face softened, filled, he had lips with warm blood in them. I swear that for a moment I saw how he must have looked as a young man. "We were going to be married. I gave her a ring, a half hoop of garnets. I told her it was my mother's." His eyes opened a slit and glimmered. "Women like to think they're sacred."

Clarry rounded on Edelstein with a furious, ineffectual gesture. "This sort of thing will electrify your readers!"

"She wore it on a chain round her neck. There was Belle, you see, we couldn't be open about it. Marianne had a lovely neck. I liked to think of the lovely place my ring was in."

I said, meaning to help Clarry, to show how harmless and predictable it was, "Of course Mrs Felice didn't think you were good enough for her daughter."

Jim crackled with joy. "No, but she thought I was good enough for herself."

"As Lovatt knew," said Edelstein. "And in self-preservation — in self-defence at least — he would deny his intention of telling her what was going on between his sister and his tutor. Was that what he meant when he said, 'There's nothing to tell'? To quote Barwell again, 'Mrs Felice had been indulged all her life and was used to getting her own way in everything.' Certainly she would see that she got it in the matter of James Burgoyne."

Clarry walked round the bed and confronted him. "I've no time for empty minds and thank God I don't have to provide entertainment for them. I see you'll stop at nothing, but I give you fair warning I'll stop you with a punch on the nose if necessary."

"Leave him be, Clarry, it's between the two of us."

"I'm the last of your family, Jim, and any muck he throws at you will stick to me. I'm starting my business career. I've got friends and enemies at the same game. We've all got reputations to keep up and mine's no better than any of theirs. But by God it had better not be worse. You hang that old scandal round my neck and there's not a board of directors that will take me seriously."

"*Your* neck?" said Uncle Jim. "Why, your own father wasn't dreamed of when it happened."

"Burgoyne happens to be my name."

"Don't worry, child, I shan't tell him anything he doesn't know."

Clarry said to Edelstein, "What the hell is the point in your hanging about?"

"This is the point," said the old man, "I'm not the only one who knows what really happened."

"Oh God."

"Who else?" said Edelstein.

"Clarry's wife knows. I told her. She said I was a cause célèbre." He giggled. "Like Dreyfus."

"That's a lie!" cried Clarry.

"She hasn't told you? I asked her not to, but I didn't expect her to keep her promise."

"With young Mrs Burgoyne it would be a matter of principle," said Edelstein, looking at me.

"I know nothing!"

"God will reward you for honouring an old man's confidence." Eyes twinkling, Jim folded his hands with a gesture of simple piety.

Clarry was gazing at me open-mouthed. I cried, "He has never even mentioned it to me!" Clarry was not listening, he was still shocked, still grasping the implication. "I don't know anything, I swear!"

"Dear girl," Uncle Jim said tenderly, "you perjure yourself for my sake. It shall not be accounted sin, but a mortal glory."

"If she knew," Clarry said heavily, "she would have told me."

"Of course I would!" I cared only about the look on Clarry's face, about changing it, stopping it. "You must believe me, you know what a liar he is."

The old man didn't care about anything. He was all-powerful, what was there to choose between the gods and him? "She came up here, bringing a bottle of that green liqueur she's so fond of."

"Chartreuse?" said Edelstein.

"Crême de menthe. She sat here drinking it and I told her everything."

"Crême de menthe!" said Clarry.

"I hate the stuff," I cried. "I never touch it."

"Isa," said Clarry. "So you told Isa?"

"She drank the whole bottle, and it was none of your miniatures. It was a pint of crême de menthe. She drank it all."

I shuddered. They all looked at me.

"It was the day you quarrelled," the old man said to Clarry. "She drank it to spite you."

I said, "We never quarrel!"

"It was a little difference of opinion," Clarry said hastily. "We've forgotton it."

"I have never wanted to spite you – "

"Tooth and nail, they tore each other to pieces. Have you ever seen a cock fight? All the secret tender parts laid bare, the breast feathers torn out. I thought it was the end of the world for them and I wept to hear them at it."

Clarry's face was grey, he looked as if he wanted to walk away from us all.

"That wasn't me!" I heard myself, as if I was taking part in a childish argument – 'You did!', 'I didn't!', 'Yes you did!', 'No I didn't!'

Edelstein coughed delicately. "Some things are best forgotten."

"I tell you it never happened!"

"It's all over now," said Clarry.

"Are you married?" Uncle Jim asked Edelstein, who nodded. "Is she beautiful?"

"To me." Edelstein was gently deprecating.

"Beautiful women are the devil." For once he did not grin. The last resource failed. His lantern skull went dark as if it was already full of earth. "Isa was a beauty, but Marianne was the most beautiful woman I ever saw."

"Was? Isa?" Edelstein looked at me.

"He's talking about Marianne Felice," Clarry said sharply.

"Who else?" It occurred to me that after the devil had had his fun the worst could still be to come. Malice and enmity connect, damnation is private. "She was beautiful when she laughed. Other women split their faces, they could be crying or snarling. Hers lit up. I tell you, I'd give my soul to be with her on the funny side."

"But you weren't," said Edelstein.

"If I had been, I'd still have it."

"What would you still have?"

"Ask Isa." He did not look at me.

"He knows," I said to Clarry. "He's known all along."

"Ask Isa, tell her I sent you," the old man said to Edelstein.

"Sent me?"

Clarry seized me by the shoulders and shoved me at Edelstein. Edelstein, obliged to retreat, finished up against the wall, Clarry's fist in my back pinning me to him.

We clung together in painful intimacy, Clarry crying, "Isa can tell you nothing!"

## VIII

"He lost an eye," said Hillgren, "and couldn't afford a glass one, so they fitted him up with a wooden eye. It was painted bright blue. He was shy, and thought it gave him a bold bad look. One day he screwed up his courage and took the shade off and went to a dance, one of those parish hall hops where there aren't enough men, and the non-crackling stand in rows. Not to push his luck, he picked out the ugliest girl in the room and asked if she'd care to dance. She was so thrilled to be asked, she looked up at him and said. 'Wouldn't I!' and he shouted 'Hunchback!' and ran out."

Bealby laughed, the others smiled. Clarry drank down his gin and tonic. "If you think about it," said Hillgren, "it's a parable."

"A what?"

"First he loses an eye, through his own folly, or because of some criminal act: he may have been spying through a keyhole when someone pushed the key in. That makes him deprived, handicapped, incomplete. Who can afford to be that, in this rat-race? We all lack something, but this fellow is half-blind, and he doesn't look so good, which puts him sexually at a disadvantage."

"Some women fancy a one-eyed man."

"Lady Hamilton fancied Nelson."

"He's too poor to buy a decent glass or plastic eye, and, ashamed, covers up the wooden one. For weeks he shuns his fellows, hides himself like an animal."

"Doctor," Kremer worried, "is it recommended to put a wooden object into a socket of flesh and bone?"

"This isn't a surgical case history, it's a sick joke for our sick times." Normally a pedantic and exclusive man, Hillgren now talked with less than partial regard, with hardly more than a passing reference, to his audience. "He couldn't do right, do you see, he was doomed. He makes up his mind to face the world and goes to

163

a dance. What a field for his first battle! Nature in the raw, all competitive flesh, no spirit, no perception — and what the poor devil needs is to be perceived."

"Don't we all?"

"He does the wrong thing, but it's his thing and he can do no other, in choosing the ugliest girl in the room, out of cowardice, or call it humility, and kindness — for certainly an innate generosity made him pity and seek to encourage someone worse off than himself. That, too, works against him. Had he been less sensitive, coarser, more selfish, he would have gone up to a pretty girl who would not have been so grateful."

"She'd have told him to sod off."

"It wouldn't be so bad as being mocked."

"He wasn't mocked, though."

"He was bound to think he was. From the moment of his conception he was Woodeneye. So are we all, woodeneye, woodenleg, jellybelly, from the cradle to the grave. We do what we must. Every man is his own best enemy. Dichotomy is the message."

Hillgren finished his whisky. It was his third, he must have come to the club straight from evening surgery. He looked tired and was almost certainly supperless.

"It lets us all off the hook," said Clarry.

"And were it as simple as that," said Kremer, "would make nothing of your profession doctor."

"It is simple," Hillgren insisted. "I do what I have to do — like everyone else. That's where it's compounded."

"I do not subscribe to your conclusion, but I'm not surprised that you should reach it. Encapsulation is the basic principle of organic matter. For my part, I cannot accept the illogicality of God."

"Bully for you," said Bealby.

"God might have something bigger in view than your life-cycle or mine," said Hillgren.

"A grand design? Our function to fulfil it?" Kremer smiled. "God does not need people."

"Why did you start this?" Bealby wanted to know. "I don't come here for theological discussions."

Why indeed? Hillgren was eminently clubbable, he did not coerce or even seek an audience: he usually sat with a few cronies, listening with a slightly abstracted air as if he were making notes.

He smiled at other people's jokes, remembered their names and family situations, but did not bear their failings in mind. He neither avoided nor brushed off, yet he managed to be selective. He was said to be a disappointed man. He had gone into medicine late in life, with what intention nobody knew, but nobody believed that it was simply to be a G.P. Altruism did not sit squarely on him, and for his fellow clubmen it was not a viable concept anyway. The general impression was that something had not worked out.

"Now, I'll tell you one you haven't heard," said Bealby. "About the nuns and the lion-tamer."

"Another Scotch, please, steward. A double." Towards people like Bealby his abstraction simply deepened. But now he stared round at them all and a general accusation in his manner became particular. He seemed to be looking for somewhere to put it. "Have you seen my daughter lately?"

They were startled. It was as if he had stepped out of character. They watched him down his fourth whisky and Bealby said, "The lovely Louise? Have you lost her?"

"What does that mean?"

"What I say. She is lovely."

The whisky in Hillgren sought offence. He scanned face after face for a wink or a leer and finding none, could not pick a fight. Two scarlet discs appeared on his cheekbones. Normally of a white, powdery complexion, as if his skin secreted talc, the unwonted colour changed the impression he gave. He looked febrile and feminine. It was noticeable what slender hands he had, what spreading hips, and grey headmistressy curls above his ears. Kremer, who avoided scenes, withdrew to the fringe of the group.

"What's happened to Louise?"

"I haven't seen her for months."

"Shouldn't know her if I did."

"About a week ago."

Clarry did not say anything. He was amused at the change in Hillgren who always pretended to be more than human. Though not a moralist, Clarry had a layman's jealousy and relished the thought that the same old primitive firewater could shoot down the medical man and all his expertise. The hint of womanliness was slightly sinister.

"Where did you see her?" Hillgren turned on the last speaker, Charles Moffat, who could be counted a friend of his.

"In the arcade. At one of those Benaresware and Chinese junk stalls."

"Alone?"

"Except for the other customers."

"Did she speak to anyone?"

"Not that I saw. I had only a passing glimpse, I was double-parked and in a hurry."

Hillgren tapped his friend's knee. "Think what she was doing. Try to remember, it's important."

"Why?"

"Never mind why, damn you!"

Moffat raised his brows and glanced at the others. Kremer moved away out of earshot.

"At that precise moment she was examining one of those openwork shawl things. Holding it up."

"For someone else to see? Someone with her?"

"That wasn't my impression."

Hillgren threw himself back in his chair, muttering something which Moffat, his brows still arched, chose not to hear. But when Hillgren signalled again to the steward, Moffat stood up. "I'm going your way, I'll drive you home."

"If you've got anything to tell me, you can tell me here and now."

"About what?"

Clarry turned away. He was surprised at Hillgren: he would have expected the man to hold his liquor and, being a doctor, his tongue. He heard Hillgren saying, "Do you think I'm a fool? You all know! You're all in this conspiracy of silence. Who are you shielding? It's one of you, isn't it? It's somebody here."

Clarry followed Kremer into the lobby. "What's it about?"

"He has a daughter."

"And?"

"She is all he has. No wife. No sons."

Hillgren's raised voice penetrated to the lobby. "I'll find out, I don't care who he is, I swear to God I'll find him and I'll break him!"

Kremer, smoothing his smooth hair and brushing his speckless shoulders, looked at Clarry in the mirror. "A man has been seen in Miss Hillgren's company. Hillgren wants to know who he is."

"How old is she?"

"She is in the same class at school as my own daughter. The

average age of the class is fifteen."

"And the man?" Have you seen him?"

Kremer shrugged. "How should I know?"

"There's no need to be cagey. I'm not Hillgren's enemy, or his particular friend, for that matter. I don't really give a damn."

"It is true I have observed Miss Hillgren with the same person on two seperate occasions. Perhaps he is the man her father is concerned about, perhaps not. I have also seen the same man in the company of a member of this club."

"And which member would that be?"

Kremer put on his coat and made a business of settling into it. "Miss Hillgren should marry."

"At fifteen?"

"It's a question of maturity. Which she has achieved."

"Then she can take care of herself. The sort of girls who go for older men are invariably the predators."

Kremer smiled. "How pleasant to be their prey."

\*   \*   \*

Someone was in the shrubbery. Clarry saw the bushes wagging and when he switched off the engine a deliberate rustle moved towards the house. He stood for a moment, listening.

"Tony?" The rustle stopped. The tassels of lilac hung stiff as cardboard in the beam of the headlights. "I know you're there." He seemed to have picked up a pip of anger, he couldn't think where from or why, but it was ready to grow. "Come out or I'll pull you out!"

Another pause, it could be a cat or dog. He picked up a pebble to lob into the bushes. The lilac shook violently, something scraped the holly, and Tony Burgoyne came out into the glare of the headlamps. Clarry tossed the pebble at the boy's feet. "What were you doing in there?"

"Nothing."

"Then why not answer when I called?"

"Because I was doing nothing."

"You can do that indoors."

" I can't, actually. I was looking at the stars."

"Why didn't you say so?"

"It sounds sissy."

"I know you're not."

"That's because of what you take me for."

"Sometimes I take you for a bit of an ape."

"You take me for your son. But what else? I'm somebody myself, you know, in my own right. We're not exactly the same mix, so it doesn't follow that what you're not, I'm not, and what you are, I'm going to be."

"Whatever you're going to be, you won't be sissy. That's kid's parlance."

"What's the word for an adult siss?"

"There are several. You'll know them when you know what you want them for. Would you like to put the car away?"

Tony slipped behind the driving wheel and pressed the starter. "Where's everyone?" Clarry called above the revving engine.

"Mother's upstairs and Robert's whereabouts unknown, probably in the arms of some girl." Tony put his head out of the window, "He's at the difficult age."

Clarry slapped the side of the car. "Get away. Neither of you has ever been anything else."

It wasn't true. The boys had given no difficulty: if they found any, they themselves resolved it. Clarry had wondered what all the fuss was about raising children. Normal children, of course. People he knew were always complaining that Peter wouldn't wash and Johnny wouldn't work and Crystal told lies — someome actually had a girl called Crystal: to expect her to speak the truth was tempting Providence.

He stood in the hall, listening. The house was quiet, if it hadn't been he might have gone straight out again. He had been known just to walk round and round the block feeling craven, wronged, angry, afraid, murderous. If he came in for the final scene, the calm after the storm, the exhausted lull, the little miracle of recognition which he hadn't earned, he got the smile, the love, he got it all, coming in from outer space it must seem, after everyone else had coped.

Almayer never resented it. She was the one who was devastated. And she was the first to recover, to hope and believe that if it had been bad it was for the last time, and if it hadn't been so bad it was because the worst was over. 'The time before,' she would say, 'the time before this it went on much longer, it was much *deeper*. There has to be a turning point.' She clung to that belief, but no doctor had ever told them there would be an end. Except the one end.

He sat down and opened the newspaper. He had little prospect of reading, it was just a gesture. Carrying on the pretence, he got up and went to say goodnight to his daughter like any other father.

At the top of the stairs was her door. In the centre of the panel a transfer of a nosegay of wild roses, delicate and pretty. He had put it on just after she was born. Farther down the panel was a little black engine with a bright green belly, and beneath it a comic dog treading on its ears.

Words came into his head: 'For what we are about to receive, the Lord make us truly thankful.' He pushed open the door.

Almayer looked up with a smile. "You're just in time. We've had the Three Bears and the Little Giant and she's ready for Nod."

He kissed his wife's hand, without gallantry, just with gratitude for what it accomplished. "A fair day?"

"Quite beautiful."

"Hallo, Goldilocks." He bent over the bed.

"Orgghh," said his daughter.

Almayer smiled. "That's Father Bear or the Little Giant speaking."

"Father Bear is me." said Clarry. He walked two fingers over the pillow and knelt them by her cheek. "Here's Little Giant saying his prayers."

She had collected their worst features: his jaw, Almayer's nose, but she did not get her lint-white hair from either of them.

"Diddiddiddiddi – "

"Yes, darling. Kiss him goodnight."

Clarry put his face down to hers. She had lovely eyes, the whites pure white and the iris a deep mysterious blue. She should have been wholly pure, mysterious and lovely, but she was seventeen and her mental age was four.

"Kiss, kiss – a big kiss." Showing her, Almayer touched their lips with her finger. Then he received a kiss on his chin: she was so pleased to understand, she went on planting kisses all over his face, fierce, smacking kisses with lips bunched hard.

Almayer laughed. "Save some for tomorrow, my darling."

He drew gently away. His prayer for her was that she should not know love. To give her the capacity for that would be to give her a private and incommunicable pain besides the pains they knew of and tried to suffer for her.

He watched her settled into her pillows, a knitted rabbit beside her, the sheet folded down, the rail of the cot drawn up. The shock of hair sprang from her forehead like the dry blond grass which neither breaks nor bends.

"Go to sleep, sweetheart, it will soon be morning."

She did not like the night. They kept a dim light burning but she could feel the darkness outside the house. Sometimes she got up and looked and howled, on a note of fear and wonder.

He blew a kiss. "Goodnight, Nonny, sweet dreams."

She sat up and threw her woolly rabbit.

"What a way to treat poor Bunny." Almayer let down the side of the cot and gently pressed her back into the pillow. To Clarry she said, "I'll stay till she drops off. She's a little overdrawn."

He went downstairs and put the newspaper on his knees. Time was when he had asked what they had done to deserve it. He asked what Nonny had done, but there was nothing, she could never do anything to deserve what she had to endure. Silly questions, asking for silly answers. He no longer asked. He no longer wanted to know about her. Uncertainty was essential to his state of mind, which was the best he could achieve in the circumstances. He had lived so long on a razor's edge that now it was the only way to live.

Everything had gone wrong at her birth. It was premature: Almayer's own doctor had been called away, the midwife was detained by the breakdown of her car. There was a series of complications, minor at first, but as each one was mishandled and luck never held, the decision had to be made to save the mother and sacrifice the child.

Against all odds, Nonny was delivered alive, tiny and perfectly formed, the longed-for daughter. She survived, wrapped in cottonwool and kept in a heated box. They were told not to worry, the wounds on her head would heal and the scars would not show under her hair. She thrived, she became beautiful. The fine silken floss which grew into a charming but obstinate crest did not conceal the dark red weal across her scalp. But the redness, they were told, would fade, and of course her hair would grow longer.

Of course. And at two years old she was a sturdy, pretty child, eager for life. Perilously eager, they feared when, at three years, she was not only grabbing at whatever took her interest, but was hardly sustaining that interest longer than it took to get her hands on the object of it. Her life and theirs — Almayer's most of all — were lived in a flux of shifting, toppling, spilt and broken things. There was an enormous sense of rejection and frustration which the family was called upon to bear. The child herself seemed ready and willing to sort through the whole world for whatever she wanted. They were told to bear with her, it was a phase quite common in bright children, it was the pressure of the eager mind before any material judgment had been formed. She would soon begin to discriminate.

At the age of four she broke out of the little pen they had made to keep her safe while Almayer's back was turned, and, leaving piles of endlessly desired and rejected toys behind her, she went into the kitchen where she desired, and grabbed, the blue and gold flame of the gas-ring. The burns were superficial but it was then, when the need to explain, or at least to convey to her a warning, became urgent, and the impossibility of doing so became evident, that they took her to a specialist.

They were told that there had been damage to the meninges and loss of the cerebro-spinal fluid which protected and nourished the brain. 'We know,' Almayer had said, 'we've been reading about it.' Then they would know that if for any reason the supply of this fluid was disrupted, the brain could not develop.

"Damage?" Clarry had said, his mind flying at tangents from the word like water from a splash. Sustained during the process of birth, they were told. Almayer cried, 'Was that my fault?' The answer came that she had merely been one of the instruments. 'One?' They were told, with a wryness that twisted them, that there had undoubtedly been others.

Clarry contrived to settle it in his own mind long ago. Time had been against them and time was still their enemy. There was no escape from the inexorable passage of minutes into days into weeks into years into Nonny's life-span. A single error, not human, had brought her to her botched and beggared existence as logically as any normal growth. A biological slip, at the beginning no more serious than a white feather in a black bird — it had taken on itself wrong after wrong after wrong, multiplied mistakes and compounded failures until there was nothing to say, except that she had been born too soon.

Tony put his head round the door. "What's your reaction to the news that I've scraped a wing?"

"That you'll get no pocket-money till you've paid for the respray."

"No hysteria, no panic, I'm glad to see. It's allright, I was only testing your chloresterol. I must say it's a good thing I haven't scraped it, for I owe money right, left and centre."

"Who's the centre?"

"Roskill of P.T. I owe him a quid for a bet on a race."

"Horses?"

"No, ladybirds. I'm sure he gave his a booster-shot of lavender."

"A pound is a lot to put on a ladybird."

"I know. He was being Irish and boasting and made a big gesture and I had to fall in with it."

"He's pretty vague, he won't remember if you haven't paid."

"And if I pay he won't remember and he'll ask me for it again. It's not the point though, is it?"

"No. But he'll have to wait till the end of the week. There can be no advance. Who's on the right and left?"

"Oh I don't owe that kind of money all round. Just odd pence, it's a question of credit, really."

"Credit?" Almayer, coming into the room, gave him a sharpening glance. "Have you been getting things without paying?"

"Well, I had the excitement of the ladybird race without paying."

"He's talking about personal credit," said Clarry. "And not being a bad risk."

"Honour sounds so stuffed," said Tony.

"How does ladybird race sound?" Almayer shook a cigarette out of a packet. "All day I'm trying to believe my ears. Can't I stop now?"

"Yes," said Clarry. "Relax."

"How's she been?" asked Tony.

"She? Your sister's been fine."

"Hey Nonny, Nonny, no."

"Don't!"

"Don't what," Tony said sulkily. He knew, though he had not been born when it first came up.

Clarry had realised what a short screw they were on when Almayer had cried, 'Don't call her that — surely you can see it makes nothing of her!' 'Not to me,' he said, and, to play it her way — 'It means she's unique, there's no-one like her.' But he was not sure what Almayer's way was. He continued to call the child Nonny, and so did the boys.

"Shouldn't you be working? Haven't you got a maths test tomorrow?"

"French. Ce n'est pas la même chose."

She stood holding the unlit cigarette, at a loss. Clarry knew how disorientating a session with Nonny could be. Nonny was totally absorbed, her complete self, with little recourse to anyone beyond. She was pretty nearly self-sufficient, except in the practical and material sense, of course. Left alone, she would die, because she could not do what was necessary to stay alive. But she would probably never notice that there was nobody with her. Such absorption was itself absorbing, and after a while one's own existence was lost in the immanence of hers.

He lit his wife's cigarette. "The day's over, come and talk about it."

"What's there to talk about? We don't have a full social round."

"We want to hear what you've been doing."

"Does it matter?" She spoke without bitterness, puffing at her cigarette in the amateurish way she had. He did not resent anything, for of course what she and Nonny did bore no relation to what went on, and Almayer was entitled to any joy she had of it. "This makes a week of Day One."

Day One was a good day, the best they could hope for: without mals, grand or petit. There were Days Two and Three, and a fourth which they did not specify. Day Four was the abyss.

"A Week One," he said. "That's terrific." They could count the Weeks One on the fingers of one hand.

"Will we get to Year One?" Tony said.

He was young and rash or he would not have asked. Among themselves they had no pretences, they either dropped into the abyss en famille, or they got out of the house until the worst was over. It depended on how strong or how lucky they were.

Clarry saw no one to blame, not even the doctor who had told him, 'We have saved your wife.' The arachnoid mater — 'rather like a spider's web' — in his child was broken. He imagined the tattered filaments lying across a little dried-up orange that was her brain.

"She has a dress sense," Almayer said. "You didn't know?" She smiled at them. "She tore the sleeves out of her brown cardigan and it looks much nicer as a waistcoat."

"She tore the arms off her brown monkey," said Tony.

"That was destruction, this is construction."

"Seems she doesn't like brown," Clarry said.

A door slammed upstairs and they sat waiting for the next sound. Clarry even heard and dealt with it, ghostlike, in his head.

"It's been such a good day!" Almayer looked at him as if she were drowning.

"I'll go and see," said Tony.

Clarry went to her and picked up her hands which were gripped in her lap. "It hasn't been so good, has it?"

"By her standards it's been lovely — quiet, yet full of interest."

He did not know how much Nonny enjoyed the other sort of day. After the pain which passed in a winking, which could, in fact, be seen to lift on the flick of an eyelid, she took her revenge. She would, D.V., have been fun-loving and spirited, and sometimes he detected an awareness of what she was about.

"By my standards — they're not mine really, they're other people's — it hasn't been so good." Almayer let him gently open her clenched fingers and lace them in his. "How much longer? She's seventeen, she should be growing out of it."

"Perhaps she is. A week of Day One is a start. The pattern's changing."

"For a week, a month, a year? It has to be for ever!"

Doctors said they were afraid it was unlikely: the brain specialist, unafraid, said categorically that it was impossible. Almayer clung to her belief that Nonny would grow out of it and ordered their lives on that basis. 'Later on we shall have to move somewhere there's a good school for her. We'll take the children abroad when she's better...'

The specialist had spoken to him in private. 'The end may come at any time. The child is subject to severe seizures, there is great strain on the heart with an ever-present risk of embolism and partial or complete paralysis. Drugs will relieve the epileptic symptoms, but it is my opinion that she would need such massive doses that she would be reduced to a near vegetable.' 'My wife thinks she will get better.' 'Your wife is deluded, Mr Burgoyne. I shall not say sadly, for the delusion may help. We each have our own way of facing the truth. In some cases, denying it is as good a way as any.'

For Clarry there was only one way, and so far as Nonny was concerned they were on a collision course. Once embarked on, once that first move had been made, seventeen years ago — and who could say positively whose move it was? — there could be no retracting.

He held Almayer's hands in his. "It will take time."

"Time she's losing, time she'll never make up." She did not notice when the ash from her cigarette fell on their linked hands. "I want her to be well and happy and pretty like other girls."

Clarry could not imagine Nonny any way other than she was. He loved her that way, and if he could have lost her suffering for her he knew that he would have been happy with her, flawed and perilous as she was. And no one could beat that for utter bloody selfishness.

He blew the ash off their fingers. "I think she's happy enough."

"Enough for what?"

Tony came back. "It was the wind banging Robert's door. She's sleeping like a top."

"Happy enough for now," said Clarry. "We've got to take it step by step."

Tony, dropping into a chair and hanging his legs over the arm, sang, " 'Every little breeze seems to whisper Louise...' "

"What?"

" 'Birds in the trees seem to twitter Louise...' It's his favourite song."

"Bob's?"

"He's sweet on Louise Hillgren."

"The doctor's daughter?"

"Is she sweet on him?" said Almayer.

"Not while she's got Tom Beach."

"Tom Beach!"

"I thought you'd know, him being a senior pilot."

"I'd like to know how you know," said Clarry.

"I've seen them together on Rushett Common."

"Together?"

"Walking around — you know."

"We don't," Almayer said sharply.

"A chance encounter," said Clarry.

"Holding her hand. He takes her cakes from Fullers. I saw the name on the box."

"Were you spying on them?"

"Certainly not. I go on the Common to fly my models and I take the binoculars because when a Fokker fighter lands in a gorse bush it's practically invisible. I happened to be panning around with the glasses and those two got in my sights."

"I'd rather you kept off the Common," said Clarry.

"OK," Tony said blithely. "I can fly in the park just as well. But they won't be going there any more because Louise is going to stay with her grandmother in France."

When he had gone to bed, Almayer said, "I've noticed how moody Bob's been lately. If he's in love, that explains it. What do you make of Tom Beach?"

"It's none of my business, or wouldn't have been if I hadn't heard Hillgren swearing vengeance. He doesn't yet know who it is dating his daughter but he'll find out, and then he'll make trouble."

"What can you do?"

"I could warn Beach."

"You sound doubtful."

"It's a bit dodgy. Beach and I are not on buddy terms."

"How old is Louise Hillgren?"

"Fifteen. Beach is forty."

"I should think the damage has been done by now." They looked at each other. Almayer gave a downward smile. "That's something *we* don't have to worry about."

\*   \*   \*

Beach came to Clarry's office a week before his routine instrument rating check. He was untidy as usual, his tie sideways in his collar, his sandy beard pricking through his cheeks. He took the officialdom out of a uniform, made his captain's stripes look like hoopla rings.

"I shan't detain you." He consulted his wrist, on which there was no watch. "It's a question of leave taking. Time off, not goodbye."

"What's your entitlement?"

"None. That's why I've come."

"Of course you can take a few days."

"I want a few weeks."

"Why?"

"I have my reasons."

"They'll need to be good and I'll need to know them. We're operating a tight schedule."

"After this check, I want to go off for a bit."

The periodical tests were a strain. In addition to normal flying procedure and handling of the aircraft infallibly, if not impeccably, carried out, pilots were required to go through abnormal manoeuvres to meet some situations which they devoutly hoped they would never find themselves in.

"Feeling apprehensive?"

Beach grimaced. "I don't know who the instructor's going to be, but if it's the one who monitors the way I blow my nose I'll fly upside down from La Guardia to Shannon for him."

He seemed sure of himself, his mockery was not of the sort with which some men tried to hide their dislike of the pilot test. Clarry made up his mind not to mention Louise at this point. Perhaps after the test was over. A personal worry or preoccupation could affect Beach's concentration: poor showing could result in his being grounded: a major bungle could crash the plane.

"We might manage a week."

"It's not enough."

"Not enough for what?"

"To visit my sick grandmother." Clarry looked at him sharply. Not only was he not bothering to make it stick, he was expecting Clarry not to be bothered, and to bend the regulations for him. "At her age, it could be fatal."

"It's your age I'm worried about."

"I'm in my prime. I shan't let the line down. I've had pretty nearly all of it, you know. Made touch-and-go's, then a butterfly — engines cut and propellor feathered — belly-rolls, instrument failures, jammed under-carriage, turbulence, careens. I can handle them, and any little Hitler on my flight deck."

"I wasn't thinking about the check." It was noticeable that he did not ask what Clarry was thinking of. Clarry felt himself warming. He said, "Leave her alone!" The tightening of Beach's skin was so abrupt as actually to cause his ears to move back. Clarry added, "Your French grandmother." Now the fences were all up:

177

Clarry was disturbed to see Beach's face keep its own untidiness and yet manage to become completely anonymous. "That's my advice. Maybe I shouldn't offer it, it's none of my business. But it comes into my job. I meant to wait till your check was over and then give you a warning. You've pushed me to it by asking for leave. I think I know what you want it for."

"The hell you do."

"You're asking for trouble."

"I thrive on trouble."

"It won't be your sort, you won't be fighting an engine. You won't be fighting — not even your own shadow. You'll get chopped."

"I don't know what you're talking about."

"I'm talking about Dr Hillgren."

Beach got up to stretch his anger in the confined space between Clarry's desk and the window. "Why the hell can't people leave me alone?"

"Oh, come on," Clarry said impatiently. "Look at it from his point of view, as a father — "

"I've never been one, so I can't."

"Then look at it from mine. I work for an airline, in flight personnel. It's as bad for us to lose a pilot as a plane, and it could be the same thing if one man's good and the man who takes his place isn't good enough." Clarry unlocked his hospitality cupboard and brought out whisky and glasses. "You're a senior flyer with years of experience and an unblemished record. Perhaps you're aiming to be Chief Pilot. Whether you are or not, if you want to stay in the air you shouldn't make an enemy of Hillgren."

"What can he do?"

"He can do you harm."

"You a pal of his?"

"No. I happened to be there when he said he would break you." Clarry pushed a drink across the desk. "It's not worth it."

"How do you know?"

"I know that your relationship with this girl — "

"Worth is something I can't get for money, nor from any job." Beach poured the whisky down his throat. It seemed to chill him: shuddering, he dropped the glass on Clarry's unsigned letters.

"You're old enough to be her father."

"If I was, I could keep her with me."

Clarry said, disgusted, "I'm sorry, that was a mindless bloody thing to say. I don't know what you and the girl have got going and I don't want to. But I'll tell you what I think. I think you should cut it right out, stop seeing her, stop thinking about her."

"I can't."

"And let it be seen to be done. I'll arrange for you to be based at Shannon." It was probably too late. Beach could go to Timbuctoo, but Hillgren would not forget, or forgive.

"I need her."

"Get yourself a woman."

"I have."

"Well?"

Beach looked at him. He seemed to have to make an effort. "The woman is blonde, pretty, loving and faithful."

"But no fun."

"The greatest. Everyone says so."

"But not you?"

"In bed she's blonde, pretty, loving and faithful. And efficient." He added, with a slow, unpleasing smile, "Like a slot-machine."

"And this girl? What's she like?"

"Like me."

"Is that an asset?"

Beach said soberly, "Like being me, myself. Do you know what I mean? When I'm with her I fill my skin."

"It's the usual sensation." Beach frowned, and again seemed to be making an effort. For God's sake, thought Clarry, I'm the one who's doing that.

"It's not sex and it never will be. I've never laid a finger on her."

Beach picked up his cap and went. The interview was not over, his whisky glass left a yellow ring on Clarry's letters. The top one would have to be typed again.

\* \* \*

"Louise Hillgren? I don't really know her," said Robert.
"You know her enough to lose your heart to her."
"What!"
"And I hear it's a legitimate loss. She's pretty, isn't she?"
"It's not true."
"She's not pretty?"

"I'm not — I don't — " Robert picked the words with distaste — "feel anything for her. Louise Hillgren? Good Lord!"

"She isn't your type?"

"A type implies a selection. I haven't made any. Women are the unnumbered sea, how would you pick one? *Why* would you?"

"For all sorts of reasons. I daresay yours will be much the same as mine."

"Why should they be?"

"Because we're short on the same things."

Robert frowned. "She's quite pretty, quite nice, and quite intelligent. That means altogether quite — not just quite. It's too much." Not for some, obviously. Perfection, if that's what it was, thought Clarry, drew imperfections, if that's what they were, as still water drew flies. "I can guess who told you. He's quite the little voyeur. When I know what I want," Robert said scornfully, "I go and get it, I don't watch it through field glasses."

"Tony? He only cares about aeroplanes and football."

"Then maybe it's Tom Beach he's watching." Robert pulled a face.

Clarry said steadily, "Maybe. I don't want Beach's name mentioned, or hinted, to anyone else, by you or by Tony, in connection with the girl. Is that clear?"

"You can't stop it coming up. They all know."

"They?"

"All the kids. Oh they don't hear it from her, she doesn't confirm or deny it. She never talks about him. Or about anything that involves her. You know what I think? I think nothing involves her."

"So you've tried?"

"Tried? I don't have to, she's only a schoolkid." Clarry surmised that a few delicate intentions had been trampled and was sorry. "Twenty to thirty's the ideal age. Women should never be any younger or any older."

"Sooner or later every age is the ideal age for a woman. For me," said Clarry, "it's been from one month to two years for quite some time."

Robert sat down in the chair, hauled his knees broodingly up to his chin. "Fifteen is the age of ignorance. Louise keeps quiet and people think she's clever. All she's really doing is hide her ignorance."

To Tom Beach, with a bag of Fullers' cakes on Rushett Common, that ignorance was bliss. To so utterly implicated a professional tin god, paid to take life and a hundred tons of fast-flying metal in his hands and put it gently down far from home, the uncluttered mind, the total lack of concern would be refreshment and a huge relief. He could love and envy it, he might long to destroy it. The footprint in the snow, thought Clarry. We all want it to be ours.

"Did *you* get what you wanted?" said Robert.

"Eh?"

"If you don't know why you chose, you must at least know whether you chose well, whether it's worked out."

Clarry leaned over and smacked him. It happened fast, the mark had not quite come to fruition — a stinging red rose — before Clarry's anger had passed. He felt no compunction and said cheerfully, "People your age don't ask people my age that sort of question."

Robert's face reddened all over to meet the mark of Clarry's hand. "I suppose it is rather basic."

"It's bloody impertinent, and a son who asks it of his father, or his mother, is asking for a hiding."

"I'm sorry. Of course you can't answer."

"I don't choose to."

"C'est la même chose."

From fairly deep down a grain of alarm and despondency shot to the surface. "It's not the same thing at all! What's the matter with you two?"

"We two?"

"You and Tony." The grain burst: somehow, somewhere, a connection had been made. "I'll answer your question — for your sake, mind, not mine, in the hope that it will do some good." As a general anodyne, because for the life of him he did not know what was wrong. "Yes, I chose well and it's worked out."

Robert gave him a wary glance. "There's nothing the matter with me, or with Tony. He's just a kid. We're part of the working out, aren't we?"

"There have been no mistakes. That's more by good judgment than luck."

"Sure."

"You'd better believe it." Robert nodded. For God's sake try! But Clarry forebore to shout, it was convention, he thought, it

181

was himself who was snide.

"I've got to go, I'm meeting some people." Robert stood up from the chair, but remained beside it, looking unsurprised, as if he had been aware of it all the time, at Nonny's knitted rabbit which he had been sitting on. "They're people who know you. 'Your father runs an airline,' they said, 'so are you going to be a pilot?' I told them, 'My father doesn't fly and I shan't, either.' "

He was afraid in the air. Clarry hadn't realised it until he found him being sick in the airport lavatory before a cross-Channel hop.

"I hope you put them right about my running the airline."

"In a manner of speaking you do."

"No, not in any manner."

"The point was — " he snatched up the rabbit — "they said you were God and was I going to be Jesus Christ. It was me they were quizzing, to see how far they could go. They weren't concerned with facts." He kept trying to crush and contain the rabbit in his fist. In a burst of anger he threw it across the room. "Why won't she realise!"

"She?"

"Toys, dolls, shoosher-puffers, bow-wows — Nonny's not a baby! Why won't she admit it?"

"She?" Clarry felt the cold clutch of alarm.

"It makes me sick, all the baby talk. Nonny's growing up."

"Growing up?"

"Whether she likes it or not. She doesn't like it, and the reason's obvious."

"If you're talking about your mother — "

"My mother — and my sister. Nonny's seventeen, is there any reason why she should be treated as a baby?"

"You know there is."

"And there are reasons why she shouldn't!"

"What reasons?"

Robert flushed. "You've only got to look at her."

His fear was apparent and Clarry said soothingly, "Allright, you've made your point."

Not that he felt soothed. When Robert went, he sat picturing his daughter.

She was adolescent. It was something he had refused to recognise. Under the dresses of gingham and printed lawn, the Peter Pan collars, the narrow childish bodices, she had breasts. Her arms and waist had thickened, her face had changed from the soft mask at times untenanted — retreated from, never totally abandoned. At times, lately, he had glimpsed Almayer in her face, and that, too, he had refused to admit. For the likeness was not of the young Almayer, nor of Almayer as she now was, but as she might become. Nonny's undamaged body was going right ahead with puberty, but her flawed brain could not use the process to advantage. In her first womanhood she looked elderly.

He thought, in a fury, that it was one of Nature's jokes, not just merciless — obscene. He got up, dropping the Sunday paper and putting his foot through the front page.

In the kitchen, Almayer was making breakfast. She did not look at him — why should she? She had seen him already this morning: he had taken tea to her in bed and now the fried bread was sticking to the pan and the tomatoes had burst and the whistling kettle was screaming.

"No tomatoes for me," he said. All the same, he wished she would look up. There was nothing like a hot stove for cutting her off. He waited to share his disquiet. He did not know what he was going to say. "Where's Nonny?"

"In the garden with Tony. I'm worried. She's been so sick." She turned down the gas.

"She's been sick before."

"Not like this."

"Something disagreeing with her." She said wryly, "She isn't exactly selective." When she was in an empirical mood all sorts and conditions found their way to her mouth.

"This is different."

"She's growing up." Almayer glanced at him and began chipping and turning the fry with a spatula. It had been easy to say, but he knew that it wasn't enough. "Physically, I mean." Was there any other way — that he could have, might have meant? Didn't it all, normal or not, depend on changes in the body?

"I know. She's a woman, has been for more than a year."

"Oh God."

His dismay touched her to brief pity of one who has learned to accept the unacceptable. "She's also a little child."

"Should we treat her like one — always?"

"She has the brain of a child and the emotions of a child."

"Has she?" He said fearfully, "God knows I'd like to think so."

"In everything that matters she *is* a child. Everything, that is, that matters to her."

"How can you be sure?"

"Because she is my child."

"Maybe we should try to treat her more as a grown person."

"What do you suggest? We give her lipstick? Powder? High heels? Send her to parties?"

"Of course not. But we could talk to her — not baby talk —"

"Baby talk is what she understands. I know her, I know how her mind works. You may not think there's much to know —" Almayer sat down at the table, pan in hand — "You don't know how marvellous it is, the most marvellous thing in the world, to be able to get into her mind. To be free of it, to understand completely, to share — we do share everything — her little pleasures and fears —"

"Little?" Checked, she stared at him. He put his hand on her arm. "That's what I'm afraid of."

She emptied the contents of the pan on his plate. "Leave the tomatoes if you don't want them."

He ate them without noticing. He was trying to decide was she right, or was Robert. They could both be right and both be wrong. Only Nonny was entirely right, Nonny was the expert on Nonny. He watched her with Tony in the garden, lifting her knees, laughing, stamping on the daisies. She clung to the small boy's hand, looked down at him with trust and inquiry, a child in everything that mattered to her. If Robert was right, Almayer could be righter.

On Sunday mornings he took her off Almayer's hands. After breakfast he dressed her in her duffel coat and tam o'shanter which she at once pulled down over her eyebrows.

They went to the Museum gardens. The Museum itself had been the local stately home: in the grounds was a boating lake and a bandstand.

Nonny loved the water but she never remembered that it was there. Each time she saw it was the first time: her enchantment, sometimes joyful, sometimes sober, was always new. She could hardly be got away. Clarry used to take her through the shrubbery up the hill to the bandstand, past the swings and the seesaw which she could not use, into the rose-garden and then, and only then, down to the edge of the little lake.

On winter mornings there was an added chill from the water and sometimes a thin chalky vapour, and Clarry, standing on the bank, stamped his cold feet and called to her. But she would never leave until she was taken by the shoulders and her back turned on the water and she was led away. 'I can't make out what fascinates her,' he said to Almayer.

'The light and colour. And there are the ducks, and the fish.'

'She never tries to touch it. She runs to and fro along the bank, or just stands and gazes. I think she's mesmerised.'

The bandstand was a small pretty thing, painted white and eau-de-nil. A man was putting out chairs ready for the afternoon concert. Nonny laboured along at Clarry's side, she had never moved gracefully or easily, and now she was holding on to his hand with both of hers and making walking difficult for them both. She was excited, uttering the sounds which he had never been able to relate to speech. They seemed to go farther than speech, and to mean more. He felt that they were the shape of what she was feeling, and that if she could get it across like this in a cry, she must have the edge on them all.

But Almayer translated her. Nonny, she said, had her own vocabulary, based like everyone else's: the connections were remote, the derivations obscure, but it would be an odd thing — and terrible, as Almayer pointed out — if she did not know what her own child was talking about. 'After all, I'm with her every day, every minute, I know what's in her mind. The words she uses aren't so very different.'

'Words?' he had said once, and only once, because she had cried, with a bitterness which shocked him, 'She's human, isn't she?'

When they reached the bandstand, Nonny ran to the man who was placing the chairs. She ran, holding out her arms. He drew back and looked at Clarry as if she were a boisterous dog to be kept under control.

Clarry called, but she already had the man by the waist. Startled, he beat down her hands, thrust her away and snatched up a chair which he held, legs out, like a tamer facing a lion.

Clarry ran to her and took her by the shoulders, expecting a struggle. She made no resistance. She turned under the pressure of his grip and began to walk away down the hill.

"Bloody marvellous!" shouted the man in the bandstand. Clarry held up two fingers.

They went into the rose-garden. Nonny refused to take his hand. She stood pressing her chin on her chest. Her lower lip swelled.

"Nonny, Nonny." He tried to look into her face but she pulled the tam o'shanter right down over her chin. He could just see her eyes glistening through the holes in the knitting.

"Always remember, my love, nothing matters more than you." He squatted on his heels beside her. "You don't have to grieve. We'll do it for you, we'll take on the big griefs and the little miseries. You're excused, just be happy any way you can."

She ran from him. He thought she could probably see enough through the knitting, but she was headed in the direction of the lake. He was obliged to run after her.

Children on the swings screamed as she passed. The woolly pom-pom of the tam o'shanter was now in the middle of her face and looked like a snout. He called to the indignant mothers, "It's only a joke."

Arms flailing, she ran headlong to the shore of the lake. He thought she was going straight in, for all he knew it was the start of a fit. He shouted as he ran, twisted his foot on a tussock of grass and went down.

He fell heavily and lay on his back, winded. The clouds swooped at him with a sound like singing kettles, and covered his nose and mouth. At the same moment they became, with swiftness and cunning, the self-same colour of his own linings – the strong, thick rose colour inside his lips.

When he opened his eyes it was raining. He tried to sit up. He felt groggy and sick. He must knock off the whisky sandwich for lunch, take more exercise, keep himself fitter. Like Beach. He thought, struggling, why Beach?

His arms gave way, the clouds sounded like underground trains in a tunnel. He fell back with his face to the rain.

"Are you all right?"

A girl was standing above him, her long hair blowing in the wind.

"Where's Nonny?"

"She's here."

He got up then, without too much difficulty. Nonny was

standing quietly under her woolly mask.

"Missed my footing. It's easily done." He was glad that the clouds were now giving off only a hiss, like air escaping from a bicycle tyre. Confused, he reached for Nonny's hand, turning to her for help. It was probably the first time ever. "Let's get out of the rain." He said to the girl, "Your hair — it's getting wet. What a pity." He felt almost tipsy.

She shook her head. The hair lifted like a curtain and folded about her shoulders. "T'will endure wind and weather."

"Thanks for rescuing Nonny."

"I didn't rescue her, she was standing looking at the lake."

He said sharply, "She's all right." But the girl was entitled to something more. "She's quite harmless."

At times Nonny became violent and did damage. The harm was never first-hand or intended. It wasn't even done by her, but was picked up, acquired by others from her innocent acts.

He led Nonny into the shelter of a tree. The girl followed. "People get nervous because they don't know what she's going to do. They think the worst, I suppose they think of the worst *they* could do. But she'd never do anything bad." This girl hadn't even seen her face: for all she knew, Nonny was as vicious as they came. He thought of the children screaming, the angry mothers, the roaring sky. The girl had been outside all that, yet part of it. More likely it was part of her. "Like to sit down," he said. "Feeling a bit undecided."

The rain was needling down but the ground under the tree was dry. Nonny squatted beside him. He leaned against the trunk and looked at the girl. Qualitatively she was good looking. What he could see of her was good — eyes, nose, mouth, skin — any of it would be someone else's best. He would take a bet that everything he could not see was good too. He touched Nonny's mask. "It's what's known as pulling the wool over your eyes. Do it myself sometimes." Her kind of looks would not stop a room, but inevitably the room would be drawn to her. "Why don't you sit down? We're going to wait and see if the rain stops."

It wasn't fair. No one had any right to a hundred per cent perfection, fifty per cent was enough. He gripped Nonny's hand, it should be fifty for each.

The girl sank to her knees on the grass. Then she sat to one side, her legs laid one upon the other, the polished bones of her ankles disappearing beneath the hem of her skirt, her hands in her lap. She really did accomplish the movement, and he was tempted to ask her to get up and do it again so that he could have the pleasure of seeing it.

Nonny whickered like a puppy and put her hand up to his face. Her fingers, blundering into his nose, made his eyes water. "All right," he said to her, "you're all right." The girl's perfection might tell against her. What could be worse than being perfect in an imperfect world? It could make her as suspect as his poor Nonny. Perhaps she was to be pitied.

"She must be hot under there."

"No — don't —" he said, but the girl stretched out her hand and gently lifted the woollen hat.

When Nonny understood limitation she fought it: when she herself imposed it she fought, literally with tooth and nail, to maintain it. Often her limits were secret, the family knew they had overstepped them only by her reaction. In this case, the inference was obvious, she did not want to be looked at, yet here was a stranger coolly stripping off her limitation and discovering her to the world. He waited for the explosion.

The girls looked at each other with frank curiosity. Nonny liked what she saw. Her face, suffused and wet from the heat of the wool, broke into a smile.

The girl settled the tam o'shanter squarely on Nonny's head, deftly tidying back her cotton-coloured hair. Then she sat on her heels with an air of having given Nonny every chance, and made her appraisal.

The rain began to step down the leaves. It was getting past the dry barrier and soon there would be very little shelter under the tree. He could see the lake busy with rain, and the sky was a steady working grey. "Going to get wet," he said.

The girls appeared to be engrossed in each other. Nonny, yes, he could understand her gazing and gazing, but what about Miss Hundred-per-cent? What was she thinking? How did she feel about Nonny's five per cent?

His anger mounted as he looked at her. He could have cried, 'Bloody marvellous!' as the chairman had. For she had every reason, and no right, to feel superior. There sat Nonny, nodding and grinning, and there, but for the grace of God, sat she. Nonny, bless her, had no way of thinking, as she gazed on that tranquil beauty, that there but for the malice of the selfsame God, sat she.

"Going to get wet walking across the park." He drew up his knees. How did it go? A twist and a push and up on your feet.

"I think she's worried about you," said the girl.

"About me? Nonny doesn't worry about anyone."

"Why not?"

"She doesn't have to. It's her privilege. We do all the worrying for her. Don't you think she deserves it?"

"I don't think anyone can do that for anyone."

"My daughter isn't anyone, she's a special case."

"She has feelings, like everyone else."

"But nobody else can hurt them. If we can't make her happy, we can't make her unhappy either."

"Don't you want her to love you?"

She was still looking at Nonny. Had she directly faced him, asked him, he would have had to let himself go and ask *her*, did she think he wanted any of it? For Nonny, for any of them?

He got to his feet, steadying himself against the tree. He could hear the rain ferreting about on the leaves. The girl, too, had risen while his back was turned. He was sorry to have missed that. Nonny held up her arms to him.

"I think she has the heart for it," said the girl.

\* \* \*

"I don't want to see him," Clarry said into the intercom. "Tell him I'm engaged." He depressed the button again immediately. "No, you'd better send him in."

Damn this. Damn Beach. This was his office: the disadvantage was, or ought to be, Hillgren's. He stood up, held out his hand across the desk. To say nothing somehow gave the impression that they had an appointment, so he wished Hillgren good-morning.

"Nice of you to see me." Dry, soft, doctor's fingers briefly touched Clarry's. "I shan't keep you long, I know you're busy." He glanced round the room, but his curiosity was fleeting, and he began to put back the skirts of his overcoat preparatory to sitting down. He did not, however, seat himself until Clarry drew forward a chair.

"Would you like coffee?"

"Thank you, no. I must not trespass on your time."

Clarry pushed his cup aside. "I've just finished my third this morning. It keeps me going."

"A stimulant is ipso facto a depressant. What goes up must come down." Recollecting himself, Hillgren managed a smile. "Unless it sticks on the ceiling."

"What can I do for you?"

"I want Tom Beach's address."

"May I ask why?"

"He is the man who is pestering my daughter."

"Pestering?"

"I know no other word for a man who forces his attentions on a child."

"Even if that were true — "

"It is true."

"I can't help you."

"You mean you won't. That is what it amounts to."

"Beach is an employee of this company. So am I. What it would amount to would be a breach of trust."

"To tell me where he lives? My dear fellow, I can find that out anyway."

"Then why come to me?"

"I should like to know something about him."

"Do you seriously expect me to talk about his private affairs? Even if I knew what they are?"

It was conceivable that Hillgren expected it, or had simply not thought thus far. He said, "Of course not," with the impatience of one required to turn aside from important considerations to admit someone else's point of view.

"All the information I've acquired and hold in these files is relative to the company's concerns and is strictly confidential. My commitment is to the company, they pay my salary and I should be little use to them, or in any other business as a staff officer if I leaked details of personnel to all and sundry."

"I am not all and sundry," said Hillgren. "I seek your help as a friend."

"The rules of my professional conduct are no less binding than yours."

Hillgren nodded without conviction. He obviously felt that Clarry had to be humoured. "Louise is all I have. There are no rules

I would not break for her sake."

"I can understand that."

"You can tell me, without breach of confidence, what kind of man he is, appearance, manner, class. Such information is readily available from anyone who knows him."

"I suggest you get it from anyone. Anyone but me."

"You won't help?"

"If you'd like to talk to him I might be able to arrange it."

"Talk — to a man like that!"

"But you don't know what he's like. You're asking me."

"He's a monster, a pervert!"

"Perhaps I should tell you. Perhaps not telling you what isn't on the files is where the confidence ends and the breach begins. How do I know what's best for someone else? You're lucky in your job — "

"Medicine is not an exact science."

"Nor is personnel management. We say to a pilot, 'Don't trust yourself, trust your instruments.' That's what I call being let off the hook." Clarry meant to laugh but something had happened to the muscles of his face. They refused to obey. He feared he was grinning and tried to adjust his expression with his fingertips.

"Well?" said Hillgren, watching.

"Beach is one of our most experienced pilots, sober-sided, ordinary. He is not the life and soul of parties nor is he the odd man out. He runs a second-hand car. He looks as if he sleeps in his clothes, otherwise his appearance is passable."

"The man in the dirty mackintosh who molests children?"

"Why don't you talk to her — to Louise?"

The two discs of colour appeared in Hillgren's cheeks. He touched his pompadour of hair with the gesture of a woman seeking assurance from her looks. "I have tried. Of course I have. But Louise is old beyond her years, though in the essentials still a child. She will not admit the seriousness of the matter, she chooses not to grasp it." Having her cake, thought Clarry. He supposed that Hillgren, being a doctor, knew what the essentials were. "I am sending her to her grandmother in Brittany. It's the last resort and God knows I don't want to do it. The thought of being without her is more than I can face."

"She'll soon get over it. Out of sight, out of mind."

"She will remain there as long as it takes to break this man and run him out of her life."

"I know how you feel, I should feel the same if it was my daughter." They stared at each other. "If that were possible," Clarry went on steadily, "I should want to kick his face in. But I believe, I do believe, there's another side to this business. I think you should try to see it, or if that's too much, at least to admit it's there. Talk to him, tell him he's got to leave her alone."

"By the time I've finished he'll wish he'd never set eyes on her. I shall discredit him utterly." Hillgren rose up and leaned across Clarry's desk, balancing himself on his polished finger tips. "Never think I can't. It may take time, but I shall do it. In view of your connection with the man — "

"Yes?"

"I hope none of it rubs off on you."

Clarry knew that he should be angry. After all, he was being threatened, an attempt was being made to intimidate him, about a matter with which he had little enough to do and about which he had already done what he could. It wasn't that he doubted Hillgren's intention or capacity to do damage: he just couldn't get excited about it.

Hillgren paused at the door. "By the way, have you taken medical advice?"

Clarry stared at him. "My God, what do you think? We've had specialists, hospital tests, encephalograms — the child's been turned inside out —"

"I meant about yourself."

"Myself?"

"The seizure you had in the park. You should see your doctor."

"How do you know about the park?"

"Louise told me. She didn't know who you were, but when she described your daughter I surmised it was you."

"Seizure? That was Louise in the park?"

"If I were you I should take care of myself."

When he had gone Clarry said "Ah!" He was thinking about Louise. He found that he could appreciate Hillgren's problem, and Beach's. One way and another he had thought a lot about the girl in the park. The memory of her kept coming to the surface of his mind, one morning, even the clouds reminded him. He had thought, this is her sort of day, cool and white. Yet she had made him angry, he did not like remembering how angry. It was only later that he understood that the curious intimacy of his anger was because it was directed against himself.

Now he knew why. And was bitterly ashamed. As well he might be. For he had been comparing the girl with Nonny. Coveting her perfections for Nonny. Somewhere, somehow, some evaluation had been done: a cold commercial instinct had checked the goods, item by item, with the account rendered, and come up with the information that he was being grossly overcharged.

He went to the window and watched Hillgren emerge into the street. Hillgren walked away briskly, and then his steps faltered. He hesitated on the kerb, someone running for a bus bumped into him and he rocked stiffly like a skittle. Clarry felt sorry for him, for anyone who tried to tell Miss Hundred-per-cent what she should do.

Beach, who had been rolling around for forty abrasive years, wanted to stop somewhere, to be caught and held, even if only by the need to work out where he was going. 'I've never laid a finger on her.' Clarry believed him. Purity was part of the mystique, the hocus. Beach with his holy grail, Hillgren with his crystal daughter, grown men insisting on perfection — and little Miss Hundred-per-cent had yet to learn that nobody was perfect. Fifty per cent would be a state of permanent war: twenty-five was for the Schweitzers and Mahatmas: fifteen was average, was the ordinary, abiding, but not quite salt of the earth: five per cent was real. Five per cent was Nonny.

He rang for his secretary, and when she came he asked if coffee depressed her.

"No, but it gives me the collywobbles."

"I'll have another cup, extra strong."

The girl raised her brows but she brought him fresh coffee, hot, dark and bitter. He emptied most of the sugar-bowl into it and drank, wincing at the tigrish sweetness. He could guess what Hillgren's taking care would entail: no splendours, no miseries, and positively no stimulants.

As a matter of fact he had never felt better in his life. The stumble in the park last Sunday, the 'seizure' as Hillgren had called it — he had certainly been seized and shaken up — had done him good in some arbitrary way. He didn't want it to happen again, not like that.

His secretary rang through. "Your wife's on the line."

He picked up the receiver. They all spoke at once: the girl said "You're through, Mrs Burgoyne"; he said "Almayer?" and Almayer said something which he did not catch.

"Sorry." There was a click as the extension was switched off. "Almayer?"

"Will you come home."

"What?"

"At once. Please."

"What's happened? What's wrong?"

"Just come home."

"It's Nonny, isn't it? She's had an accident — she's ill — "

"It's not that."

"What then? Look, I can't come now, I've got to report to the board in half an hour — "

"Clarry, I need you."

"I'll come as soon as the meeting's over. It won't last long, but I do have to be there. It's important — "

"If you don't come I shan't be answerable for the consequences." She hung up.

He rang back. "Tell me what's wrong."

"I can't."

"I've got a forty-five minute drive, I'll be worrying all the way."

"I can't tell you over the phone," she said and hung up again.

He continued to hold the receiver to his ear. She would never summon him so peremptorily without reason, but the fright she was giving him seemed to have met and joined with something which was already there. Something total.

He pressed the buzzer and spoke to the girl. "I'm going home."

"Is something wrong?"

"I think so."

"What about the engineers' report?"

"Get Mr Marlow to present it."

"The board will want to ask questions."

"So do I."

He took the report out to her in her office. As he hauled on his top coat he said, "It's raining cats and dogs!"

"Raining?"

"Can't you hear it?"

The girl shook her head. He went to the window. The roofs

and pavements were bone dry. "Funny, I'd swear the rain is swilling down."

"I can't hear anything."

"It must be in my head – the coffee making my blood boil. I'll have to cut down."

"Are you allright?" the girl said sharply.

"Ask Marlow to make my apologies."

Traffic, they said, built up at lunch-time. He could not see how that was possible, unless it ceased to move at all. Inching along in first gear, he kept telling himself at least it wasn't her, it wasn't Nonny. The smallest mercy – perhaps he should cling to it. The boys were equipped and they were going to get their fair, or unfair, share of trouble, whatever he did for them.

But not so soon! He cursed Fate, Providence, Destiny, what have you: not yet, it shouldn't happen to them yet, they were too young.

'I need you,' Almayer had said. Of course. People said their hearts stopped, and he sat in a traffic block, between an articulated lorry and a bus, while the lights went through their cycle, amber to red, the regulation pause, then amber again, and green, without a single beat, one single drop of blood being pumped into his veins.

Something had happened to Almayer, something she could not talk about over the phone. The lorry moved, his foot stamped at the accelerator, the car bucked on the handbrake and his heart hammered to make up for lost time.

In the suburbs he encountered children coming out of school. Waiting for them to cross, he calmed, and drove the rest of the way prepared for anything. It was possible to anticipate the worst without knowing what it was, to get the drama over and be ready for whatever action should be necessary.

When he finally pulled up outside the house he was not frightened, only incidentally bothered by the lightness, the almost irresponsible airiness under his ribcage.

Almayer was waiting, at the window in a straight-backed chair, her knees together and her hands in her lap. She was making a procedure of it, sitting as if uninvited, in her own house. Clarry thought, with a rush of relief, that it must be something he had done. She did not move to greet him.

Suddenly he was as ready for the best as he had been for the worst. He had done nothing that he could not handle. Then he saw that she wasn't angry, she was desperate.

"What's happened? What is it?"

She looked at him without hope. She was holding on, as if speech, even opening her mouth, might dislodge her. He went to kneel beside her chair. "Something's happened to you." She moved her head, but so little he could not be sure if it was a shake or a twitch. "Are you sick? In pain?" He saw how her dry lips had stuck together. How long had she been sitting there with her mouth so tightly closed?

"It's her."

"Nonny?" The old fear rushed at him, but he made a stand. "You said it wasn't, you said Nonny wasn't ill – "

"She isn't."

"Where is she?" He couldn't help looking all round the room, though if she had been there he would have known when he came through the door. "What's happened to her?"

"She's upstairs, asleep. She's tired, I shouldn't wonder." He was startled at the bitterness in her voice.

"You're having a bad day – but you didn't get me home to tell me that."

"She's pregnant."

"What?" Almayer looked at him silently and the word, which had hit only the surface of his mind, began to sink in. "*What?*"

"I didn't believe it. My little girl – my baby – I actually said, how can my baby who doesn't even know – "

"What makes you think – God, it's crazy!"

"Dr Reed made me think. She's not been well, I told you she's been sick, often in the mornings. Of course it never occurred to me. I took her to the doctor, he made tests and the results are positive."

"It's impossible!"

"It's quite possible. She started her periods when she was fifteen, like any other girl. They've not been regular and we thought that was one of the side effects of pheno-barbitone. When she missed, I didn't worry. Dr Reed says she's been – about ten weeks."

"God!"

"Do get up, you look so silly kneeling on the floor."

"I am silly, I've been knocked silly!" He hit at the arm of the chair with his fist. "Do you realise what you're saying?"

"That she is preparing to bring a child into the world. A child like herself? Perhaps, perhaps not. How do I know? It won't, it mustn't happen. Dr Reed will operate at once."

"Operate?"

"An abortion." She got up from the chair with what looked like impatience. He felt his inadequacy to her and, above all, to Nonny.

"But how? Where — when did it happen?" He did not think the answers would provide a loophole, an alternative, but the questions had to be asked. They were all there was to choose between himself and a dumb beast faced with disaster. "You never let her out of your sight!"

"I can't keep her with me every minute of the day. Sometimes — I need not to see her. Can you understand that?" She had picked up a cigarette and was tapping the end on her thumbnail. Clarry, snatching at all the strings, knew that he must be careful: she wasn't calm, she was wrought up: she had got there before him and she was ready to fly apart. "I wanted everything for her — health, looks, brains." And she had always seen the miracle coming, she had seen it as a ripening, a late development. "She has nothing, worse than nothing. You don't know, you're not here, but I tell you it isn't possible, every minute of the day, to be glad she's alive."

"Of course I understand. You see it all, you go through it all with her. Oh don't think I imagine it's switched off when I leave here!"

"In the warm weather I can take her to the summerhouse and leave her for an hour or so. She's happy with her dolls and her little radio. She dances to it, I've seen her dancing. I've put blankets and pillows on the garden bed there and sometimes she sleeps." She bent her head to light the cigarette and added, with a coolness that stunned him, "Sometimes, obviously, she does other things."

"What makes you think she'd stay there? In the summerhouse? She'd wander off, into the field, or the wood, it would happen there. She could have been raped — "

"I always lock her in. She couldn't get out."

"Suppose there was a fire? She'd be trapped — "

"There's nothing in the summerhouse to start a fire, no matches and I took away the picnic stove. She likes it there, I watch through the window to make sure she's happy and doesn't need me. Then I turn the key and leave her."

"How long for?"

"Half an hour — an hour."

"You leave the key in the lock — so anyone could go in!"

"Someone did."

"And raped her."

Almayer drew hard on her cigarette. "She would have fought tooth and nail if it was anything she didn't want."

He knew that: many a time, those terrible scenes with Nonny fighting and biting and scratching, having to be held down like a wild animal, had left him shattered. "But who? Who would — who *could*?"

"Anyone, any passer-by." He could not believe what was happening, he could not believe her. "It could have been one of the village boys, a farm-hand, a tramp — "

"For God's sake!" He put his hands over his face.

"We shall never know."

"I'll find out!"

"How? How will you find someone who was perhaps only passing this way, weeks ago?"

"I don't care who he is, where he is — I'll find him." Rage had burst his heart and now it was thrashing about in his chest like a flat tyre. "I'll find him and I'll kill him!"

"We shall never know."

"You don't want to!" He blundered about the room, snatching at the furniture. "I don't understand you — don't you care what's been done?"

"It's done. There's no point in recriminations."

"You think I'll stop at recriminations? Tick him off and let him go? I tell you I'll kill him — " He had caught at her arm in his anger. She cried out and he felt a stickiness. When he opened his fingers he saw raw deep scratches along her soft underarm from wrist to elbow.

They avoided each other's eyes. He stood gingerly holding her arm. This he knew about, this was familiar. Her blood was on his fingers and he felt no more anger, only a fist of pain and sickness in his stomach.

"They're only scratches," she said.

He knew what they were, he had seen them before, on his own

198

flesh and even on Tony's. They were the marks of the beast that lived, kennelled, in the tender bones of his daughter. The tiger in a matchstick cage.

"That wasn't grand mal. You were trying to get something out of her."

Almayer pulled her arm away and began to pace about, drawing hard on her cigarette. "We could always talk, she and I. I knew what she wanted to say, she didn't even need to try to say it. I knew what she felt, I knew what she was going to feel." He thought, in the womb maybe, but Nonny wasn't still there. "Sometimes it was enough for me, it was all I wanted. Oh that was wrong, of course it was — I was having the best of the bargain, wasn't I? But it doesn't happen to everyone."

"It doesn't happen to anyone."

She wasn't listening. He might as well not have spoken, not been there. "I wanted it never to end, even when she would be well and living normally — I thought, then I'll have more of her, only it will be different. Better. I thought, she'll have everything, and I shall share it with her."

"Living her life?"

"It's all over now. She won't talk to me, she won't listen. She just laughed about something of her own — *with* someone of her own."

"She's always done that."

"She's laughed with *me*! When I got her home from the doctor's I knew that whatever I felt I mustn't let her see. And at first she didn't. She started laughing, but when I couldn't raise a smile, she was angry. She cried with anger. I cried too, I could do that — but she didn't want me to. She wouldn't let me cry, she went for me. She tried to kill me."

Day Four, day of the abyss, of the beast with five fingers. "She did see, she saw that you were upset and she wanted to stop it. She didn't know any other way, she must have been frantic. It wasn't you she tried to kill, it was what you were feeling — "

"Well, it's over, it will never be the same again. And it's been over, it must have been, ever since — " She shrugged. "Ever since. It was over and I didn't realise. I still thought we were part of each other. I've been going on with everything for the two of us. Like a stupid horse that's always been one of a team and doesn't understand it's pulling the cart alone." She stopped moving about to gaze at him. "She's been living a life of her own."

"She was raped. By some Tom, Dick or Dirty Harry who unlocked the door of the summerhouse and overpowered her."

"She would have torn him to pieces. There were no signs of a struggle, not one mark of violence on her. She was willing. She must have been." The dead cigarette went to and from her lips with a regular clockwork motion which alarmed him. "Which is worse? That she didn't enjoy it, or that she did?"

"For God's sake!"

"Whatever she felt, I felt nothing."

It wasn't for God's sake, but for theirs. "Do you know what you're saying?"

He knew that he had to get out, right out. The valve in his head was blowing and the important thing was to keep going, no matter where. He needed to run, like a cat trying to get away from the scald.

But running, actually moving fast along the pavement, he felt a warning, more of a conscience-strike really, of missed beats — one, two, three, ten, maybe twenty. Could he survive a default of twenty?

Came the answer, not if it should be double what he went through in the park. But why should it be? He paused to consider why, when all he had done that day was to twist his ankle on uneven ground, and fall, he should be left with a very present nightmare. So present that at this, of all moments, he was not thinking of Nonny or Almayer, but of clouds. He could hear them roaring.

The weather was sunny, someone had said to him, hours ago, 'What a lovely day!' There was no cloud. His ankle was weak: he should watch it, or what a case he would make, sprawled on his back in the street, clutching at last Sunday's sky.

He found that he did not want to think about Nonny, he could not bear to. Or Almayer: he was going to have to settle her part in it to his own satisfaction, or dissatisfaction. Whichever way he looked at it. She had locked Nonny in the summerhouse and left her. He did not know whether he would be able to discount that, or whether he should.

How much did he expect Almayer to stand? Every minute of every day, every day of the week, every week of the year, split living between the ordinary and an aborted world?

How much did he expect Nonny to stand, a prisoner, at the

hands of the sort of creature, sub-human, sub-beast, who would outrage a child? He leaned against some railings. Why did they say 'sick as a dog' when it was so easy for a dog? He felt he would bring up his heart.

It was market day, there were stockmen and smallholders in town: coming out of the pubs, knotting on corners, their lorries and trucks dropped caramel-coloured mud and dung straw. After the market the small growers, scratch-farmers, took their unsold produce and hawked it in the suburbs. One of them, any one, could have found Nonny in the summerhouse, turned the key and walked in and used her. To relieve himself, to amuse himself.

Perhaps he should go into the pubs and ask did anyone sell beans or cabbages or potatoes or salt pork, did anyone sell anything to a house outside the town, on the St Albans road, a house with a garden backing on fields, and a summerhouse painted white, and in the summerhouse a girl, younger than she looked, a girl of seventeen, who was about four years old, locked in, with the key left in the door — two months, ten weeks ago? Did anyone know of anyone selling anything on the St Albans road? Or driving, and stopping, and getting out, and walking? Anyone in the public bar of the Duke's Head, the Running Horse, the White Hart? Anyone in the saloon? If the man was a commercial, that's where he would be, with his gin and tonic. Then there were the transport cafés and the milk bars and the old railway arch: he should seek out the boys, go into the cinema and stand up in front of James Cagney or Jane Russell and ask, did one of you rape my daughter?

Nonny, Nonny, no. All her life they had been saying it: they didn't even know how long her life had been — four years or seventeen. It had made no difference. She was beyond them. They could forbid her nothing, refuse her nothing, spare her nothing. That was the sum total of their failure. Of his failure, anyway: he could not, should not, try to answer for Almayer. He had not been adequate, not nearly up to Nonny. The fault had been his and he had let the child take the blame, as well as the hurt, of all her shortcomings.

But Almayer had worked and worked and never spared herself to match up to Nonny's need. If she was inadequate, what was he?

Years ago when it was just beginning, when they first knew

that they were in for something, and Almayer was blaming her own body for the child's injuries, he had quoted some doctor's statistic: 'There's one born every eight minutes,' thinking, in his confusion, that it might help to know they were not alone. Almayer had rounded on him, crying, "It's every eight *hours*! Why will you belittle her?"

He found himself walking past the nice old houses behind the church. Hillgren had his plate up on one – 'Dr Stuart Hillgren', greenish letters cut into well-polished brass. He and Hillgren were in the same sort of trouble. He knew now what was in Hillgren's mind, he was organised to take what help he could from it.

Hillgren need not know what was in his mind. Talk without telling, that's what he would do, not mentioning Nonny. Where else could he take his thoughts of her? He rang the bell.

Surgery was over and it was Louise who opened the door. She waited, polite but reserved, as a young girl should be, confronting a stranger. At once he had doubts that he and Hillgren were on the same course. Looking at her he knew that they weren't even in the same craft.

"Is your father at home?" He said quickly, "It doesn't matter if he isn't. Another time will do."

"Won't you come in?"

"Not if he's busy – "

"I'm sure he'll see you."

In he had to go. But not to the surgery or the waiting-room. She took him into a room off the hall, little more than a cupboard. Coat pegs set into the walls testified that that was what it had once been: a desk, a leather armchair and a lead safe almost filled it.

"This is his own place. He comes here to read or take a nap. And I do my homework here. We don't go upstairs much, except to eat and sleep."

It seemed a cheerless existence. Of course there was no woman in the house. "If he's busy I won't wait."

"I'll tell him you're here."

Clarry wished he had not come. What was he going to say? He had no excuse, he had only his need to talk about Nonny, to know what she had gone through, what she would have to go through. To hear that she wouldn't be hurt and that it hadn't mattered so much – that she would leave the never forgetting to him. Then the knowledge would be acceptable.

He had to take it anyway, he had no choice: his only hope was to take it all.

He sat in Hillgren's chair. Something was kicking around in his chest, and seeing that he had walked quietly, steady as a policeman, up the hill, it could only be the rage in his blood. It might serve as an excuse, he could pretend to be concerned about himself.

Louise came and stood in the doorway. He wondered how Beach could be comfortable, held in her full round eye as in a bubble. A man wouldn't be forgiven for being one hundred-percent, nor would a woman. This girl got away with it because she wasn't old enough to know better, or because she was young enough to get to know a lot worse.

"How's Nonny?"

His hackles rose immediately. "Why?"

"Why was she crying in the park?"

"She's not like other people, she doesn't cry." He heard his voice as if it was being thrown at him on the wind. Louise raised her brows. "Except when she's in pain," he said through his teeth.

"She wasn't in pain, she was unhappy."

"Of course you know all about it."

"Don't you?"

"You tell me."

"Mr Burgoyne, I know nothing about your daughter. I didn't even know she existed until Sunday."

"Didn't Robert tell you he had a sister?"

"Robert?" The full bubble gaze slanted along her nose. "I scarcely ever speak to Robert."

"Then why do you say she was unhappy? What do you know? You must know something!"

"There's something to know?" She perched on the desk, positioned the hem of her skirt midway between modesty and advantage. He did not blame her for showing her knees, only for the nicety with which she did it. "If you hide your face it's usually because you can't hide what's in it. She isn't very good at hiding her feelings, is she?"

"She's altogether different."

"But she has feelings."

"No."

"You mean because she's as she is?"

"She can't be hurt by what people do or don't do, by what they say, what they think. She doesn't have to care. She's too young."

"Too young?"

"Only physical violence can hurt her and we save her from that. At least, we have always tried. What happened happened because of my carelessness and selfishness. I'm the one to blame."

"To blame for what?"

"There are people who would hurt her. You wouldn't believe it but there are people who would hurt a babe in arms."

"She's not a babe in arms."

"She is nearly."

She laughed, a sweet, bell-like note. "What an extraordinary idea," and he thought it was high time she was put across someone's knee and spanked. Hillgren should have done it long ago. "Of course I can see it would be easier."

"Easier?"

"To deny her love," she said crisply. "But you can't."

"Don't you think she's got enough to cope with, without caring about other people?"

"I think she was born with the capacity and you can't stop it growing."

"People put you through hoops. All your life. You too, you'll have to go through them."

"Hoops?"

"Don't worry, you'll do it beautifully."

"I shall do it for love," she amended, without coyness or embarrassment, rather as if she were finishing a shopping list. "So will your Nonny."

That smile of hers, chopping him off at the knees, also chopped Nonny, but for a fleeting second he had the impression that she was chopping herself too. "Love?" Not pain, not terror, not rape?

"What else do you expect?"

In the summerhouse an idyll, a rapture, a blaze of joy? "Christ!"

The cry offended her. She said coldly, "You don't want her to grow up. That's quite natural, my father's just the same." Little Miss Hundred-per-cent — he could see that, after all, her pretty knees were intact. "My father feels it very strongly, having no-one else."

"Where is he?"

"He must have gone out through the surgery."

"I shan't wait."

"He won't be long. Is it about yourself?"

"Myself?"

"Because you're not well."

"I'm perfectly well."

"Why do you want to see him?"

"I don't."

He turned to the door but she said quickly, "He's been talking to you, hasn't he?"

"We both belong to the golf club."

"Did he tell you he's sending me away?"

"To your grandmother's."

"Did he tell you why?"

It was marginally his business but he had not thought that any useful purpose could be served by talking to the girl, a schoolgirl with her feet off the ground. He thought now that the feet were dancing, and out of his reach. "For a holiday, I suppose."

"My grandmother's bedridden. Her house is fifteen miles from the town. You can't see out of the windows, and you can't go out of the house without an umbrella, because of the sea spray. The sea's never quiet, they call that part of the coast the Bed of Death because so many ships have been wrecked there."

She spoke with the faint amusement which she seemed able to direct unerringly at him. She did not stop to differentiate, to acquit him of what did not come within the margin of his business. She probably thought he had made it all his business — as an adult, and her father's friend. She said, "I shan't come back."

"You mean to live there permanently?"

"My grandmother is eighty-five, what permanency can I expect with her?" She put a hand under her hair and threw it briskly over her shoulder. "My father doesn't realise that if I go, there'll be nothing to come back to."

"Why will there be nothing?"

"Because I'll take it with me," she said, smiling.

Clarry was aware of some mixed feelings of wonder, resentment and pity. She was so sure of herself. God help her. And God help Beach. "Your father will miss you."

"If he wants to keep me a little longer he should let me stay here."

"Look," said Clarry, "I know you won't do anything that's not in your own interest, but before you do it, won't you stop and think whether it's in anyone else's?"

"If you mean Tom, our interests are the same."

"Your father could be a good enemy."

"Of Tom?"

"It's quite natural — isn't that what you said? — that he shouldn't want you to grow up. Certainly not to the age of forty."

"Forty?"

"Beach is forty-two. Your friendship could do him a lot of harm."

"Only people's minds can do the harm."

"Your father's, chiefly."

"Are you saying my father has an evil mind?"

"I'm saying he's concerned about you, he blames Beach and he's out for revenge."

"What can he do?"

"He can punish him," Clarry said soberly.

"For talking to me? For meeting me on the Common and walking about and talking? That's all we do."

"I don't honestly think it makes any difference — "

"He won't believe me."

"If he did, it wouldn't change his attitude towards Beach. Or his intentions."

"The poor man thinks that Tom and I are lovers. He imagines it." The depth of knowledge in her smile raised a prickle under Clarry's collar. "Do you think we are?"

"Beach doesn't think of you like that."

She stood up and delicately stretched herself, ankles to shoulders. It was beautiful to watch and was somehow a winding, rather than an unwinding. "But he will."

## IX

From inside, looking out, it is possible to be deceived into thinking that the house is in a gracious countryside, extensively but delicately wooded with birch and beech and sycamore. In fact it is in a new town that has grown to a present capacity of 150,000 and is still expanding, on an old coal streak this side of Warrington. Walk to the front gate or to the end of the back garden and there are the pylons crossing the valley, the trunk road hanging on callipers of white concrete and blocks coloured pink and blue and yellow high-risen above the dignified grey stone pile of the multi-storey car park. It is Tony's home. And hers.

"Don't you mind?"

"Mind what?"

I could see that she didn't. She doesn't have strong feelings about extraneous things. Where she lives would be extraneous, so is what she wears. Her clothes are terrible.

"When I was first married, Clarry and I lived in what was called a garden city. It wasn't either a garden or a city — but this is a non-returnable town. When they've finished with it, it will have to be dumped in the sea. Like plastic bottles."

"You've only been here three days."

"Three more won't improve it for me. I think I'll go back."

"You won't be expected."

"I daresay not, which is the time to go. Carème is always trying to start some new system."

"Carème — it sounds like French candy."

"The original Carème was Napoleon's cook."

"It sounds caressing, and degenerate. You're aware of Frenchiness, sweetness, sexiness, and corruption."

"Oh come! It's not her real name, it's only old Doris Moody giving herself airs."

"They're in it too, the airs and graces. Is she attractive?"

"She may have been, years ago. I daresay she had quite a pretty face. Now it's pouched like an old glove. So is mine."

"But fleecy-lined."

"What?"

"The glove."

"Why don't you come back with me? Until the week-end, till Sunday? We could go to some shows, there's son et lumière on the river, there are the shops, and galleries."

"Galleries?"

"Anything you'd like to do." I didn't know what she liked to do. How bizarre that I didn't know. Once I heard her say, 'No, not that,' but she had never declared herself, as other people do. And I had no hearsay to go by, no history. Until I met her I took no interest, heard no details, asked no questions. It was one to me whether he married a girl or an ape.

"We're glad you came," she said. "It has been as if half the world stayed away."

"Not to Tony. My sons had no use for me once they were born."

"We did not feel complete." She was smiling, but I had noticed that she took her time about changing her expression, she went on using it after it was past its prime, and frequently past its relevance. At least I wasn't deceived into thinking I knew what she was thinking — that was a kind of honesty.

"You felt that?"

"Tony said so."

"He wants the best of both worlds. And frequently gets it." This house in its capsule of trees and sky — when the clouds come over his garden, they become country clouds. I've seen it happen, the grey stuff that bags between the tower blocks becomes dove-coloured and lucent over the tops of his trees. And he has only to step outside his gate to enjoy the amenities of town-living — business, shops, motorway, an airfield. "He got you," I said.

"I'm not even the best of one world."

"You're very personable." Her face has the pious immaturity of that picture of the Sforza girl, the one with a plum in her mouth. Her nose is too long and under her skin, laid end to end, are the confetti freckles that go with her auburn hair. "And you're working at your marriage."

"I don't have to work at it, I love Tony."

"*You* didn't feel incomplete because I didn't come."

She raised her brows — confirming the assumption? Why should she care whether I came or not. "We have some nice things in the shop. We have wild silk – viridian, peacock, flame."

"Wild?"

"There's a shade of yellow, almost gold, with a hint of green. With your colouring it could either work miracles, or murder. You should come and see."

"What would I want with silk?" She twitched the woollen dress which she had worn every day since I came. It hangs on her as indifferently as a blanket on a bedrail.

"Silk would be wonderful on you. You're the right shape for silk."

"My shape is the same as everyone else's."

"Not quite." I had seen her undressed and thought, because words had been necessary, and only the best would do, of the 'still unravished bride of quietness'. It was, it must have been, appropriate somehow or it wouldn't have come to me. Tony is not quiet – he's not a ravisher, either.

"Two arms, two legs and a torso," she said. "It would hardly be a revelation."

I found that my cigarette packet was empty and threw it into the hearth. She went with good grace – the best in the world – to pick it up. Why that should anger and distress me I did not know. "I'll leave this afternoon. Take the two-thirty train."

"Without seeing Tony again?"

"At best we should argue, at worst we should quarrel. Irreconcilably. I feel like saying unforgivable things. If they were said to me I wouldn't forgive them."

She sighed. "I wish – "

"What do you wish?"

"That you two – After all, you are mother and son."

"Actually," I was rummaging in my bag for another pack of cigarettes, "you can't be bothered. I'm a nuisance. Now that I'm here I ought to run to pattern, behave predictably like a mother and a mother-in-law. But wishing won't make it so, not with Tony and me. We've had thirty years to reach this degree of misunderstanding."

"I did so hope," she said wistfully, still wisting, because it must seem to her a legitimate and a laudable hope and no-one, certainly not me, should rob her of it.

"Square pegs go into square holes. I think you'd prefer the

mother-in-law problem than no mother-in-law to speak of, even as a music hall joke."

"We wouldn't joke about you."

"If I conformed, how much easier it would be!"

"I hoped that you and Tony would be able to talk. Is it because of me that you can't, because I'm there? I could leave you alone, go to bed early, you needn't come out to help me with the dishes. I never expected you to do that."

"Talk? About what?"

"Perhaps you've never had time."

"Is that what he said?"

She shook her head. "But if it's had to be by the by, with everything going on, perhaps you've never really known each other. You could have missed each other. He isn't easy to know. I took a short cut."

"Am I easy to know?" She did not answer. She thought, of course that I was deliberately missing the point. "Talking won't bring us together, and we don't really want to be together. We've been spared that, and we wouldn't be good for each other. Tony asked me here for the look of the thing." I had found a cigarette and the first draw gave me sufficiency enough to say, "Whether you come with me or not, I shall take the afternoon train."

\*   \*   \*

She did not come to see me off. I dislike goodbyes on railway stations. A year ago, when I first saw her, not then knowing who she was, in a temporary gap among the crowds at Euston, a girl with the face of a Sforza, a long-nosed, white-skinned, secret face, I thought there is someone for me – not being sinister or unhealthy, I simply felt we had a future together. And then Tony appeared from somewhere and took her arm and brought her to me. 'This is Min, we were married this morning.'

I gave him no credit for her. I have not thought good for you, there must be something in you, something of me. If there is, I don't want to see it.

He never calls her Dominique, which is her name. The ugly diminutive he uses could identify a polish, or call a cat. I suppose he loves her in his way, his system of loving is different from mine.

I thought a lot about her after I saw her first, so briefly, as they were passing through London to their honeymoon. I accepted his invitation to stay last weekend with the fixed idea, the resolution, of taking her from him. If I say she 'appealed' to me, it does imply a felt want on her side, and that she has not shown. But certainly I was ready to supply it and, thereby, my own. I thought her wasted on Tony: she seemed to me a rarity, a special person who would meet, and perhaps surpass, my requirements. They were, putting them simply, to have someone else to think about. I wanted to take her away, appropriate, encourage, realise, and see her fulfilled. It was wicked waste, with so much mediocrity in the world, for her to add herself to it, a provincial young matron, unseen and unsung. I planned to dress her, style her and put her where she would disturb and enchant. It was a whim, my mind as well as my heart was set on it.

I found a corner seat on the train. I seemed to have been much longer away than a few days, it was more like a month of Sundays, dating from the moment when I realised I had come to the wrong place.

Tony, my younger son, is, if anything, more of a stranger to me than Robert, who accepts the inevitable. We have less to say to each other than strangers, it has all been censored by our common past. The most ordinary question, asked for politeness's sake, pretending interest, but not involvement — which neither of us want — tends to come out at the wrong moment, in the wrong voice and the wrong context. If I am not feeling guilty, he is. We are close enough for me to know that.

I'm told it's a matter of genetics. A child collects mastercells from its parents, more or less from each, and these decree how and what the child will be. One would expect, in the nature of things, that children would be nearly blue-prints of their mothers. Mine are not even flesh of my flesh. Robert has pores like an orange. Tony's chin, when he has not shaved, is dark blue. I am thin-skinned and brown haired.

My daughter was part of myself, a part I had never suspected. I could never have gone so far without her: she pressed on to the very end, to heights and depths which were the illogical end of all my illogic. I did not need to wonder why she did anything, her extremes were the same as I flew to in my dreams — and my nightmares. I knew what she thought and feared and suffered,

211

and what her joys were. She was the extension of myself, on my wild side.

As the train drew out, a girl ran along the platform. I got to my feet and was thrown against the knees of the other passengers. And it wasn't Dominique, not even someone like her. "Sorry," I said, and sat down again. I had been so ready to forgive, only too eager. But not any more. Dominique is a fool and one should not excuse fools. They are dangerous.

The woman in the opposite corner said, "Are you going to smoke that cigarette?" and I was tempted to reply that I was going to eat it.

"Do you object to my pipe, madam?" a man asked her.

"Oh no, I love the smell of pipe tobacco. I always say to my husband I'm sure it contents me as much as it does him. He smokes Balkan Sobranie."

"I can't afford that," said the man.

"Are you smoking nosegay? It must be, the smell is like new-mown hay."

"This is a smoking compartment," I said.

"And if I have reservations about what is smoked I ought to play safe and find a non-smoker, oughtn't I? But I was so taken up with goodbyes I'm afraid I dumped my luggage in the first empty corner."

The train was passing the secondary modern where Tony teaches. He showed me over the place, an E-shaped block: on the middle prong sits a barrel of glass which reminded me of the Crystal Palace. Tony said it was a thoroughly modern building, only completed two years ago, fully equipped with electronic educational aids, at a cost of 1½ million pounds of taxpayers' money. Right in line, Tony says, with the forward-looking policy of the school.

To me it looked old before its time. Everything is chipped, cracked, fingered, kicked, and scrawled over. The boot, I judged, had been put in the day it opened. But Tony is proud of it. He wears jeans and tee-shirts to class and he knows about pop groups and sweetie drugs, black bombers and goofballs, and treats his pupils as equals. I asked if they treat him as their equal: he said they think he has been mentally side-tracked, but, he says, if he can get them a little way along the track with him it will all be worth while. It seems little to ask, surely not enough. I think he means to become headmaster. If he does mean to, only an act of God's sabotage will stop him.

"You feel as if you're being torn in two when you say goodbye." The woman opposite was a talker: talk glistened on her lips and her jaws were full of it. I leaned back and closed my eyes, but it is no use pretending to be withdrawn into sleep yet still conscious enough to smoke a cigarette. I opened my eyes and she was waiting. "You never know if you're going to see them again."

"Who?"

"Your loved ones. A goodbye is a little death."

Something died when I said goodbye to Dominique. I don't know what, but I'm better without it. I have had the wish: I am — I must be — a degree better for not having done the deed.

The woman opposite said, "I'm going to a little resurrection."

I do not relish some of the discoveries I have made. I tell myself they are a phase and they will pass. But then I have to ask, a phase of what? What will come after?

"I am going home to my family. Parting is a death, so meeting must be a resurrection."

It was only hope that died when I parted from Dominique, hope of acquiring her. I wanted her for my unresolved and selfish ends. Certainly there was a prospect in that, but the real thing was the ploy itself, the actual getting her away was what fascinated me. I believed I could do it: I forgot, I chose to, how strong the physical bond is at her age.

"Part of me has stayed behind," said the woman. "I am not quite all here." She laughed. "They tell me I always leave something behind, a little bit of myself for them to be going on with. I feel the pull very strongly just now. We didn't have much time together. Three days, that's all."

What should have died is still alive. I am a nearly old woman and my son's enemy. That's something I have found out. The reason why, I don't know, but I have one. No doubt it will come into the next phase.

"If I was to keep travelling up and down," said the woman opposite, "shuttling back and forth between here and London, I'd end up in shreds." I looked at her, I could hardly do otherwise. She had a deep pink face, thickly powdered, the colour unabating down her neck to her speckled bosom. Her hat was a strong cooked green, she wore a coat of some yellow toy fur, and sat with her knees apart. "There you are," she said, "that's living."

Dying too, she had said: she was some kind of fool, but not Dominique's kind. Dominique does not know how to dress, either. One day she will see the need and she will try. She won't succeed, with that or with other things she will suddenly see the need for. It is always too late when people like Dominique look at themselves. I cherished, for an instant, a vision of her, her nose beaked, irrigated with the scarlet threads of middleage, the same woollen dress braced over her spreading thighs.

The woman opposite had not even tried. "I came down to Blackley on a flying visit. 'Baba, if only you could fly!' they said. 'We'd have a whole day more of you.' And the children cried, 'Darling Baba, you're never to leave us.' 'Never's on Wednesday,' I said. I had to come away. My husband's waiting at home for me. That's what I mean when I say I'm going to a little resurrection."

Between my sons and me there has been war. Robert has other and bigger battles now. When we meet and I see how tired he is, I am sorry for him. I should like him to be at peace, with me at least. But he is my son and I know I am still his enemy. I can see it in the back of his neck, and in his hands, hard, finny hands that never touch me. I can smell it on his skin. He has stopped fighting me but I know that he will trust the whole world before he trusts me.

Tony is different. He knows what he wants and, without yet having amounted to much, he has the better of everybody. He does not fight, but he will certainly have to be fought. In a material sense he has less than Robert. His is a junior teaching post and not well paid. His house is mortgaged: his car, though it is his own, and not a company car like Robert's, is second-hand. Robert's wife is the only child of rich and indulgent parents: Dominique's father was a bankrupt. Robert has three children, Tony has only Dominique.

"Everyone calls me Baba. I suppose because I'm small and chubby." Beyond the train window streamed a banner of grass. Fields, trees, hedges, were gone by before we had reached them. "I wish I was more rangy. But things relax, don't they? All over, they give up, there's not the same incentive." Her knees gapped wider. Smiling, she plucked at her chin. "Even up here."

I turned my eyes away. As we ran through a cutting the undigested green filled the windows. "I don't like travelling with my back to the engine," I said.

"The best age is the age you are. I try to believe that even this one —" she leaned forward — "and any to come — I shall reap what I've sown, and if it's not enough, I have only myself to blame."

She might have sown a daisy or two, a bit of fescue, but no wild oats. And yet, those knees, could she have such knees and be modest? It was a schism I had observed before. Matrons in their soft hats and hard-won faces, sat placidly chatting, their gloves and handbags disposed in their laps, and underneath, all unbeknown, apparently, those rapacious knees, ready to spring, to grapple, ready for God-knew-what. This woman's emerged, faceless but grinning, from directoire knickers. The elastic bit into flesh as taut as a tyre and pink as a pig's.

"It makes me feel sick."

"What?"

"Travelling backwards."

"Why didn't you say? I am so sorry, I didn't realise — we'll change places. You take my seat, it doesn't matter to me whether I'm going or coming!"

When we had exchanged corners her renegade knees at once spread wide. I said, "I could do with a drink."

"Water?"

"Whisky, preferably a double."

I could tell by the way her face fell that she wasn't a drinker. "I'll go to the dining-car and see if I can get something."

"It doesn't matter."

"Oh I don't mind!"

"Don't bother."

"It's no bother if you really —"

"I don't really. Half-past two is the wrong time to start: it's too late and too soon."

"Oh." The information was of no use to her. She could not apply it, she was one of those people who can go along with you only if it's to somewhere they've been themselves. "Was that your daughter who came to see you off?"

"Nobody came to see me off."

"Goodbyes are awful, aren't they? Did you see my crowd? Such a rag-taggle! They all had to come, even the baby — did you see the baby? He won't be parted from his potty, he loves it so, he carries it under his arm like a little top hat."

215

"When we get to Euston, perhaps you'll join me for a drink."

"My husband will be waiting for me. I expect he's setting out now, this very minute, to get to the station in time. He'll be much too early, but he dreads missing trains."

"Missing you," I said. She gazed at me in panic. Her neck darkened, her face became beefy. "He can join us in the bar at Euston."

"I'm so sorry — it's not possible. But you are so kind to ask —"

"I am a busy woman, I run a business which wholly engages me. I have no time for personal relationships. You will be quite safe, I shall not try to intrude on your family circle."

"You mustn't think I think that!"

"It isn't kindess on my part, it is courtesy. You may reject it if you like."

"It *is* kindness!" Her distress was disproportionate and made us ridiculous. She had tears on her cheeks. "You are so *very* kind. But my husband doesn't drink, and nor do I."

"My husband drank himself to death."

"Oh —" She drew back, with a wholly respectful gesture, into her corner — "dear."

"He had the choice of living and waiting for his heart to burst, or of blowing it up himself."

Why in God's name did I bring Clarry into it? For that foolish woman? No, I brought him in for myself. I needed him. I need him at times that are not times but holes, like the hole on the train, before anything has happened. After it's happened I can usually manage, but before, I feel the need of him, even when I don't know what's going to happen. He had said, 'Don't think I've anything arranged, I haven't. I'm not ready. And if I do what I'm told, and just wait, I'm bound to think I ought to be let off the hook. I'll have earned a remission but I shan't get it.' I tried to tell him that if he lived to think that, he would be having a remission. He said what was the good if he wouldn't know until it was nearly over.

"Your husband had a heart condition?"

The name for what he had looks like a spider. I can still see it, hanging in its corner. "It was fifteen years ago. I have forgotten."

He did not tell me he was dying. He had been doing it for weeks before the doctor rang me and said couldn't I at least help him cut down the drinking. I rushed to Clarry's office, I was frantic, and I burst in when he was dictating letters and asked him point-blank if he was trying to be a saint. He understood at once, and looked sheepish, and I thought then, and still do, that he had enjoyed keeping me in the dark, having that advantage. It was just about the greatest anyone could have over anyone else, and the most unfair. I do so hope he had some pleasure out of it. He said he'd told his secretary, and when I asked why he hadn't told me, he said that he thought I knew.

I lost my mind then, I went crazy and we had the biggest row of our lives, heart or no heart, and that secretary of his kept proffering a box of pills as if she was trying to tempt him to sin.

"It's terrible to be alone." She edged towards me, we were knee to knee.

"Oh no," I said, "it's fine to be alone, it's a revelation, truth at last, no-one to modify and distort, no-one to cover up for, no-one to hide from, nothing to hide. Free, naked and unashamed." I spread my hands to avoid the touch of her pink chippolata fingers. "It's natural. You start alone, you finish alone. In between — the getting, having and losing — is just refusal to face the fact."

"I'm sure it's not. We're members one of another the Bible says —"

"It says we're sheep, too."

"I'm wanted —" She now looked like a pigeon with gaudy neck puffed up. "Isn't that natural?"

"It doesn't help, though. No one can come into your skin with you."

Distressed, she cried, "If we were meant to be alone, we shouldn't have learned to talk!"

"I'm quite content. I have come to terms with myself. I have no expectations, no more foolish desires, no more fears. No one makes my heart ache, or flutter, either. It's the bonus, the only one, for getting old. God gave us that when he gave us little apples."

She was ready to cry, and had begun to dissolve after the manner of her kind. I could tell she would weep with her whole body. But her knees still smiled.

"There's nobody but you for you and me for me." I shut my eyes. My visit was to have been a gesture rewarded, an anomaly remedied, so that Tony and I could be seen to have touched fingers. That would cover the family relationship: nowadays there is no need for more, there is a kind of caste system as rigid as the old class one. Caring, really caring, is a private, nearly pubic, thing. I could hear Tony saying. 'My mother doesn't like this part of the world. She calls anywhere north of the Chilterns the Blacks Country.' And anything else that occurred to him to say to tickle, charm or tease his present company. The only reason he wishes to be tied, or rather, looped, to my strings, is because for a man going where he is going, a family background is desirable. I had decided that my leaving early would not affect his image-making. I had been to see him and had stayed in his house, enough for the look of the thing. He has never wanted more: I should say he has a horror of more.

Did I actually hear a certain word at that moment, or did it just follow, like Pavlov's dogs' saliva, from my own conditioning? 'What about love?' I think I heard, between a thought and a whisper.

Certainly I was not prepared to consider it. I blinked open my eyes with a degree of violence which seems now like an inkling of what was to come. There remained a split second, no more, during which I saw the woman opposite lean out of her corner. Her face shone with some thought, some victory — some appetite for some meal she was about to make. I can see it now — as avid as her knees — in every pore a private solvent of tears, sweat, organic wet.

Then something happened which was in itself physically shocking. The consequences brought more subjective pain, but this was enormous, crude, and wanton. The train, which must have been going at a good ninety miles an hour, was suddenly halted. I suppose the brakes were fully and violently applied, and I swear the repulse of all that tonnage of hurtling metal went right through my bones. My stomach recoiled, I would have vomited, but was not given the chance. The woman opposite fell on top of me, my suitcase tumbled from the rack on top of her, and the breath was knocked out of my lungs. There was a shrieking of brakes and a crashing of couplings, and a sense of compression over and vastly beyond my own windedness.

I was aware of people pitched into each others' seats and hanging on as if they had got to them in a game of musical chairs.

Hundreds of mushrooms, the contents of someone's burst carrier-bag, ran over the floor of the carriage. I went on gasping for my own breath and fighting for my own survival. I believe I fought the other people, for at that moment there simply wasn't enough breath for all of us.

The train stopped dead, really there was a deadness, as if a huge animal had been brought down: followed an utter silence, and then came a sound, a ball of voices rolling towards us along the length of the train.

By my own efforts, I got the woman opposite off my chest. She made no attempt to help me, I managed to push her aside, and she slid into a kneeling position with her head in my lap. The green hat had come off, her hair, the colour of ironmould, clung in tendrils to the nape of her neck.

I resented that innocent looking nape, lying in my lap as if she was kneeling to confess, to beg forgiveness. I shook her by the shoulders, tried to lift her head. She had a horribly heavy head. I cried out, told her to get up. She did not move, except I thought she pushed her nose deeper between my thighs. In a panic I beat her head, thrusting it away as if it were a rat.

Indeed it was evil and harmful to me then: everything has its capacity for harm, and on occasions shows it. On that train the plain everyday things were all showing it together.

It was only when she slid off my knees that I suspected she was unconscious. She lay across my feet and then I worried about getting free, I thought I must be free to move, I was afraid of what might happen next. The train had stopped, but that did not guarantee safety. We could be run into by another train, we could catch fire, explode. Any minute I might need to save myself. I was crying to her to get up, though I knew she couldn't hear, scolding as I would any obstruction, animate or inanimate, that I was trying vainly to shift.

Someone heard me and came to help. The man with the pipe — he had it in his hand, broken. I remember he held it out to show me with, I thought, disproportionate dismay, before turning to the woman at my feet. He raised her head. I saw that her eyes were open, so she wasn't unconscious after all. I leaned over and shouted, "Get up!"

She wouldn't move. The man took his hands away from her head and put them under her armpits. He hauled her into her seat without ceremony and she fell over sideways. She looked up at me, her face pink and wet, I swear it was still arranged around the word 'love'.

The man crouched down between the seats and put his ear to her chest.

"She's allright," I said, "she didn't hurt herself, she fell soft, she fell on top of me."

"I think she's dead," said the man with the pipe.

\*     \*     \*

They looked at her and then took her away. To the nearest hospital, to a doctor, said the man with the pipe.

"Then she's not dead?"

"Yes, I'm afraid she is. They'll want to know why."

"Why?" I said. "Why?"

"Some sort of seizure, perhaps. Heart perhaps. Or it could have been a blow."

"There was no blow. The luggage fell out of the rack, but that couldn't kill her."

"If it caught her on the right spot it might — on the back of the neck."

"I don't believe it!"

"Like a karate chop. Quite lethal."

They took our names and addresses, they asked if I knew who she was. The man with the pipe said there would be an inquest. We were in the dining-car, drinking brandy, on our way again, they couldn't delay the train, it was running beside an estuary of white mud. There were a few gulls stooping about, like shoppers, to itemise the emptiness. It froze me. Death will be everlasting space.

"She was sitting in my seat."

"If she hadn't been leaning forward at that particular moment she'd have a headache now."

"I should have been sitting where she was. We had changed places."

"Lucky for you."

But I shouldn't have died, I shouldn't have been leaning towards her, asking about love. The blow, if it landed at all, would have landed on my head. I didn't even have a headache. Wasn't that pushing luck beyond the definition of the word?

"Purely fortuitous. Tragic, of course, but fortuitous." He laid the bits of his pipe on the table and stirred them with a sad finger. "If I'd had this in my mouth I'd have damn nearly swallowed it, but I shouldn't have broken it."

"It's not the same thing at all."

"Yes, it is," he said soberly. "It's the same, to the nth degree."

When we got into Euston I took a cab to the shop. It was past closing time, but I knew that Carême would be there. She always stays to redrape the stands and enter the takings in the day book. She loves counting money: being bad at figures it takes her a long while.

Through the shop door I saw her rewinding a bolt of Dacca muslin. I rapped with my knuckles: she looked up, frowning. Then she came with the muslin in her arms and stared through the glass. I thought she wasn't going to let me in, she has some funny ideas.

She unlocked the door and the first thing she said was, "You were going to be away for a week."

She had taken off her shoes. She used to do it during shop hours and I had to speak to her, I can't bear the rubbery sound of her stockinged feet. I don't like the look of them either, and I'm sure customers don't. She rubs her feet together the way some people rub their hands.

"I changed my mind."

"Why?"

"I don't like the north of England, or the north of anywhere."

"It's rained here too."

"There was an accident on the train. The woman sitting opposite me was killed."

"God." Her hands stopped, the instep of one foot went on moving slowly up and down the calf of her leg. "You allright? Not hurt?"

"She fell on top of me."

"Heart attack?"

"I told you, there was an accident. The train suddenly slowed and the luggage fell on her. She fell on me — she died on me."

"You're upset. Why didn't you go straight home?"

Because my flat is empty, there's no one there. What a fool she is! "I need a drink."

"I never drink on the premises." She carries a bottle of gin in her flight-bag and she knows that I know. We eyed each other, she was bristling, her hackles had risen as soon as she saw me. "Go home and rest. Take a sleeping-pill."

Take the bottleful, sleep the week out, is what she means. "How have things been?"

"Fine."

"Did the metal yarns come?"

"Came and went. I sold the last today."

"We must order some more."

"I already have."

I looked round the shop. It seemed smaller and amateurish, like the corner grocer's. "You've put out more stands."

"To show the Thai silks. They're worth it."

"There's no room to move. People want to see what they're buying."

"They'll buy what they can see. The colours attract them, quite a few sales have started with people looking through the shop door."

Carème wants the shop, she loves it, and everything in it — she loves the fluff in the floor-boards. While my back was turned she had exulted in her possession.

"Tomorrow — " I said. Tommorrow I would arrange it my own way.

"There's no need to come in, you know. Finish your holiday."

"Holiday!"

"Well, you should rest."

"It's late closing tomorrow and you'll be shorthanded."

She shook her head, her feet caressed each other. I thought they might turn to and help, she might have trained them to use a pair of scissors. "I've organised for my niece to come. She's just left school, a bright girl, soon found her way about."

"You've employed her — without telling me?"

"I'm not paying her, if that's what you mean." She finished winding the muslin and carried it to the shelf. "She's getting the experience, isn't she? At her age everything's experience. Grist to the mill. Of course if you think of keeping her — "

The last thing I want is Carème's relations round me, my shop to be her family business. "There isn't enough to occupy the two of us."

"I find plenty to do." She wet her finger and used it as a magnet to pick up pins. "You're the one who talks of being shorthanded."

"She was in my seat."

"What? Who?"

"The woman on the train."

"Try not to think about it."

"She was killed. And I should have been sitting there — where she was."

"Why should you?"

"We had changed places. Because I felt sick travelling with my back to the engine she gave me her seat. It could so easily have been me. If I had done what she was doing —" I could have had a reason, it did not have to be the same as hers. "If I had been leaning forward, sticking my neck out, at that very moment — Perhaps it was meant, all along, to be me."

Of course I wanted Careme to laugh. She only blinked. There was a pin stuck to her lip, she picked it off, indignantly. "It wasn't meant to be you. Obviously." I think she thought I was getting at her, accusing her of something she could not refute because to deny the wish she would have to admit to the thought. She must often have the thought, plays with it before she goes to sleep, dreams how handy it would be if I went away for good and left her the shop. "Every cloud has a silver lining."

"You go," I said. "I'll lock up."

"I've still got one or two things to do."

"Do them tomorrow."

"You're the one who should go home, Mrs Burgoyne. You're not yourself."

"God, how would you know! I'm sorry — I want to make a phone call, a personal one. You run along."

She fetched her coat and put it on with a kind of disgust. Fretfully, she cast around for her bag and last of all, squeezed into her shoes. That must have been painful, for her feet were so swollen that her insteps rose up like soufflés. At the door she paused to look back, but not at me — at the shop.

It's indecent the way she covets my shop. When I was four years old my father took me to the seaside. I didn't like it, the sand was cold and wet and I was afraid of the emptiness. I kept my back to it and my head down, and made a sandcastle. Father helped me, he said it was after the style of Windsor. A girl watched us from the edge of the sea: she squatted, rapt, with the water coming in and wetting her clothes. She grudged me every spadeful of sand. Then father and I went away to get something to eat, and when we came back my castle was stuck all over with pebbles and bits of seaweed. It wasn't mine any more. I can't stand that sort of thing.

After Carême had gone, I seized the extra showstands and tossed them into the stockroom. I left the silks heaped on the counter and went to the telephone.

I had to call up someone who would laugh, and cry 'What nonsense! What a fool!' I didn't mind my friends knowing I had such a thought and all that it implied. Let them imply, so long as they laughed. I planned how I should say it, to start them laughing. But the saying scared me, hearing the words. My own voice crying, 'It was meant to be me,' was shocking and conclusive as no-one else's could have been. Speaking the words to Carême had not demolished but certified it. All I could think of to do now was to re-shock myself with the sound of a deadly truth in the hope of getting it denied, and a grain of comfort from the denial.

I sat beside the telephone my hand on the pickup, and none of my friends was loud or ribald enough. It would take a lot of ribaldry if 'What nonsense!' was not to blow away like a shout in the wind.

One morning, years ago, I was awakened by a wonderful joy: wonderful because it was in no way connected with me. I had not gone to sleep with it nor, as far as I could remember, had I dreamed it, and I had no claim to it, nor cause. I got up and went to the window and drew back the curtains. The weave of dark had just begun to thin. There was a smell of mint in the air. I put out my hand and felt the dew falling. That was probably the happiest moment of my life.

I went back to bed. Clarry was lying with his eyes amazedly open, his mouth too, as if for that 'Woof!' with which he countered anything surprising. He was already cold. Sometime before midnight, soon after we had gone to bed, he had opened his eyes to death, there was no time for him to counter, or properly acknowledge it. And I had slept on beside him.

When my daughter was dying they did not tell me until it was too late to reach her. 'We have to use our discretion. It was kinder,' they said. 'Kinder who to?' 'To you, Mrs Burgoyne. It would have been – distressing for you,' 'What about her? What about her distress?' 'We would, of course, have consulted Mr Burgoyne, but in the circumstances it was not thought advisable to call you. You must understand, she was not aware —' 'I've always known what she's aware of.'

I have not seen anyone die. You don't see a major event if you think you're seeing a minor one. I saw that woman fall, I felt the weight of her, that's all I felt. I did not feel her die.

I dialled the number, and as I listened to the ringing tone, Clarry laughed, from somewhere before and beyond it, cried, 'What bloody nonsense!'

"Tony Burgoyne speaking."

Relaxed and trim in his easy jeans and crew-necked shirt, my son is pared down to the essential, he is all there. I wonder who counts his hairs and scales him up every morning.

"Yes, well," I said. It is the sort of thing he expects from me, and in the brief pause he recognised and adjusted. The line bristled with his adjustments.

He said, "Why did you leave so suddenly?"

"There was suddenly no point in staying."

"Point? We asked you to come, we were glad to see you, we tried to make you welcome. I didn't know there was a points system."

"I'm sorry."

"I asked some people in tonight to meet you."

"Are they there now?"

"Yes. It has made me look rather silly."

"What did you say?"

"I said it's made me look silly -- "

"No, to them."

"That there was a crisis at the shop. You were called away. What else?"

"That's allright. You can tell them I have just called you from the crisis."

"But there is no crisis."

"No. I suppose I left because I ran out of things to say."

"Women do that?"

It wasn't his sort of quip, the fact that he made it, indicated that he was put out, put off his stroke.

"It was my fault. You mustn't blame Dominique."

"She's the last one I'd blame."

"The things I ran out of were things to say to you. I've never

225

had many." He did not comment and we waited in silence, each at our end of the wire. My end was quiet as the grave. Yet the wire was not silent, the wire was buzzing. Other people were talking on it, communicating, shouting, laughing, crying.

"There was an accident on the train," I said. "A woman was killed."

"An accident? On the train or to the train?"

"There was something on the line."

"The train hit something?"

"The driver jammed on the brakes, we were travelling at speed, at least a hundred miles an hour, and he jammed them on and we were all thrown about."

"The brakes on those diesel electric trains are activated by compressed air."

"I don't care, we were all knocked silly. But the woman opposite me in my compartment was killed."

"How was she killed?"

"The luggage fell on her."

"And?"

"I don't know. She was hit on a vital spot. Weren't commandos taught to kill with a chop of the hand on the back of the neck?"

"Were you hurt?"

"Not really. I was shocked, physically and mentally. A thing like that coming out of the blue, it was a kind of rape."

"Rape!"

"Of circumstance, yes."

"Aren't you overdoing it? The train braked for some reason known to the driver, luggage carelessly stowed on the rack fell, incidentally striking a person who was in the act of dying, or had already died."

"It was my luggage." There was a pause for him to take in where that took us. "It killed her. My suitcase killed her."

A sound came over the line, an exhalation. It was either a smile or a sigh. "I don't think a suitcase, weighing a few pounds, falling a few inches, could rupture the cervical vertebrae."

"It was *hurled*."

"Those trains are fitted with regulators. Think of a pan of boiling milk – "

"Milk!"

"How is rises, then sinks, fast and silent, Deceleration on the

Pullman is no less smooth."

"It was like being shot out of a gun!"

"We're talking about *loss* of propulsion. Ah," he said, "why are you laughing?"

"Because you've only gone as far as the facts." I had intended him to bring me all the way back. I thought he could if he would, I am free to think he can do anything he wills — it is never disproved.

"I'm glad you're amused."

"I have the right!"

"I really mean glad — I mean *glad*. You should relax. You've blown up this mishap on the train out of all proportion. You're hyper-tense. We'd noticed."

"We?"

"This is only the second time Min's seen you, so she's never known you otherwise."

After I had hung up, I smoked another cigarette, though I knew I would worry afterwards that I might have left a spark to smoulder in the shop. I threw the butt down the lavatory, switched off all save the display lights, locked the door, and hailed a cab. I was actually sitting in it when I told the driver to wait while I went back, opened up the shop and checked for a smell of burning.

"Now?" he said when I got back into the cab.

"Now." We rocked along the Fulham Road and something which had been at the back of my mind, behind the fuss about the cigarette spark, came to the fore. I rapped on the glass partition.

"What is it?"

"That suitcase." I could see it propped beside him. "It's not mine."

"It's the one you had with you."

"I haven't a label, a plastic window-thing like that on my case."

"You ought to have a label."

"My case isn't strapped."

"You ought to have a strap."

"That's not my luggage." He plunged into a gap in the traffic outside the Brompton Hospital. "I want my suitcase," I said.

When we slowed for lights, he leaned down and turned over the label.

"Imshi, 2 Palmyra Terrace, NW6. That's not you?"

"No." In the confusion on the train I must have picked up, or been given — yes, someone had put it on the rack and carried it along the platform at Euston, the man with the pipe, with the pieces of pipe stowed away in his pocket — the wrong suitcase. I had taken it into the shop, thought about it, talked about it, but I had not examined it. The last thing I wanted to do was examine that case.

"Where's it to be?" said the driver. "Want to go to Kilburn to sort it out?"

"Now?"

"You've got Jimshi's luggage, he might have yours."

"I suppose it's possible. Do you know where the place is — what is it — Palmyra Terrace?"

"I was born there."

"Born there!"

"Thirty years a cabbie and I can say I've been born everywhere between Buckhurst Hill and Strawberry Vale."

I know I'm walking on a thread like everyone else. It's been twitched from under me a few times. But my tragedies have been destined and private, and there's a strength, if not a comfort, in knowing that liability is limited to oneself. I had never before been conscious of the frivolity of disaster. The events on the train, each one touching off another, did not have even the coherence of a lighted fuse. The whole thing was evitable from the start. If the obstruction on the line, whatever it was — a brick, a cow, another train — had been inches away, or minutes, a woman would not be dead. "Jimshi? Kilburn?"

"Do you want to go?"

"It doesn't matter."

"You don't care about your luggage, but he could care about his. Suppose he's got his prayer-wheel in that bag?"

"Oh allright. Kilburn."

Palmyra Terrace was a row of those solid, mum little houses built for the deserving poor, for the artisans, a hundred years ago, equipped with two windows, a door and drainpipe apiece, and a slate roof for the lot of them. Attempts to break out and be individual had merely confirmed the unity of the row. The houses carried their poster paints and white-straked walls as a toolbox carries the chips and splashes of its trade.

At No 2 there were window boxes with little wicket fences. The door was sky-blue. It opened before I took my finger off the bell. I thought, they were waiting. A shadow slipped away quick as a blink, I could not swear I had seen anything, I just knew there was someone else there.

A man stood politely holding open the door, an English gentleman at the door of his house, his castle. Except that his skin was the wrong colour.

"Mr Imshi?" He inclined his head in a composed and gracious movement. "Is this yours?" I pointed to the suitcase.

He glanced at it and immediately looked at me. "No."

"Your name and address are on the label."

"That is possible."

"It's a fact. At least do me the courtesy of examining it."

He stooped and took up the label with delicately trembling fingers. "Yes, this is my name and this my address."

"So whose case is it if not yours?"

"It is my wife's."

I felt myself pinned by his stare which was now neither composed nor gracious. "I should like to see her."

"Why is this case in your possession?"

"It's a long story."

"I wish to hear it. If you will, accordingly, step into my house?" He held the door wide. I went in, left him to pick up the case, which he did, with a whistling sigh.

"It's not my fault," I said. He had slipped past me and held up a curtain of wooden beads, recalling to me a gentle girl who used to sit with me when I was a small child and tell her rosary. For the clicking of the beads in Mr Imshi's hall I had a second of quite uncalled-for happiness. "I was given this case by mistake."

He waved me, really waved me as if I were perched on his hand and could be committed to the air, into a front room. It smelled of beetles: if there were any, they had to live a secret life, for Mrs Imshi was obviously house-proud. There was a lot of deep cold polish, not a speck of dust to be seen, and everything was accurately, was geometrically placed, chairs right-angled, pictures parallel, rugs bisecting, and each cushion balanced on its corner, forming a rhomboid.

"If this is your wife's suitcase, it's possible that she has mine."

"Please." He indicated that I should sit down.

"I have a taxi waiting."

"It is most certainly my wife's. Here, concealed, are her initials." He unbuckled one of the straps and revealed the letters 'E.I.' burned into the leather. "The question, if you will excuse me, is not whether she has your luggage, it is why you have hers."

"There was an accident on the train. The luggage was thrown about and I got the wrong case."

"Train? You have been with my wife on a train?"

"I don't know your wife. But I do know there was no Indian lady in my compartment."

"She has not colour."

Between the rectilinear curtains was a cloud. It was the only shapeless thing in sight. "Where is your wife?"

"I do not know."

"She hasn't come home?" He shook his head. "Why not?"

He spread his hands, palms up, as if for rain. The cloud did, after all, have shapes, it had several, one inside the other.

"This alarms you," he said. "You fear for your luggage?"

"Your wife, what is she like?"

"She is English lady."

"But what does she look like?"

"She is looking like English lady."

"Is she thin or fat, short or tall? What colour is her hair?"

"I cannot tell."

"Why not?"

"I do not know how she is, only how she was."

"Was?"

"Excuse me." He placed his hands, palms together, before his chest. "I shall speak plainly. At a certain age the aspect advances most suddenly and considerably. I am myself aware of physical adjustments. Here a little less — " he touched his thinning temples, "here a little more," and, delicately, indicated his waistcoat. "It is the time of life. I would prefer the lateness not to be so signified. It is not all vanity, for there are accompanying debilities and assuredly others will come."

"Perhaps she's still at Euston, looking for her case?"

"I have not seen my wife for five years. Certainly changes will have taken place in her appearance, relevant, of course, to the fact that she is female."

I took a chair. I was tired, and if I was on dangerous ground I might as well be sitting as standing. I no longer minded about spoiling Mrs Imshi's geometry, it was probably Mr Imshi's, anyway.

He sat opposite me, his hands in the praying position. "If she is at the station, she will eventually come here?"

His anxiety was unmistakable but I didn't like the way he was referring it to me. "Well, where else would she go?"

"It is true." He fetched a breath that whistled out of his nostrils and left his chest flattened and his shoulders bowed.

"Please," I said, "if you can't tell me what she looks like now, tell me what she used to look like. When you last saw her. There can't be all that difference, and I must know."

"Why?"

"There was a woman on the train. We talked, we exchanged seats — you see, my luggage was on the rack above her and hers was above me." Am I here to tell him that his wife is dead and that it was my fault, my luggage that killed her? That she died in my place? That she will never come home, the woman he and all those people in Blackley are waiting for? She left them something of herself and they'll get no more, the supply has been cut off. What will happen to the supply now? Terrible, she said, to be alone. "If it's her case I brought here, it must have been your wife I talked to. Almost certainly."

"She has left me. I do not wish her return."

"You weren't going to the station to meet her?"

"I have had no communication with, or concerning, her."

"She said, this woman on the train, that her husband would be waiting at Euston."

"She was not happy, certainly not." He was gazing at me earnestly, almost raptly, he still thought I shared his anxiety. "But she will return here if she is not happy elsewhere."

"Perhaps she's coming to see the children."

"Children?"

"Or did she go to them, in Blackley?"

"We have no children."

"No family?" He shook his head. "No dependents? There's nobody — relying on her?"

"She wished for children, she prayed, she sacrificed."

"Sacrificed?"

"She offered her most treasured possession. Her hair. It was the colour of saffron and descended to her knees. She cut it off and burned it. It was her belief that my gods also must be appeased."

I thanked mine that I hadn't to tell him his wife was dead. "It couldn't have been Mrs Imshi I spoke to on the train. That woman, whoever she was, was positively fecund, and had no imagination. Her hair was ginger. She wore a green hat. Ginger people always wear green."

"My wife did not regain her hair. It became a bad colour and she was obliged to dye it." I glimpsed a crescent of white eyeball. It could have been sly, but it was desperate. "There has been hope, every day becoming stronger, every year reborn. It will take great trouble to die."

"Hope?"

His smile was a pained and painful fixture. "That she would find."

I felt that it was logical he should not say what. With a woman like Mrs Imshi there was no knowing, there could not even be any wishing. Simply to find, was all one could ask for her. "And that she should not come back?"

"I can do nothing." He bent his head and a bald patch as big as an old penny shone in the centre of his skull.

"Perhaps she won't," I said. "Perhaps she'll change her mind."

"She will come."

I stood up. "I've kept my taxi waiting long enough. I'll telephone tomorrow to see if my suitcase is here." He did not move. I could smell the desolation off him like a breath of fog. "The woman I talked to, the one with the big family and devoted husband, was killed."

"Killed?"

"There was an accident. My luggage fell, it struck her and killed her. Perhaps they'll keep it as evidence."

"It was not your fault."

"It worries me. There were so many people waiting for her!"

"People do not wait long."

He opened the door into the hall. The suitcase was there, in the middle of the floor. Beside it crouched a girl, very slight, and wearing a yellow sari. Her black hair, unbound, fell around her like rain. She had her hands over her face and was rocking to and fro.

Imshi knelt beside her. He put his arms about her and they

swayed together, he with his forehead resting on the top of her head. His desolation, faced with hers, became a tenderness, almost a comfort. There was something improper in my being there, watching them. He murmured to her, in their language, I supposed. I couldn't make out the words.

Then he lifted his head and said to me, "She fears that if my wife returns she will be sent away."

With reason, I thought. Who could allow those slender hips and twining arms, those ankles ringed with silver, that café-au-lait skin?

Weeping, Imshi put his face down into her hair. "O Baba, O Lal."

\*   \*   \*

Tomorrow I shall ring Dominique. Tony will be at school and I shall talk to her. I shan't ring Imshi, I don't care about my case, there is nothing in it that isn't replaceable. I'd just as soon — I'd sooner — not see it again.

It wasn't up to me to tell him his wife is dead. I'm not official sources: you don't tell people things like that if there is a margin of doubt.

No, but I'm sure. That was Mrs Imshi on the train. Loved and envied she wanted to be, and I believed that she was.

Dominique will laugh. 'You envied her?'

She was needed and I was not. She was taken and I was not. It seemed to me that I had cheated Fate, but Fate had got the better of me just the same.

'Fate knew that you don't like travelling with your back to the engine?'

Fate knew that there was no-one waiting for her, no family, no children crowding to the station, greedy for the days she spared from her loving husband. There was no resurrection.

'You think Fate is working for you?'

I think that was Imshi's wife who sat opposite. Everyone called her Baba, she said. But not for a long time.

Baba is a dear child, a reed, a suppliant, shedding sweet brown tears because she fears that her capacity for doting is to be lost to Mr. Imshi and her bright shadow will be chased from under his elbow. He wept for that too. He wept for her, and for himself. Most of all for himself, for he knew what was coming to him.

They are going to be happy, those two. Such a God-stroke, releasing him from everything except memory. I wonder will he suffer for joy. To him it will seem an act of deliverance, and because of whence it comes, it may seem a secret judgment. If he's not careful, he'll be left with Mrs Imshi after all. The Baba of the big knees. And not even the hope he once had that she might find and be happy, somewhere else.

'Why should you concern yourself?'

About Imshi and that girl, Baba Lal, who will twine round him like a vine and melt on him like dew? He might brush her off. Poor man, there are layers of conscience, degrees of obligation. Don't I know what the dead can do!

'How absurd you are!'

Dominique and Tony have discussed my absurdity. He calls it something else. Deviousness. He once told me that I was devious and I said did he mean cunning, and he said no, it was a private con, nobody else could join.

I shall say to Dominique if she finds me absurd, does she find me transparent, showing all I've got? She will say, 'If I could see all that, I shouldn't find you absurd.'

Not knowing, she will not know how I had been wanting someone to cry, 'What nonsense!' and a straw to clutch at. Sweet are the uses of absurdity, I shall say.

I'll tell her about the metal yarns. She will look wonderful in gold thread. She must come and choose some for an evening dress.